TURBULENCE

COLLECTION

JORDAN CASTILLO PRICE

First published in print in the United States
in 2013 by JCP Books.
www.jcpbooks.com

This book is a work of fiction. The characters, incidents, and dialogue are drawn from the author's imagination and are not to be construed as real. Any resemblance to actual events or persons, living or dead, is entirely coincidental.

First Edition

ISBN-13 978-1-935540-59-5

Cover art by Jordan Castillo Price

DEDICATION

Special thanks to Sharon Cox
for patiently fielding my aviation questions
and Amanda Corlies
for sharing her zookeeping experience

CHAPTER 1

I probably should have put my affairs in order.

The pool filter chugged to life and slurped down a hefty palmetto bug as Marlin Fritsch gazed out over the artificial blue waters. Maybe he should draw up a last will and testament. There was probably some website where you could do that, right? There must be. You could do anything online. Though what would having a will really accomplish? Material possessions—house, car, 1972 custom-finish Strat, sweet midnight pearl Harley Nightster—once it was all said and done, did it really matter how his friends and family divvied it all up? Those were physical things, and Marlin was so much more than a physical being.

His bare toes curled over the lip of the sun-warmed, faintly slimy tile that edged his pool. There was fear, and that came as a surprise to him, but he accepted the fear without judging it...until the urge to pray came upon him.

Prayer? Really?

Rather than beating himself up for exhuming a childhood superstition, he turned that prayer urge inward, and reminded himself he was an expression of Source consciousness, about to embark on a journey toward pure positive energy. And that it was the right thing to do.

The only thing to do, if he accepted his role as the Guide.

He closed his eyes and saw amber on the insides of his eyelids in direct contrast to the bright blue chlorinated water, and he ran through the email he'd scheduled to go out to the other crew members later that morning, once his task here was done.

```
To: CaptainK, cc. Dallas.Turner
From: Atlantic_Marlin
Subject: Flight 511

travelers in dark,
when the blazing sun is gone
find the tiny light
```

He didn't suppose either of them would recognize that it was haiku… and, with a growing sense of stillness and clarity, he didn't suppose their recognition mattered. They were on their own journeys, each of them.

And his was just beginning.

Marlin closed his eyes and found his center. He breathed, and stood in gratitude for his strong and capable physical body, and his sharp mind, and his sweet Harley. Once he was in vibrational alignment with Source, he took a single small step forward and dropped into the warm water with barely a splash. The kettlebells strapped to his weight belt, one over each of his hips, pulled him down to the pool's bottom, where he folded his legs in lotus position and focused hard on his center.

There it was. Shining. Dimly at first, but growing brighter. Like the evening's first star.

Marlin Fritsch held the image of that bright point of energy firmly in his mind's eye…and he exhaled.

His earthly life fled him.

As it did, a power surge caused a circuit breaker in his house to fail.

His computer shut down, consigning his final haiku to his hard drive.

***

Heat blazed from the tarmac, painting the distant aircraft in shimmering waves. South Florida in July was not for the faint of heart. Not only were temperatures loath to fall below ninety, but the humidity was thick despite the ocean breezes. Heatstroke was a legitimate concern. If you stood still too long, the soles of your shoes could melt and stick you in place—so ground crew said.

Paul Cronin was fairly confident melting shoes were an urban legend.

Besides, he wore leather-soled shoes, not rubber or synthetics.

He crouched under the aircraft (where the heat of the tarmac didn't radiate through the soles of his shoes, thankfully, due to the shade) and checked each of the antennas. All secure. Fuselage drains? Clear. Fuel drains? Boost pumps? Dry. Starboard landing gear? No leaks, no excessive tread wear, nothing unusual at all.

A few yards away, a pair of baggage handlers leaning against the shady side of a cart were engrossed in a discussion of how fuel economy was killing the American automotive industry. Paul felt their eyes on him. Aviation was an old boys' club—an uncomfortable fit for a gay man, especially one as obvious as he was. Not that he had *GWM seeks long-term relationship* tattooed on his forehead. But the type of guy you'd find loading a plane, or servicing a plane, or flying a plane tended to like their cars fast, their steaks rare, their women blonde, and their co-workers manly. Paul's mannerisms, while not particularly lavish or effeminate, pinged the sensors of these macho types in such a way that he showed up on their radars, bright and clear, as openly and unequivocally gay.

Let them look. He was the First Officer of this flight, and it was his job—nay, his duty—to ensure the safety of the passengers and crew. If the baggage handlers wanted to look askance at him while he performed his preflight inspection, that was their business. He wasn't about to let their opinion of him affect his performance.

Paul straightened up, ignoring the way the conversation seemed to ebb every time he moved. He approached the starboard engine and scanned for obstructions. All clear. Landing lights, clear. Flaps and rudder undamaged. When he rounded the plane, despite his best effort to avoid them, one of the baggage handlers caught his eye. The man wore the typical navy coveralls and bright orange vest. His protective earphones hung around his neck. He was stocky, maybe even chubby enough to look deceptively "jolly" to his friends. But now, squinting across the wing at Paul, he managed to seem forbidding.

"What do you drive?" he said.

It could have been an honest inquiry, an invitation for Paul to join in the old boys' club, at least for the few more minutes before he returned to the crew lounge to meet with the Captain and go through the flight plan. Except it didn't sound like an invitation.

It sounded like a challenge.

"I have a hybrid," Paul said.

The chubby baggage handler shook his head ruefully. The other one actually scoffed.

Paul turned away and resumed his inspection, backing up a step and re-checking the rudder to ensure the distraction hadn't caused him to miss anything. What he should have said was, *What does it look like I drive? A regional short range commuter jet.*

But he hadn't thought of that.

And even if he had, he probably wouldn't have had the guts to say it. He'd never heard of ground crew actively harassing a pilot, but he couldn't ignore the potential for a more insidious type of backlash. Waves of negative energy that would cause him to crash the plane? No, nothing like that. Paul didn't believe in woo-woo psychic phenomena any more than he trusted the Captain not to assail him with boring personal details all the way to Atlanta when he should be paying attention to the instruments.

Ground crew could talk trash about him, though. And the journey from First Officer to Captain was a long, tedious slog, even without the help of nasty rumors and hearsay. The more enemies he made, the longer it would take.

He rounded the tail, which put him in full view of the two guys who were staring at him openly now, and deliberately went over the port side of the jet just as meticulously as he had the starboard…no, even more. Because he refused to let these men rush him or distract him. He had a job to do.

Landing gear, check. Lights, check. Flaps, check. Valves, check. Around the cockpit—*go ahead, stare all you want*—and another check of the starboard landing gear just to be thorough…what was that?

A small round spot below the brake line looked marginally darker than the tarmac around it.

Paul hadn't actually seen it drip, but judging by the position, it could very well have come from the hydraulics that powered the brakes. He touched the spot. It felt dry—and, in fact, he couldn't even be sure it was a spot anymore. Brake fluid on hot tarmac evaporated notoriously fast. He inspected the lines carefully, shining his flashlight, searching for cracks, splits or leaks. He found none.

Still, even though it was gone now, he was certain he hadn't dreamt up that spot.

He called Operations and requested a mechanic while the baggage handlers shifted to follow the shade, and changed the topic of discussion to a reality series Paul had never heard of, since the erratic schedule of a pilot wasn't exactly conducive to keeping up with TV. Within a few minutes, a golf cart pulled up and a man in jeans, steel-toed boots and a work shirt stained with grease climbed out, squinted, hefted a clipboard and a tool box, and began ambling toward the jet. His eyes lit on Paul and took him in, and then the amble eased into something more of a swagger.

Ground crew were macho, but union mechanics oozed so much testosterone it was a wonder they didn't drag a pheromone-laden trail of it in their wake.

Paul squared his shoulders and looked the mechanic in the eye as he approached.

The mechanic glanced at the jet's tail number. "I just checked 'er over this morning. What's the problem?"

"Leakage from the starboard brake lines."

The mechanic scowled and made his way toward the landing gear. As he passed Paul, the burnt metal scent of welding wafted off his work shirt. He had a neck tattoo...though between the tan and the stubble and the old, blurred ink, Paul couldn't have said for sure what the indigo blobs were supposed to be. The mechanic squatted beside the tire and said, "The *starboard* lines?"

"That's right."

"You're sure."

Paul didn't dignify that with a response.

The mechanic held up his clipboard in front of the line, which would capture the spray of a pinhole—if a pinhole spray did exist. Apparently, it did not. He studied the ground, double-checked the line, then treated Paul to a disgusted look and said, "I cleared this craft for flight this morning, and I stand behind my—"

The crack startled them, small, like a cap gun, and blindingly fast. The mechanic fell back, stunned. A gash opened on the leg of his jeans, as crisp and straight as if it had been cut by a pair of scissors. A slim red line at the same angle appeared in the center of the slit, widening quickly as blood began to flow. Beside him, the ruptured hydraulic line hissed, snapping wildly from side to side, spraying brake fluid like an angry cobra.

As the baggage handlers stoically circled the aircraft to begin unloading the air mail cargo, Paul hit redial, and requested that Operations send down a medic.

CHAPTER 2

It was day four of Dallas Turner's weekly ordeal. Flight 511 ran like clockwork, Monday afternoon through Friday morning, Fort Lauderdale to Bermuda and back again, and Dallas managed the passengers of that flight with the precision of a drill sergeant and the sensitivity of a burn unit nurse. Now it was Thursday, and the final trip to close out the week was just about to get underway. With his whole weekend spread out before him, Dallas could pretend the creep of anxiety he felt across the back of his neck and in the pit of his belly was nothing but a mild curiosity as to which pizzeria he'd order in from when he got back home Friday, and what might be new and exciting on pay-per-view.

The unease was so negligible, in fact, that it vanished entirely when he stepped into the crew lounge restroom and found a tasty white man bending over the sink in a pilot's jacket and a pair of briefs.

"Ever heard of gravity?" Dallas teased. "Even coffee's got to abide by its laws."

The pilot's head snapped up and he met Dallas' eyes in the mirror. He blushed, pink on porcelain. "No coffee. I, uh…had a run-in with a brake line."

And even better…judging by the lilt in his voice, the pilot in his drawers was gay. Contrary to popular belief, male flight attendants were not *all* big, flaming queens—though Dallas had served shoulder to shoulder with his share of gay FAs. Gay pilots, though? Not as many in the rotation as Dallas might have liked.

He treated himself to a longer look at the pantsless pilot. First Officer's stripes on his jacket. Slim. Glasses. Clean-shaven. Rusty brown hair tousled with a bit of product. But the blush? That was the clincher. Adorable. Dallas had only dated a handful of white men, but their appeal wasn't lost on him.

It was a lot harder to make a black man blush like that.

He parked his rollerbag beneath the hand dryer, sashayed up to the sink, and pinched a feel of the trouser's fabric. "Wool and hydraulic grease, hm?" He met the pilot's eyes again—still in the mirror, since the mirror seemed to make the fact that one of them was clothed and the other in his underwear okay. And since it allowed Dallas to be more flirty than he would have dared otherwise. His flirtiness was not lost on the gay pilot, whose smile went slightly coy. Good to know some things you never lose the hang of. "A scrub in the sink won't get that out for you, baby. You need a good dry cleaner. I can recommend a local business…what did you say your name was?"

"Paul."

"Dallas—that'd be me, not the city. I know a place, here, in Fort Lauderdale, not Dallas-the-city. If you're going to be here long enough to use it."

Paul dropped the pants leg he'd been scrubbing with a frustrated *humph*. "I have no idea. Right now my flight's grounded, but Scheduling hasn't cleared me to go back home, so it might only be delayed."

Time enough for a quickie.

Prior to joining the crew of Flight 511, Dallas would have acted on that impulse. But that was before he was forced to confront The Meaning of Life head-on. Besides, Paul didn't strike Dallas as the type of lay who would press for something so quick n' nasty…although given the way his gaze kept wandering back to Dallas' reflection, he probably wouldn't refuse the offer. Tempting. But not the best idea. What good was a set schedule, anyway, if you didn't take advantage of it and actually try to get to know someone instead of just sucking him off in the toilet stall? "Where's home for First Officer Paul?"

"DC…when I'm there. I keep a crash pad in Boston, too."

Major hubs, unlike Fort Lauderdale. Flight crew tended to get involved in a transient sort of way, but with the set schedule of Flight 511...well, a man could dream. Couldn't he? Dallas was just about to ask Paul for his card when another idea entirely occurred to him. "I take it from the fact that you're standing here at this sink that you're on your last pair of pants. What are you, a thirty-two? Just so happens, Mr. Dallas Turner flies prepared." Exactly like the rest of Flight 511's crew, right up to the weight limit, since you never knew what you might end up needing.

"I couldn't take your—"

"Oh, but I insist." Dallas whisked a pair of black AVA uniform slacks out of his rollerbag in the blink of an eye, then held them up with his pinkies extended, and said, "Besides, I'd be crushed if I thought you didn't want to get in my pants."

✣✣✣

The news on the bigscreen TV failed to hold Paul's interest. The crew lounge recliners offered no comfort. Even the complimentary sandwiches weren't calling to him like they usually did, because all he could think of was the phone number in the pocket of the pants that weren't even his. And the sexy FA with the knowing look in his eyes.

If other men hadn't started trickling into the restroom when they had, who knows how far things might have gone, then and there?

Disappointing, not because Paul was looking for a quick hookup—but because Dallas was absolutely fascinating.

While there were scads of gay black men in the DC clubs, it always seemed to Paul they had their own clique, just like he had his: professional white thirty- and forty-somethings, two doctors, a dentist, a real estate agent, an accountant, and him, the pilot. But he had something in common with Dallas that went beyond who stood with what group at which end of the bar. Paul might be more at home in the cockpit and Dallas in the cabin, but they were both AVA flight crew. They both knew what it was like to live out of a suitcase, and fly the red-eyes, and have their plans ruined when a bid didn't come through like they'd been expecting it to....

Although Dallas mentioned he had a regular schedule. He hardly seemed old enough. Thirty-five? No older than forty. Maybe it was a racial thing, and he was older than he looked.

Paul leaned his recliner all the way back and settled an open magazine over his face. The racial thing. It seemed silly in this day and age that there even was any sort of "thing" to be aware of...but not only had Paul never dated a black man; no one in his clique had, either.

How exciting.

He shifted the waist of his borrowed pants and fidgeted in his seat. Sleep would be out of the question. He was already coming down from an adrenaline rush from grounding that morning's flight when he'd found himself being cruised in the restroom. Strange, how similar exhilaration and anxiety could feel. He was drifting, trying on various first dates—what sorts of things would Dallas be into? Movies? Clubs? The beach? Long, romantic walks? Oh, so many options spread out before them, a buffet of possibility just waiting to be tasted.... Paul's phone rang.

Dallas?

He checked the number on the phone. Not Dallas. Scheduling.

So very many possibilities...unless he got reassigned and couldn't meet up with Dallas tomorrow after all because he'd ended up in Seattle or Minneapolis or Atlanta. Paul answered, "Cronin," though what he was thinking was, *Please, please, please say* I'm *off-duty.*

No such luck. They had an assignment for him.

Just as his heart was about to sink, though, he absorbed the details and realized it was an easy little flight. A quick hop to Bermuda, overnight in a hotel, and back to Florida again in the morning. Not only would that spare him from getting a room in Fort Lauderdale for the night, it would also allow him to accumulate his weekly flight time-quota. All that, leaving him plenty of time afterward to catch up with Dallas—alone.

All the time in the world.

Paul specialized in Embraer ERJ-170 regional jets, and though the ERJ-135 waiting for him was slightly smaller, he had plenty of hours under his belt with this scaled-down version, too. That particular specialization was the most likely reason someone with more seniority hadn't yanked the flight out from under Paul's nose. The 135 held fewer passengers than the 170, plus the Captain, the First Officer and only one FA, so it would be a tiny crew of three overnighting in Bermuda. Normally, the anticipated downtime in such a cushy locale would have been the highlight of Paul's day. Now, he couldn't wait for the morning's return flight.

He strode onto the tarmac in his borrowed slacks, enveloped in a haze of anticipation so brilliant, the stares of the ground crew slid off him like he was made of Teflon. Just in time for a preflight check, then he'd run through the flight plan with the....

There, on the tarmac...was that the Captain? Doing the preflight? Weird.

Weirder still, it was a woman.

At least Paul wouldn't have to listen to her talking about watching Nascar and scoring with FAs all the way to Bermuda. Hopefully not, anyway.

Paul approached as she held up the clear plastic cup of jet fuel and squinted at it, scrutinizing the contents for contaminants or water. He cleared his throat and said, "Captain? I'm Paul Cronin. Here, I can, uh...."

The Captain's eyes darted from the fuel sample to the First Officer's stripes on Paul's jacket. Those eyes looked sharp. Small and agile. She wasn't a pretty woman; her skin was leathery and her cheekbones were prominent, and her graying blond hair was caught back in a bun that looked like it was stretching her browned skin over those cheekbones far too hard. No, not pretty. But the air of someone competent—damn competent. "You're the substitute FO," she said.

"Yes. Paul Cronin."

"Right." She shifted the cup to her left hand and thrust out her right. Paul shook. She shook hands like a man. "Kaye Lehr."

Once she released Paul's hand, he held it out for the fuel. "I can take it from here."

Captain Lehr gave Paul a hard look—though what it meant, he had no idea. It wasn't as if he was stepping on anyone's toes. It was his job, after all, to do the aircraft's preflight. She should be running through her Jeppesen charts, making sure everything in the cockpit was working correctly and double-checking the payload. And it wasn't as if he was taking a tone with her—the kind of tone the mechanic who'd needed three stitches in his leg had taken earlier that day with Paul. In an attempt to appear "helpful" rather than bewildered, Paul gave his best harmless-yet-earnest smile and stretched his hand farther still in a gesture of supplication.

Captain Lehr considered that hand…and frowned. Here Paul thought she'd looked intimidating before. "Nothing personal, this doesn't have anything to do with you. I've been flying the same flight, with the same crew, for quite some time. Since my customary FO isn't here for the preflight check, I prefer to do it myself."

Oh, now suddenly everyone at AVA had a regular schedule but him? "And it has nothing to do with you either, Captain, when I say that I'm unaccustomed to flying any jet I haven't examined. So I guess we'll need to do it together."

The Captain gave him a long look, down, then up again. And then her mouth tightened into the grim shadow of a smile. She handed him the fuel sample without a word, then turned and shone her flashlight into the starboard engine.

Captain Lehr scrutinized the jet just as fastidiously as Paul did, but neither of them found any issues. The craft was clean as a whistle, not so much as a dot out of place—and Paul would have noticed, had there been one. And if, by some off-chance he'd missed anything, Lehr would have spotted it with her shrewd little eyes.

Though nothing would have escaped Paul's attention to begin with.

"That's that," Lehr said, once her white-glove treatment was finished. "Crew meeting in ten, and then we board."

The crew meeting on a three-person flight crew, especially for such a short flight, wouldn't be anything formal. Anything unusual about the weather, the passengers or the flight would be discussed. Captain Lehr struck Paul as someone who did everything by the book, maybe even beyond the book, so he told himself it wasn't strange at all that she didn't just do a casual run-through with him while they were both walking back to the crew lounge. And he also told himself it wasn't strange that she didn't do small talk. Some people kept themselves to themselves. And if Captain Lehr was one of those people, it would make for a peaceful flight. She also didn't strike Paul as the type to "debrief" the crew in her room with beers and shots once they'd landed—and that was fine, too. He could catch up on his sleep and be well-rested for tomorrow's rendezvous with....

Dallas.

The flight attendant stood in the crew lounge at a window overlooking a taxi lane. He was framed gorgeously by clear blue skies—pale green uniform shirt, black tie and uniform pants, close-cropped hair, closer-cropped goatee, and deliciously dark skin. He turned, noticed Paul, and brightened. A wide smile spread across his face, then eased back just a bit as his eyes went sultry with promise.

And then he saw the Captain, and his smile drained completely away.

"This is our FA," the Captain told Paul, "Dallas Turner." She cocked her head to indicate Paul, and told Dallas, "Marlin's not here. It was either cancel the flight, or get a sub."

"A sub," Dallas repeated blandly. He glanced at Paul, then looked quickly away.

Disappointment stabbed at Paul—because although he hadn't yet gotten around to fantasizing exactly how his greeting from Dallas would be when they finally got to see each other once more, now that they were right on the verge of being alone, shouldn't it be at least a bit more enthusiastic?

"At flight level 310 we should make it to Wade in ninety minutes..." Captain Lehr began, and as she spoke, in her dry, inflectionless voice, Paul told himself to get a grip. Because of course Dallas wouldn't fawn all over him in front of the Captain—especially the one in charge of his regularly scheduled flight. Three was as small as it was possible for a commercial crew to be; it wouldn't do for Dallas to go upsetting the balance by getting flirty with the First Officer while he was on duty. It simply wasn't done. Not by a professional.

Besides...the Captain was usually the only one who got to bunk alone. Chances were, with Paul and Dallas being the same gender, when they overnighted in Bermuda the airline would put them in the same room. Alone. There'd be plenty of time for smiling and flirting...and maybe more.

They'd arrive at Wade International Airport by dinnertime and wouldn't fly back out until after breakfast. And not a 5 a.m. bagel on the run, either. A leisurely breakfast.

Maybe even in bed.

Paul arranged his expression in a dutifully professional semblance of concentration as Captain Lehr ran through the particulars of the flight. But inside, he was absolutely giddy with eagerness. Only an hour ago, he'd been hoping to be relieved of duty so he would be able to stay in Fort Lauderdale and meet up with Dallas tomorrow. Now, it was as if the forces of the universe had conspired to allow the two of them some privacy even sooner. Not that Paul believed "the universe" had anything to do with it. He was an AVA pilot, and Dallas was an AVA flight attendant, and they were both in the same airport with a craft in need of a substitute First Officer. All perfectly logical.

And, he had to admit, perfectly fabulous.

No doubt it would be a flight to remember.

CHAPTER 3

Passengers turned and stared, as passengers tended to do, as Paul, Dallas and Captain Lehr strode toward the skybridge, trailing their flight bags behind them. From the front row facing the gate counter, a passenger jumped up and approached the flight crew, a woman in her late fifties wearing mom-jeans and a royal blue T-shirt appliqued with red and white stars. She made a beeline for the flight crew and latched right on to Paul's rollerbag arm. "You're the pilot?" she said breathlessly.

He was "a" pilot. No doubt she was trying to determine if he was the Captain, and couldn't tell from their stripes that Kaye Lehr outranked him. And no doubt the passenger had assumed Paul, despite being far too young, was the senior officer because he was the only Caucasian male. Captain Lehr didn't break stride, though Dallas did slow a bit, spreading their tight walking formation into more of a drawn-out line.

"I'm flying the plane," Paul told the woman. It seemed easier than trying to explain seniority and rank in the few moments he had before boarding.

It was a good enough explanation for woman in the patriotic T-shirt. She nodded, then said, "So we're flying *around* the Bermuda Triangle, right?"

Paul caught himself before he laughed out loud, directly in the woman's earnest face. Barely. "There's really no such thing." He did his best not to sound condescending, but it was hard. Damn hard. "There is no 'triangle,' it's just a term someone used in a magazine article in the 1960's to describe the waters off the east coast of Florida."

"But everyone knows—"

"Besides, there's not really any other way to get to Bermuda from the States…unless you want to travel there by way of Japan." The woman looked at Paul blankly. People's grasp of geography never failed to disappoint him. "That would add about twenty hours to your flight and two thousand dollars to your ticket cost. Not to mention the environmental impact. So you can see why plenty of people fly over this particular stretch of the Atlantic Ocean every day. Despite the ominous nickname."

The woman didn't seem particularly appeased, but Paul had a cockpit to inspect. He caught up with Dallas and whispered, "This is your regular flight? You're the one dealing with the passengers. I'll bet you get that question every day."

"Just tell 'em what they want to hear," Dallas said softly. "They don't know any different. Put their minds at ease."

The gate agent did a double-take at Paul as the flight crew approached the skybridge. "Where's Marlin?" she asked none of them in particular.

"Marlin won't be flying with us today," the Captain said. She yanked her rollerbag over the ramp with more force than she'd needed. Paul couldn't tell if that meant she was angry about something. He didn't know her well enough. If she was angry…was it the passenger presuming Paul was the Captain? This Marlin guy's absenteeism? Her typical state of being?

No idea.

As long as she was professional enough to not let her annoyance affect her flight, it didn't much matter to Paul. And Captain Lehr did strike him as a consummate professional. They took their places in the cramped cockpit while Dallas prepared the tiny 37-seat cabin, which would shortly be about three-quarters full. Captain Lehr ran through the systems checks (multiple times, Paul noted) and his trepidation over the Captain's unenthused reception of him on her "regularly scheduled" flight receded. He'd never seen a commercial pilot check, triple-check and quadruple-check the equipment to this extent.

Maybe she had OCD. He supposed it wouldn't be a bad characteristic for a pilot to have.

Since Captain Lehr didn't make any small talk, Paul checked his own systems again.

All clear.

Soon Flight 511 was boarded, the stairs pulled up, doors locked, and Dallas was broadcasting the emergency instructions in his gently-southern, gently-black, gently-gay cadence—cool and unflappable and completely in charge, and the sound of his voice over the plane's speakers as he pointed out the emergency exits made Paul squirm a bit in his seat…and then the realization that he was wearing Dallas' trousers made him squirm a bit more. But mostly on the inside. Because he didn't want Captain Lehr to think he was incontinent.

They taxied to the runway, awaited the tower's instructions, and soon they were hurtling forward, ninety, one hundred, one hundred twenty knots. And then Captain Lehr eased back her yoke…and they were ascending.

Nothing unusual whatsoever.

The ascent and descent of an aircraft were the critical times at which most errors occurred. There was even a rule in force—the Sterile Cockpit rule—that dictated absolutely no business non-essential to flying the aircraft could happen during these critical times. Not even stray conversation.

Paul had never seen anyone observe the Sterile Cockpit as fastidiously as Captain Lehr.

Funny, Paul had always thought that on the scale of uptightness, he was about as high as it was possible to be, owing to the fact that he was a gay man among a world of macho jerks all waiting for him to fail. Maybe that had been Captain Lehr's attitude once, when she was Paul's age. Look what she'd become now. Maybe it was time to loosen up.

Although…Paul really couldn't see himself chatting about his hobbies or playing Angry Birds on his phone while he was supposed to be flying his aircraft. It simply didn't make any sense to him. By the time they reached cruising altitude and the Captain switched off the seatbelt signs, Paul had decided that while she wasn't exactly the most affable Captain to fly under, Captain Lehr might not be a bad match for him after all.

They cruised well above cloud cover. Winds were moderate. Normally, the Captain would have told Paul to activate the autopilot by now, but instead, Captain Lehr said, "Monitor the weather." Paul tuned his headset to the weather band—and conditions were exactly the same as they had been during the flight plan. What about autopilot? Should he wait for her command to activate it? Or should he ask? She and her absent First Officer no doubt had it all down to a routine. Maybe that was the only reason she hadn't told Paul to do it. He hoped that was the reason, anyway, and not some sort of test. If it was, he wasn't about to blow it by presuming. "Autopilot?" he asked, hoping that his tone hadn't come across as critical.

Captain Lehr didn't seem particularly offended, but she responded with, "It's only an eighty-five minute flight."

"Oh, it's just…well, that's…."

Weird, was what it was.

Better not to question her. Chances were after tomorrow's return flight, he'd never work with her again, anyway. Paul continued to listen to the weather band, all clear, and re-checked all his gauges yet again. Only this time, with his internal sensors more finely attuned to spotting anything out of the ordinary, his eyes landed on the fuel gauge. The completely full fuel gauge.

A full tank? For a partially-empty flight that the Captain deemed too short for autopilot? How had she managed to talk Operations into that?

Jet fuel was heavy, and it made no sense to haul all that weight to Bermuda and back when they could top off on the island, especially since they had fourteen hours to turn the flight around. Normally, Paul would have asked. But Captain Lehr's stony silence, her extended Sterile Cockpit, didn't exactly encourage a Q&A session. Instead, he settled himself in for a silent trip, listened again to the clear and uneventful weather droning by on the weather band, and re-checked his gauges.

The sound of the Captain's voice, when she finally spoke, made him jump. "You strike me as a very by-the-book kind of pilot," she told him.

The exact thing he'd thought of her. He couldn't tell what she meant by it, though coming from her, it was probably a compliment. "I guess you could say that."

"You're just a kid. How old are you?"

"Thirty-seven—but I've been flying since I was nineteen." He'd landed his first commercial post as a navigator at twenty-three, and his first FO flight at thirty. Very young. He was consistent, and had a great eye for detail. Such as the dot he'd spotted this morning. And the brimmingly full fuel tank now.

It seemed as if Captain Lehr would follow up with something that would indicate why she'd asked. A question. Another statement. Anything. But she didn't. She only nudged the yoke as the altitude dipped, and gazed straight ahead.

Was Paul supposed to ask something of her? It didn't seem so.

Sterile Cockpit. Fine.

Airspeed, altimeter, oil pressure, vacuum gauge, everything was fine. He settled himself back and looked out into the blue expanse of sky, and pushed the thoughts of the Captain from his mind...because now they were landing in less than half an hour, which meant an hour from now, they could feasibly be at the hotel. Him. And Dallas. In their hotel room. Alone.

Paul could hardly wait.

He was in the midst of trying to come up with a funny line about the slacks he could joke about that would sound spontaneous (although it would be impossible to outdo the off-the-cuff remark Dallas made back in the restroom) when Captain Lehr said, "Would you say you're a man of science, or a man of faith?"

Oh crap, she's some kind of religious nut...and she's going to try to convert me. "Science. Definitely science."

"There's a lot of that in aviation. Pilots, from military backgrounds, or mechanical, or engineering. There's a lot to consider. A lot of science."

How long until Sterile Cockpit would technically be in force again? Another ten minutes or so. Paul decided if he just sat there for those ten minutes, if he didn't encourage her, he wouldn't need to listen to anything about how he needed to be saved—because people like that thought he'd burn in hell anyway for the eager thoughts he was having about Dallas.

So there was no sense in enduring the whole "saving" thing if he had no intention of flying on the straight and narrow. So to speak.

He turned his thoughts back to the weather band.

All clear.

A minute went by...several minutes...almost time to begin their descent. Captain Lehr lit the seatbelt sign, and Paul realized he was practically in the clear—because no one would start trying to ram Jesus down his throat in just a couple of minutes. If that had been the Captain's plan, she would have started right off the Florida coast. Paul let his shoulders relax, until Captain Lehr switched to intercom and said, "Mr. Turner... report to the cockpit."

She wanted coffee? Now?

Dallas' voice came over the intercom, "Right here, Captain," and Captain Lehr buzzed open the lock. Dallas stepped into the cockpit—Paul didn't know him well enough to read his expression, but it looked nothing like the casual, bantery vibe that a crew who worked together regularly might share. "What did you decide?" he said.

The Captain said, "He should stay with you."

What the hell was this about? The hotel?

One thing was for sure. They were obviously referring to him. Paul cleared his throat nervously. Dallas leaned over his shoulder, crooked a finger, and said, "Paul? Come with me for a sec."

Paul looked at Dallas, and then back at the directional gyro. "But we need to start our descent."

"I know." Dallas' voice sent a course of shivers up Paul's arms and down the back of his spine. Soft, yet sure. Soothing. Profoundly confident. "That's why you've got to come with me."

Paul looked to Captain Lehr—because no doubt this was some sort of joke. The first day of a flight attendant's duty, a new FA could expect a series of bizarre requests from the cockpit, all in good fun. Or air sickness bags full of Chunky Soup if the cockpit crew was a bit more cruel. Flight 511's crew seemed like a close bunch, despite the Captain's reserved personality. Paul was being hazed. Yes. He was sure of it.

"Okay guys," he said, "very funny, but we're landing in a few minutes."

Dallas and the Captain stared at each other intently. Neither of them was smiling. "If he's got his heart set on it," Dallas said, "maybe he needs to stay."

The Captain shook her head, and said, "It wouldn't be right. Get him into the cabin and—"

"Hel-lo," Paul blurted out, sounding as out-and-proud in his exasperation as if he'd caught that cheapskate Dennis the Dentist trying to weasel out of buying his round of martinis. "The 'he' you're referring to is right here. And 'he' doesn't find this at all amusing."

The other two crew members, stunned into silence by his outburst, turned to appraise him. Dallas raised his eyebrows very high. The Captain shook her head, then pulled her briefcase onto her lap. "Believe me, baby," Dallas said, falling into a less formal pattern of speech himself, "don't none of us."

The Captain said nothing. She simply pulled an object out of her briefcase and slammed it down in the center of the instrument panel, hard.

It was a hula girl. With a compass in her belly and a suction cup base.

While Paul stared, the hula girl's grass skirt twitched from the vibration of the aircraft while her upper torso, with its molded ukulele, tipped side to side.

"I'm serious," Dallas said to Paul. "Come back in the cabin with me. Only for a few minutes. Please."

The Captain began to speak, saying, "I recommend you—" but then she paused to listen to something she was picking up from Lauderdale's control tower, tuned her headset to a private channel and said, "This is Captain Lehr."

While she was occupied, Dallas checked his watch, then leaned in and put his hand on Paul's forearm, stroking it with is thumb, and said to him privately, "This is no joke. Can't you trust me? For just this one thing?"

Couldn't he? Dallas looked incredibly serious—and hadn't Paul been about to take a fairly big chance with him? Still, putting his heart out there on the line wasn't the same as toying with the lives of thirty-two passengers. "At least tell me what it's all about."

"There is no short version," Dallas said. "You just got to have faith."

Paul's professional instincts told him the same thing they were telling him when he grounded his morning's flight: that he was the one responsible for everyone's safety. Him. And yet his personal instincts told him that Dallas had such trustworthy eyes….

"Change of plans," Captain Lehr said abruptly. "He stays."

CHAPTER 4

"You're keeping him in the cockpit?" Dallas snapped. "Are you sure?" He wanted to grab that woman and shake some sense into her—and if she wasn't busy steering the damn plane, he would have been sorely tempted.

Kaye looked away from the instrument panel, which would begin its nonsense any minute now, and she met Dallas' gaze, and held it. "Marlin is gone," she said. "And so...we need Paul to stay."

"Gone?" Dallas repeated. "What do you mean, gone?" Maybe he quit... but that thought didn't ring true. He'd be the last to quit Flight 511. "Gone, as in...well...gone, how?"

Kaye checked her watch, sighed, and said, "Dead."

The aircraft shuddered—the first pocket of turbulence—and Dallas looked at the instrument panel...and then the fuel gauge began rotating toward empty as if someone had peeled open the tank and left the fuel to stream out behind them in an oily, golden ribbon.

And so it began. "How much did you tell him?" Dallas said.

"Nothing," Kaye said, very calmly. Or maybe it was resignation. "I was planning on sending him into the cabin with you."

Paul was watching the instrument panel in horror as the artificial horizon began a lazy rotation like a stopwatch, as if they were flying in a corkscrew, and the accelerometer showed they were traveling at 40 knots. And then 180 knots. And then that they were stopped.

He changed channels in an attempt to contact the tower. "Bermuda ground, this is Flight 511 in system failure, request emergency landing." Static. Dallas wasn't wearing a headset—he just knew what Paul would be hearing. Because the foolishness never varied. "Bermuda?"

The electrical compass started to spin. Right on cue.

"Fort Lauderdale, do you read, this is Flight 511…mayday…."

Dallas shook his head. *Lord, maybe you could find it in your heart to go easy on us, just this once.* I'm *not asking for myself….*

Then the second pocket of turbulence, one that nearly threw Dallas off his feet. At this point in the flight, he'd usually be telling the passengers not to mind the bumpy ride, it was perfectly normal, and they'd be landing at Wade International Airport in just a few minutes. Then he'd strap himself down for the next big bump.

"Go on," Kaye told him. "I'll handle this."

Was there even time? Barely. But…Paul. There that poor man was, scrambling to save the craft that looked as if it was fixing to drop right out of the sky. Marlin always said it spooked him, even though he knew how it was all gonna go down.

Marlin. Who was dead. "What happened to Marlin?" he asked Kaye, while Paul searched frantically for a clear channel.

"They didn't say."

Dallas couldn't have said specifically why, since Kaye was about as easy to read as a paperback that had been left out in the rain, but he was positive she knew. Hopefully the passengers had paid attention to the "fasten seatbelt" sign…and if they didn't, he'd deal with it in a few minutes. Seeing as how he was in the cockpit now, he might not know exactly how he would ultimately handle the cabin situation. But he *should* be up to the task. He always was. He folded down the cramped little cockpit jumpseat and strapped himself in. Kaye noticed him deciding to stick around, but she didn't try to stop him.

He twisted around and settled his hand on Paul's shoulder—poor thing was shaking like a leaf—and said, "Relax, baby, it'll all work out."

Hard to say if Paul heard Dallas or not. He was still combing the airwaves, looking for someone, anyone, to help them. The sight of his panic was heartbreaking. Had Dallas ever been so earnest and naive? He must have. But now he felt like a wad of gristle and bone, bitten off, chewed up and spit out. "It's happened before," he told Paul.

It sounded better than, *it always happens.*

A light appeared on the horizon, small, but growing brighter, and the next big pocket of turbulence hit—exactly when it always did—and then Flight 511 hurtled into the crystalline moment of stillness where everything changed.

***

The electronic fuel gauge was first to come back online, followed by the accelerometer, and then the altimeter. Despite the system failure, Paul was relieved to see, they were still cruising within a hundred feet of their target altitude, toward the exact heading indicated on their flight plan. The radio, however, still played nothing but static. As he scoured the dial for a working channel, he realized he heard his own name. And that he'd been hearing it, in some corner in his mind, for several moments.

"Paul, come on, now. Just relax. You're fine. Everything's fine."

Paul chanced a quick look over his shoulder. Dallas had unfastened himself from his jumpseat and now stood with one hand on Paul's shoulder—working it with gentle squeezes that only registered once Paul saw his hand, there, doing the squeezing.

"Keep following the flight plan," Captain Lehr said—Paul could hear her voice through his headset clearly, so he knew it wasn't the headphones to blame for all the static. "Mr. Cronin? Stop messing with the radio. Now. That's an order."

Paul's hand fell from the radio dial, numb.

"I'll need all your focus for our descent." She turned to Dallas and said, "prepare for landing."

Dallas gave Paul's shoulder a final reassuring squeeze, and said, "It'll be okay," then turned and exited the cockpit.

Paul swallowed, looked at the useless radio dial longingly, and said, "What's going on?"

"Concentrate on landing the plane according to Visual Flight Rules," the Captain said. "There'll be plenty of time after that to work everything out." She then muttered something that sounded a lot like, "Not that you can expect it to make any sense."

Paul scanned the sky, left and right, up and down, but despite their proximity to the airport, there wasn't another aircraft in sight.

"Begin descent," the Captain said.

Winds were moderate. Descent was normal. But the quiet from the towers was deafening.

"Landing gear," the Captain prompted. They approached the runway, slowed, and touched down with a practiced bump. Paul's heart pounded in his throat as they taxied to the gate, beating so hard it felt like it would burst right out of him. It was worse than his first solo flight—or even his first excursion on the Beltway in a geriatric Buick Skylark with a wire hanger for an antenna and a hole in the passenger floor where the puddles splashed through. They slowed, and stopped, and the Captain reached up and flicked off the Fasten Seatbelt sign, and said through 511's intercom, "I hope you've figured out what to tell him, Dallas, 'cos I'll be damned if I know what to say."

Paul slid off his useless headphones, blinked, and said, "Captain?"

There was a rap on the cockpit door and the Captain buzzed it open. Dallas slipped into the cramped cockpit and held out his hand to Paul. "Come on, take a look."

"Don't you need to…deal with the…?"

Dallas gave Paul a look so unflinching, the questions all died away. Paul unfastened his seatbelt, took the FA's hand and followed him into the cabin…

…which was completely empty.

"You unloaded the…how did you…?" Paul saw a magazine face-down on one seat, a woman's purse with a plastic bag full of celery sticks and baby carrots beside it on the other. "The stairs are still up…."

As if the thirty-two passengers of Flight 511 had simply disappeared.

Dallas was gripping Paul by the upper arm, hard. "You okay? You need to sit down?" Paul nodded his head, then shook it, then got confused and nodded it again. "Get us some air," Dallas said, mostly to himself, as he switched the actuator and powered open the door. Paul squinted out over the stairs. Tarmac, sunshine and sky.

But no engines. Aside from the shrill of gulls, it was as quiet out there in the airport as the useless radio.

"Where are the passengers?" Paul shouldered Dallas out of the way. Before he even asked if it was safe, he found himself down the stairs and out on the tarmac, turning in a slow circle in an attempt to spot someone, anyone, any living soul other than himself. "Where is everybody?"

Dallas approached, and slipped an arm around Paul's waist and stopped him from turning in his useless circles. "None of us have any idea." He gave Paul a squeeze, which Paul sort-of felt, distantly. "You're a smart man. You've got a fresh set of eyes. Maybe you'll be the one to finally figure it all out."

Paul scanned the distance. There were other aircraft by some of the gates, and in the distance, vehicles in the parking lot. But no planes in the sky, and no cars on the road. Everything was still. Quiet. Empty. Aside from Captain Lehr, who hadn't even stepped out of the aircraft, Paul and Dallas were completely, utterly, profoundly alone—which Paul had been eagerly anticipating all the way to Bermuda.

But, damn. Not like this.

CHAPTER 5

-ONE YEAR AGO-

Airsickness was part of a flight attendant's job. Hearing it, smelling it, cleaning it up—in short, *dealing* with it. On a good flight, an FA could talk a passenger down from the brink just as they started looking woozy with some distracting chitchat and a cool glass of seltzer. Unfortunately, by the time most passengers knew they were fixing to toss their cookies, the most Dallas could hope for was that they'd manage to pry the airsickness bag from the seat-back pocket in time.

And then there were flights like today's. Not just puke, but Monday morning Goldschlager puke from a weekend bachelorette excursion gone long, enveloping the cabin with its pungent cinnamon-alcohol-bile odor, its metallic flecks glinting cheerfully from the molded plastic seat frame, and the nubby carpeting...and the hair of the passenger in the preceding row.

How the girl had managed to projectile vomit so accurately was beyond him.

It was a full flight too, and there was nowhere to stow either the ralpher or the ralphee while Dallas donned his latex gloves and swabbed up the malodorous mess the best he could, and did his damnedest to sweep the whole unfortunate incident under the carpet, gold flecks and all. A second round of soda can only go so far in taming the savage beast. Despite Dallas' best everything'll-be-just-fine tone of voice and a free upgrade for the next flight of the passenger who'd borne the brunt of the accident, by the time the 747 set down in O'Hare, he was just about ready to head home to Fort Lauderdale, hang up his wings, and go fill out an application at the post office.

Even worse, if the whole thing had happened just two rows higher, it would have been that smug little bottle-blonde FA from Chicago dealing with the cleanup. She didn't even offer to hold up the garbage bag. No, Lady Clairol acted as if the whole gold-spewing incident had never happened at all—that it was as far beyond her ice-cool, WASP-y notice as overcrowded homeless shelters or global warming. But it was the strange, tight-lipped smile she gave Dallas as the two of them deplaned that really put it over the top.

It was barely one o'clock in the afternoon, and already Dallas needed himself a good, stiff drink.

Not Goldschlager, though. Anything but that.

He didn't keep alcohol in the house, not with a teenage niece smart enough to sniff out any hiding place he might come up with, but there was an Italian restaurant that served beer and wine within walking distance of his house. Not the most economical way to drown his sorrows, and very little chance of cruising anyone, either.

Which was just as well, considering he'd be lucky if he made it back to Florida by three, and that niece would be home by four.

Speaking of whom…Dallas turned on his phone, and a string of texts from his pride and joy (otherwise known as Chantal) scrolled past.

```
i will b the skankiest beyotch at prom
in my 100 dollar gown
probly get knocked up
cos i look so cheap
```

Yes, Chantal's world would come to an end when she greeted her date in a pink polyester rag. Never mind that she was so cute she could wrap herself in a garbage bag and make it look couture. Never mind that the boy would be so busy staring at her chest it wouldn't occur to him to think of what the dress cost, not until she complained about it. And never mind that Dallas was also shelling out three hundred dollars for a limo and another fifty for a boutonniere. No, never mind those things. The point was, he'd fixed the budget back in January, when Miss Thang could have scared up a little part-time work of her own if her heart was well and truly set on blowing five hundred dollars on a dress she'd wear for all of one single night.

Dallas had just replied with "u will b gor-juss" when he was startled by the distinctive sound of carry-on luggage thwapping against a coach seat. He looked up and found a passenger struggling down the aisle. Where on God's green earth had this woman come from? This plane should be empty. Not only had that useless FA from Chicago avoided helping Dallas clean up the glittery barf, but she'd failed to count the passengers as they deplaned, just taken off…probably halfway home already. Normally Dallas kept himself to himself, but this flight attendant's level of negligence was enough to make even him give some serious thought to placing a few very stern phone calls.

Dallas angled himself up the aisle to meet the passenger halfway. Hopefully she hadn't been in the restroom during the descent—not that there was anything to be done for it now. And not that the rear of the cabin had been his responsibility. Still, this passenger (maybe in her 50's, maybe 60's, hard to tell with white ladies in crispy teased hair and coral-colored lipstick) was none too steady on her feet. She could have been hurt in there. Whether she was in his section or not, a close call of that nature was simply unacceptable.

"Here, now, let me help you get that." She smiled sweetly as he took the carry-on from her and the bag dipped low. Totally over the weight limit. What the heck was she transporting, bowling balls? "Watch that spot there." He indicated traces of glitter-vomit with his elbow. "Someone had a rough flight."

He maneuvered the luggage to the front of the plane, then angled himself in the entrance of the skybridge to hand it off to the woman again (who was clearly hiding a very well-developed set of muscles beneath her baggy *I Love My Pomeranian* sweatshirt. He held out the carry-on—very *large* bowling balls—and said, "Y'all enjoy the rest of your day."

As her coral-nailed fingers closed around the bag, his phone chimed.

Dallas smiled guiltily. He wouldn't dream of checking his messages while he was attending to the passengers, but how was he to know Bowling Ball Lady was still in the cabin?

"Family?" the lady said.

"I must have a look on my face. One that says I'm being extorted for a prom dress worth a month's rent."

"Would you give it to her? If you could?"

He was just about to claim that of course he would, and send the lady on her way—but the words simply didn't come. They were too glib. And, in fact, he wasn't even sure they were true.

It wasn't about the dress. Chantal was eighteen. Fresh-faced, and even innocent, in a way it seemed Dallas and his sister had never been...probably because she'd grown up with an actual parent. That parent might have been her gay uncle who was overnighting in Fargo or Newark or Lincoln as often as not, but as long as he harped on curfew and vetted the boyfriends and scowled when her report card showed anything less than a B, it was a hell of a lot more of a parent than he'd ever known.

Dallas had given Chantal far more than a dress. He'd given her a life that his addict sister never could. And if there were five hundred extra dollars lying around just begging to be spent? "I'd take that money and put it in her college fund. Books, meals, laptop. It's all going to add up."

It was more of an answer than he'd intended to give this total stranger, but it seemed to be the right answer. She broke into a broad smile and patted his arm (though Dallas had no idea how she could hold up her bag with only one hand). "It's not about giving them *things*, is it? It's about being there for them."

Which Dallas so often was not. "To tell the truth, I wish I was there more. My schedule's all over the place."

"You might not be there physically. Emotionally, though...." The passenger took a step onto the skybridge, then paused and fished a pair of clip-on sunglasses out of her pocket and snapped them onto her prescription eyeglass frames. They stuck straight out like a visor. "That's what counts."

Maybe so…but Dallas would have preferred to see Chantal more than a couple of times a week—and not just to keep tabs on her. It seemed like only yesterday she was a surly ten-year-old who needed extensive orthodontia. Now she was a determined young lady who'd be heading off to college in the fall. "They grow up fast," he said. While that might have been a cliché, it came from the bottom of his heart.

The passenger paused and cocked her head, and gave him a look that cut right through him, and despite her Pomeranian shirt and culottes and clip-on shades, she suddenly seemed anything but silly. "You take amazing care of her…because that's what you do."

His phone chimed again as another text came in. He glanced down at it and considered shutting it off, but by the time he looked up again to see if the passenger needed anything else, she was halfway down the skybridge. He shrugged and checked his message. Scheduling, asking if he was up for one more flight, a simple overnighter from Fort Lauderdale to Bermuda and back again.

It had been three days now since he'd seen Chantal, but he was heading back to Florida anyway, and at least this assignment would leave him on his home turf. With the extra hours he'd rack up, he might be inclined to raise the dress budget to two hundred. True, she hadn't kicked in toward that budget herself, and he didn't want to spoil her…but even two hundred dollars wouldn't buy much of a dress. And you only did have one Senior prom.

Dallas thumbed in a quick acceptance, then retrieved his rollerbag and headed for the crew lounge. He needed to ensure all traces of his misadventures with partially-digested Goldschlager were gone before he made his way across the terminal to his Fort Lauderdale connection with Flight 511.

-PRESENT DAY-

In the distance, a clock tower struck two. Paul turned toward the sound and gazed across the empty tarmac as if surely he'd find evidence of some other person there, someone besides the three members of the flight crew. Not that it was logical to think a clock needed a human presence to chime. But logic seemed profoundly useless at that very moment.

"Come sit down," Dallas said in his velvety voice, but Paul paid no attention. Dry palms rustled as a light wind kicked up, and a shorebird behind the hangar called, answered by a similar call out toward the parking lot. Dallas held Paul's sleeve for a moment, then eventually dropped it, and sat down himself on the aircraft's steps.

Paul did another visual sweep of the empty hangar, empty taxi lane, empty lot, empty airport, then settled finally on Dallas, who was loosening his tie. The Captain stood above him inside the craft, arms crossed, leaning against the oval doorway.

Both of them looked very tired.

"You knew about this?" Paul demanded. He couldn't have even said of whom. Either of them. Both of them. Captain Lehr, who'd held not only Paul's life, but the lives of all the passengers in her hand. And Dallas, who'd been starring in a mental audition for boyfriend-material all the way to Wade International. "How could you not tell me?"

"If I'd had half a chance, I would have." Dallas unbuttoned the top two buttons on his shirt and blotted his forehead with the end of his loose tie. "Besides, some things you just got to see with your own eyes."

Maybe so. Still, some kind of heads-up would have been helpful. "You didn't even try."

"I thought you were a sub," the Captain said. "What good would it have done to burden you with the whole situation if you were just a fill-in?"

Logical, maybe. Even humane. But then a chill danced across the back of Paul's neck as potential ramifications of her line of reasoning occurred to him. "What are you saying—you think I'm his replacement?"

Dallas glanced over his shoulder at the Captain, who shifted uneasily.

When neither answered, Paul said, "His *permanent* replacement?"

Dallas pinched the bridge of his nose and said, "Dear Lord."

Paul turned on his heel and began to walk. Long strides, nearly a run, but stiffer and angrier than any run could manage to be. "Let him go," he heard the Captain tell Dallas. "Give him some space."

"Don't go eating anything," Dallas called after him—as if he could even stand to look at food. Especially this food. Here.

He strode straight to the staff entrance and found it unlocked. Quietly, he let himself in to the baggage area and looked around. The conveyor belts whirred, hollow and industrial-sounding in the concrete and steel rooms. Flight 511's conveyor belt was empty, of course. (Was the flight's luggage even there? Probably, since the carry-ons were. But who would unload the aircraft? And why even bother, if there were no passengers present to collect their luggage?)

Parcels and suitcases from another flight were log-jammed into the exit chute. Which would mean there were no baggage handlers present to clear away the blockage.

But there had been ground crew present at some point in the recent past to unload the cargo that was now rocking at the end of the still-running belt. Paul reached over and turned the conveyor off, and the wheeze of its stopping echoed sharply in the sudden silence.

He considered yelling "Hello?" but just couldn't bring himself to do it. He wasn't in the habit of announcing he didn't know what was going on... even though it was painfully obvious he didn't have the first clue. Instead of shouting, calling attention to himself, or kicking up a big ruckus, he decided to simply look.

He made his way from one end of the airport to the other. Wade International was small, minuscule compared to LAX and LaGuardia and O'Hare. Bermuda itself was only a mile wide and barely twenty long. It couldn't support anything larger. While Paul didn't cover much physical distance, he was thorough—excruciatingly so—wedging open doors with garbage cans or backpacks or whatever else was close at hand as he went along, so he didn't find himself locked in anywhere he'd never be discovered.

Empty ticket counter. Empty concession stand. Food? Yes—prepackaged salads and sandwiches, cookies and bagels, bottles of soda and juice and water. Completely unappetizing. Outside, an empty hotel shuttle at the curb, rear door open, luggage sitting on the blacktop half-loaded. Paul opened the driver-side door and turned the key, fully expecting to hear a dead click. Instead, the engine started. Machinery worked, then. Electric, gasoline. He checked his watch—almost two, and his heart stuttered as he wondered if maybe he was caught in a frozen moment... but then he realized his watch was still set to Eastern time, not Atlantic. And he probably had been combing through the airport for just about an hour. As he considered this, the distant bell tower chimed three. They weren't in some strange time-vacuum where combustion engines stopped functioning and the earth's rotation had stilled, then.

They were simply alone.

He strode through the cargo terminal. A forklift sat in the middle of the floor, pallet aloft, engine idling. The crew lounge was deserted, and though the televisions were on, they played only static. He walked past security and customs and out through the arrival doors, then picked his way through the parking lot. At the far end, the control tower was locked with a magnetic card-reader, but a badge on a lanyard lay in the grass not a yard away. Even so, Paul felt no urge to go look. Since no one from air traffic control had assisted them in landing, he doubted he'd find anyone inside. He circled the taxi lane until he approached the gates from the opposite side. Wade's terminal buildings were outdated. There were no skybridges; the aircraft were accessed by ramp instead. As he passed a larger craft sitting silent and empty against its rolling stairs, he wondered what they would have done if their 135 didn't carry its stairs in its door, with no ground crew to roll up the ramp. Taxi around the tarmac, chasing a rolling ramp? Or simply deploy the emergency slides?

Or maybe sit there in the cockpit, close their eyes, and wish that everything would somehow become normal again?

He made a full circuit of the airport buildings, and then found himself heading back to the place he'd started. As he neared, he picked out Dallas first, sitting on the aircraft stairs. Dallas turned his head to say something, and only then did Paul spot the Captain lying in the aisle. Paul gathered himself to run back to the plane and see if everything was okay, until he analyzed the aircrew's posture and realized that the Captain was just having herself a little rest.

Which really pissed him off, infinitely more than the sniggering ground crew back in Fort Lauderdale had.

Paul stopped far enough away that Dallas and the Captain would need to raise their voices to speak to him, planted his feet wide, and demanded, "What happened to the people?"

Dallas and the Captain exchanged a look. Paul clamped his lips together tight to keep from saying anything he'd regret since the three of them appeared to be stuck with one another.

After their lengthy, wordless communique, Dallas turned back and told Paul, "They're not gone. We are."

Yes. Okay. For whatever reason, the thought of three people disappearing felt more plausible to Paul than seven-odd billion minus three simply ceasing to be. And though the logic was flawed, it was still a comfort. Until he then wondered, "But if the crew disappeared and the people didn't…what happened to the plane?" Although the plane was obviously there—Dallas and the Captain were currently lounging in its doorway. "Did thirty-two passengers just find themselves sitting on nothing, then tumbling into the ocean?"

The Captain tucked her arm beneath her head and looked up at the cabin ceiling. Only her head and arm showed in the door of the craft. "Those passengers will be fine," she said wearily. "They're all sipping mojitos at their hotel bar by now, or booking their snorkeling expeditions, or trying to figure out how much to tip their bellhops. We landed that plane, Mr. Cronin."

"God willing," Dallas murmured.

"We must have," the Captain said, "because I always do."

"You landed the aircraft," Paul said carefully, unsure where following the branches of too many ramifications might lead him, "and yet…you're here." Or maybe they were all dreaming. Or experiencing some elaborate practical joke. Or dead. "Aren't you?"

"Part of us is here," Dallas explained, "in this place. But enough of you stayed behind to land the plane."

While Paul wouldn't dream of entertaining the notion that he'd been somehow bifurcated, the other two crew members seemed awfully certain. "Let's say I buy the fact that part of me is here, and part of me is there." Even as he said it, terms like "here" and "there" felt inaccurate…since both of them must be referring to the same physical location. "Am I two people now? One who thinks everything's normal, and another who lives on an empty island for the rest of his life?"

Captain Lehr gazed up at the cabin ceiling as if she could draw strength from the fiberglass. "It's not like that. We do the flight as scheduled, and somewhere on the return trip, we get put back together."

"But for all we know, it might go down like that," Dallas patted the stairs, "if something happened to the plane. If a storm kicked up and kept us grounded. If the two of you flat-out decided you weren't flying back."

Paul ignored the invitation to sit. "Why would we do that?"

Dallas took a good, long look at Paul. "I've only known you a few hours—in other words, I don't hardly know you from Adam. Who's to say how you handle yourself under pressure?"

CHAPTER 6

-ONE YEAR AGO-

Dallas checked a young lady's boarding pass and pointed out her seat. Not that he thought she was incapable of counting. Just that people who didn't fly for a living tended to be a bit travel-dazed by the time they crossed his path. A few of today's passengers seemed well-rested, probably those who'd just spent a week lounging on pink sand beaches. Others, who'd been snorkeling or sailing or roaming through the streets of St. George's, looked like they needed a few days' vacation to recover from their vacations. Dallas himself had experienced quite the overnight; he'd needed to let out an extra hole on his belt that morning. While Kaye Lehr had seemed all business during the previous day's pre-flight meeting and even the flight itself, once the Captain's stripes came off, she was a party animal.

At first Dallas had worried he was being wined and dined in some sort of seduction ploy. But as Kaye refilled his wine glass for the fourth time, his tongue had loosened enough for him to come right out and say, "You realize I'm gay, don't you?"

She just laughed. "You and almost every other male FA I've met." Then she topped off her own glass and called for the dessert menu. Normally the company of the First Officer would have made their overnight stay less of a pseudo-date and more of a group excursion…but Marlin Fritsch had bolted from the commuter jet before even the passengers deplaned, then rolled back in the next morning right before his pre-flight check—with tangled hair, a day's worth of stubble and a killer sunburn. That man had missed out on one hell of a meal. Baby greens. Coconut rice. Rum cake. Lobster. And lots and lots of wine.

Between the two bottles of Riesling the Captain had put away and his sneaking suspicion that the First Officer hadn't got himself a single wink of sleep, Dallas was tempted to fold his hands and petition for his safe return to Fort Lauderdale. But since he'd striven to be the type of man who wasn't begging the Lord for favors every time he turned his eyes skyward, he settled for simply crossing his fingers and hoping that between the two of them they could manage to get everyone back to the States in one piece.

The flight was mostly full, and Dallas, the only FA, had plenty of duties to keep him occupied. Now that airlines were charging for checked bags, people carried on more and more luggage these days, and forcing it all into the overhead bins had become something of an art form. Once the luggage was all stowed, he'd called out those passengers who'd reclined their seats against his instructions not to, since no renegade reclining would be allowed on his watch (ditto unauthorized electronic usage) and finally, he closed the doors and began his safety lecture. The fasten seat-belt sign came on, Dallas buckled himself into the galley jumpseat, and soon he felt the shudder of the landing gear folding up and the swooping stomach-freefall sensation of their ascent.

As the ascent leveled out, the cabin speakers crackled to life. "Gooood morning, ladies and gentlemen. This is First Officer Marlin. I'd like to welcome you aboard Flight 511 with nonstop service from Bermuda to Fort Lauderdale—which is a good thing, given there's nowhere *to* stop… unless you want to see the manatees up-close and personal."

Dallas rolled his eyes.

"Captain Kaye has assured me this will be a smooth flight, so let's turn off that fasten-seatbelt sign."

Ding.

"Aaaand now you're free to move about the cabin. And fire up your iPads. And flirt with the person in the seat next to you. Maybe you came to Bermuda with them. Maybe you didn't. But, hey, I'm not one to judge…."

Oh, please. Just shut your mouth and do your damn job. Dallas hated it when pilots started hamming it up the moment they had a captive audience in the sky. He'd never met one who wouldn't be better off leaving the jokes to the stand-up comedians. Joking about crashing the plane, though? That went way beyond bad taste. And then trying to act all sexy with the passengers? Even worse.

"You'll notice the no-smoking sign is lit. Per FAA regulations, it will remain on during the entire flight. Tampering with the smoke detector in the restroom would be seriously uncool. But if you're curious about joining the Mile High Club, that's about the only place you'll get away with it..."

Was it possible to sexually harass the passengers via the PA system? This line of banter was crossing from poor taste to dangerous. Dallas unbuckled, stood up, and readied his beverage cart—and his most blandly professional face. If he were the Captain, he'd give that First Officer a good smack and tell him to shut the hell up before he found himself on the ugly end of a big ol' customer complaint. Once the service cart was wrestled into position and the first pot of coffee had brewed, Dallas stepped out from behind the curtain and lavished a broad smile on the passengers—a smile that attempted to convey that nothing at all was amiss.

A few did seem to be listening to Marlin. Their expressions looked more puzzled than offended, though. Maybe they didn't fly often enough to know that most pilots gave the flight time, cruising altitude and weather, and spared everyone the off-color jokes. Toward the rear of the cabin, a passenger stood and headed for the restroom. Just as she closed the door, it occurred to Dallas it looked a hell of a lot like the woman he'd chatted with on the skybridge the day before. But that wouldn't make much sense. That was Chicago. This was Bermuda.

"Looks like the weather in Fort Lauderdale is ninety-five and hazy. Hot and sticky, walking around covered in a sheen of sweat...musky, like animals."

Someone needed to give that man a drug test. Hiding his mortification, Dallas turned his attention to the front row. A young businessman had his headphones on and hadn't even heard the announcement. A woman was reading a book. The woman beside her—they must be sisters, they looked so much alike—did meet Dallas' eyes, but his cool, calm and confident smile (*yes indeed, this is perfectly normal on-duty pilot behavior*) caused her nervous apprehension to drain away as she basked in the assurance of his professionalism.

"Something to drink?" Dallas asked.

The woman was just about to reply when Marlin blurted through the speakers, "Holy fuck, did you see that cirrus cloud off the aft wing? It looks just like Godzilla, I kid you not...."

Dallas looked the bewildered passenger in the eye, and calmly said, "Excuse me." Coffee pot in hand, he approached the cockpit. Whether to try to sober that idiot up or dump the steaming brown swill over his head, he hadn't quite decided. He rearranged his expression to a sterner brand of professionalism and hit the buzzer.

Marlin answered. "Ya-llo?"

"It's Dallas...just checking to see if y'all *need* anything." Antipsychotics, for instance. Maybe a straitjacket.

The cockpit door buzzed open. Dallas found First Officer Marlin pretty much like he'd expected to: dark hair rakishly tousled, tie askew, sprawled back in his seat with his safety belt flapping unbuckled beside him, gazing out the window as if there might be another fascinating shape he could find in the clouds. Kaye was another story. How she'd let Marlin carry on like that, he couldn't fathom. Maybe he thought he'd find her trussed up and ball-gagged. Or passed out from too much Riesling. What he didn't expect was to find her with a book open across the dash and her nose buried in that book. Not a flight plan or a Jeppeson chart, either.

A paperback.

"I don't suppose you brought any Irish for that coffee," Marlin said amiably.

Dallas shut the cabin door behind him, then hissed, "What I should've brought was a lick of common sense. You're busy jerking off on the PA and Kaye's reading a damn novel. Who the hell's flying the plane?"

Kaye licked her thumb and turned the page. She didn't bother to look up. Marlin took the coffee pot from Dallas' trembling hand. "Relax, buddy." He smiled broadly. "It's on autopilot."

Computer systems alone were no match for the two sets of eyes and hands that were supposed to be troubleshooting and course-correcting the flight. Autopilot was meant to be used as a failsafe for zero visibility or extreme pilot fatigue, not a giant infallible cruise-control.

Marlin might very well be the most idiotic pilot Dallas had ever had the misfortune to lay eyes on—but Marlin wasn't in charge of Flight 511. Kaye was. Dallas swung around and told her in no uncertain terms, "Just because you sprang for dinner, don't be thinking I won't report—"

Turbulence shocked the plane, sudden and strong. A split second that felt like freefall, then Dallas' head smacked the cockpit ceiling, hard enough that he saw stars. "I've got the yoke," Kaye snapped, as Dallas tried to orient himself. The passengers—how many of them had been wandering around? That woman, that old white lady we wasn't even positive he'd seen…was she still in the bathroom? The plane shuddered again and Dallas was thrown into the starboard wall. He planted his hands on the floor in something warm and sticky—blood, his first thought. Only it smelled more like chocolate. A melted milkshake.

The coffee urn bounced off the control panel, and Marlin yelled, "Aii—right in the 'nads!"

Kaye talked over him, urgent, insistent. "It's happening again—radio, compass. Damn it, everything's fucked. *We're fucked*."

Two words if ever there were any that Dallas would be perfectly happy to never hear a pilot utter.

The plane shuddered again, and although Dallas had grabbed hold of the back of Marlin's seat and stood, turbulence tossed him off his feet. His back hit the ceiling this time, and his elbow struck the wall. His head was clear, though, and so he was fairly sure it was not just his vision reacting to a smack on the head when he saw the cockpit go white.

And then it was calm.

Distantly, Dallas realized he was staring up at the cockpit ceiling, and a fire extinguisher was pressing into his ribs.

"Are you okay?" Marlin said, but not to him.

"I'm fine," Kaye answered.

"I'm getting a signal."

"Pneumatic systems starting up. Electrical online."

"Just like the pocket we hit on the way over."

"Don't say it."

"But you know it is," Marlin insisted. "What now? Heading 263...supposedly. What do you think, is that right? We're headed back?"

"As opposed to what? The idea that no time passed, it's still yesterday, and we never even arrived?"

"I don't know. I don't know anything. What the—? I'm covered in coffee."

Dallas sat up and said, "And I'm just fine, thanks for your concern."

Both pilots swung around, wide-eyed, stunned, and then Kaye began to babble. "Oh my God, where did you—? Did you—? Are you okay?"

Dallas pressed his fingertips into his elbow. It hurt, but not like a fracture. He'd have a nice bruise to show for his adventure, though. "Fine," he repeated icily, and got to his feet.

Marlin narrowed his eyes. "How long have you been in the cockpit?"

"Long enough to get some sense knocked into me." Whether that meant filing an official AVA complaint or changing careers entirely, Dallas hadn't yet determined. But one thing was certain—he would not be putting up with this foolishness again.

Marlin turned back to the controls. "And you didn't notice anything... strange?"

"Other than the two of you?"

"The tower's coming through," Kaye said, then began speaking low and urgent into her headset.

"Cabin pressure's normal," Marlin said. "Altitude is steady."

Dallas headed for the door. It looked like that bump had sobered up Kaye and Marlin just as much as the pot of coffee in the First Officer's crotch, and Dallas had passengers to see to. God forbid any of them were hurt. As he released the lock, Kaye called out, "Mr. Turner?"

"Oh, so it's *Mister* now, huh?" Dallas shot back over his shoulder. Clearly, the Captain couldn't handle her wine, and now she was embarrassed. Served her right.

He glimpsed her briefly as he shut the cockpit door behind him. The expression on her face as she picked up the pink and silver chick-lit novel from her lap and said, "What the hell is this?" was almost comical, but if she was that bad of a blackout-drunk, she had no business imbibing at all when she was scheduled to fly.

CHAPTER 7

-PRESENT DAY-

"So what are you saying?" Paul asked Dallas. "The cockpit crew's real personalities ended up in some extra-dimensional Bermuda, and an empty shell was left behind to land the plane and buy you dinner, and do whatever it was that Marlin ended up doing?"

"Rock climbing on the bluffs," the Captain said. "That was his best guess."

The three of them had taken over what passed for first-class seating on an ERJ-135: the front row. The Captain sat in the single A-seat with the back reclined as far as it would go. Dallas and Paul were in B and C, Dallas on the aisle and Paul at the window. Paul glanced out every few seconds to see if anything had changed around the terminals. It hadn't. His anger had long since drained away, leaving anxiety in its place. Anxiety, and confusion, and a burning desire to make the crew's stories fit together.

"It's not like the Kaye who bought me dinner was a zombie," Dallas said. "Or even an impostor."

"Maybe not," the Captain said, "but I never have more than a couple glasses of wine—and I'd never go out drinking the night before a morning flight. I definitely wouldn't have told an FA I'd never met before every last gristly detail of my divorce."

"Good riddance to that man," Dallas muttered. "He didn't deserve you."

"Some kind of reflection, then?" Paul ventured. "An opposite?"

"Freud theorized there were three structures that make up the personality," the Captain said. "Are you familiar? The id is supposed to be the primal part concerned with satisfying basic drives. The ego is the thing we'd call someone's personality. And the super-ego keeps everything in check. When we hit the turbulence, maybe we fragment. Maybe the super-ego ends up here."

Paul had never had much use for psychoanalysis. It was a scientific contemporary of dirigibles, after all. Id, ego and super-ego might have been impressive theories in the early twentieth century, but in this day and age they seemed as outdated as a zeppelin. Still, at least it was some kind of theory, even if it was based in pseudoscience.

He turned to Dallas. "What about you? Do you think we're nothing but super-egos right now?"

Dallas considered the back of Paul's hand on the arm-rest for a long moment, then drew his fingertip across Paul's knuckles. A shiver coursed through Paul that suggested his id (if that structure did actually exist) might not be entirely gone. "I think there's more to a person than meets the eye—I just don't know that I agree the personality is split up the same way in each and every one of us. The part of us that went on to Bermuda with the passengers isn't an empty shell, and it's not a big ol' id, either. Closest thing I can think of? It's basically us, but we're coasting along on autopilot."

Paul didn't like Dallas' theory any better than the Captain's. The thought of his body just cruising around Bermuda without his normal waking consciousness firmly in charge was profoundly disturbing. What on earth would he *do* if he was left to his own devices? Whatever it was, he doubted it would involve wine or rock climbing.

"Dallas," the Captain said, "why don't you show Mr. Cronin around the island? Our situation probably feels pretty abstract right now. Nothing like having a look with your own eyes to gain some perspective." A suggestion, but it had come out more like an order. When she tucked a pair of earbuds into her ears and started thumbing through her mp3 player, it was obvious she didn't consider it a discussion. Settling back with her eyes closed, she said, "Questa è troppo calda." A pause, and again. "Questa è troppo calda." Her accent was stiffly Midwestern.

"Guess she's through with French." Dallas stood and offered Paul a hand up, which he took, though he didn't need it. The other crew members' acceptance of the situation was bewildering to him. They should be analyzing flight records, or brainstorming, or combing through every last inch of the aircraft in an attempt to figure out what the hell had just happened to them. Not learning tourist Italian.

Although Paul wasn't entirely sure he trusted the air outside, it seemed he desperately needed some. He climbed down the stairs and stood at the foot, searching the airport yard.

Still empty.

He paced, circling the aircraft maybe a dozen times, inching toward the hangar, then the terminal, then the parking lot, each time changing his mind and veering back toward the plane. Dallas watched him from the top of the aircraft stairs for a few more circuits, then said, "Let's go look around. It might help make sense of things."

Dallas headed off in a more deliberate direction, and Paul followed, comforted by the fact that Dallas might not know what was happening, but at least he knew where he was going. "So maybe we're having a mass hallucination," Paul suggested. After all, how hard would it be to lace the cockpit with some kind of contact drug? Not that Paul knew of any such hallucinogen off the top of his head, but he'd heard about all kinds of crazy stuff in the news: cane toads, bath salts. It seemed possible some such drug might exist. "An induced memory."

"Could be a memory." Dallas rounded the corner and approached a rental kiosk with cheerful scooters lined up in a row, their red, yellow and turquoise paint jobs aglow with color like a box of fresh crayons. "Marlin did an experiment just as soon as he realized everyone in the cockpit split off from themselves and ended up here, and everyone in the cabin went about their business as usual. He jabbed himself in the arm here, and found the cut was gone after he went back through the return turbulence."

Right. Marlin the rock climber sounded exactly like the kind of macho dude who'd cut himself just to prove a point—and, really, what did it even prove?

Dallas got behind the kiosk and retrieved a key as if he knew exactly where he would find it, then crouched beside the curb and pried a couple of smooth stones from the gravel trim. He strode up to the bright white scooter on the end and placed a stone beside the front and back tire, marking its position.

"So why be so careful with the scooter?" Paul asked. "We hit some turbulence tomorrow out over the Atlantic, and this scooter disappears from wherever we leave it in Emptyland and regular reality just keeps chugging along like there's nothing weird, right?"

"As far as I can tell, that's exactly how it goes down. I must've lurked on a dozen different message boards that first month to see if the people on the island noticed things appearing or disappearing or moving around, and they didn't. Still, I never cared to take unnecessary chances."

Just like the shuttle bus back in the parking lot, the scooter chugged to life, then idled quietly. Totally normal. The seat was big enough for two, barely. Feeling awkward, Paul climbed on and clutched the seat behind him rather than putting his arms around Dallas, and Dallas rolled to a slow start. Even so, Paul immediately realized he probably didn't want to end up with a friction wound or a broken limb and zero access to medical care. He slipped his arms around Dallas, and clasped their bodies together. For a single moment, he could pretend everything actually was normal—that they'd landed normally, and rented a scooter normally, and were about to have a normal dinner, and a normal evening. Maybe even a fantastic evening.

But then reality intruded, and Paul found the desire to figure out what the hell was going on nagged at him too persistently for even Dallas to distract him.

They turned onto a bridge and drove toward the center of the island. Sea gave way to bluffs, and then a few turns down narrow streets, low, square apartment buildings of pastel-painted stucco. Laundry flapped from balconies. Doors and windows hung open and empty. A loudspeaker mounted on a telephone pole played static. The street sloped downward gently. Dallas rounded a curve, and paused.

There, at the bottom of the hill, a car, a truck and a handful of scooters clustered in a heap, just like the luggage at the end of the unmanned conveyor belt. Dallas put his foot down and waited with the scooter while Paul climbed off, numb, and crept up to the wreckage, fully expecting to find casualties. There were none. No blood, either.

In the far distance, the clock tower chimed four.

Paul turned and looked at Dallas.

"They're all empty," Dallas said. "As far as we can tell, the people here on the island effectively disappeared, just like the passengers in the cabin. Most cars roll a few yards, then stop. A few keep going. This street, this curve, is usually the worst."

"Usually?" Paul turned in a circle. Apartment windows stared hollowly back at him. "So it's not the same cars in the same position every time?"

Dallas shook his head and patted the seat behind him. Paul got on again, numb now to the feel of Dallas' back clasped against his chest. Shock, he supposed.

Dallas coasted through a confusing warren of old, narrow streets ill-suited for cars. Scooters and bicycles were everywhere, some chained to bike racks or leaning against buildings, but many simply lying on their sides in the middle of the road. The roadways opened out, grew more spacious, and the homes grew newer, farther apart, and undoubtedly far more expensive. They passed a stretch limo with a hand-lettered "Just Married" sign mounted over the rear license plate and a half dozen pink and silver helium balloons bobbing at the top of ribbons tied to the door handles. Paul was tempted to stop and let one of those balloons float free, but what if that balloon ended up getting sucked into the turbine on the return trip and stopping him from hitting that precise moment of turbulence that would take him back to reality as he knew it?

Highly unlikely...but why risk it? Paul decided he was no more eager than Dallas to take unnecessary chances.

When it seemed as if the buildings must surely give way to some open area, they rounded a corner and things did indeed open up—to a broad beach dotted with empty lounge chairs and umbrellas. Dallas paused, they both touched their toes to the asphalt to brace the scooter, and the two of them gazed out over the waves together. "The sand on this beach is good and soft. It's clean most everywhere—cleaner than the Spring Break beer pong capital where I live, anyway." The scooter's engine purred as it idled. "Miles of beach…all of it private."

Paul supposed he should question Dallas more closely, but his initial adrenaline surge had worn off, and he was headachey now, and thirsty, and no longer sure what answers he'd be fishing for. Even if Dallas could tell him definitively what had happened—wormhole, mass hysteria, or elaborate hoax—he was certain he'd probably find that explanation preposterous and proceed to start combing through it for flaws in the logic. And at that very moment, he was just too damn worn out.

Dallas took Paul's hand and wrapped it around his waist, then pulled away. They rounded the south shore of the island and headed back up the other side. There was a sameness to the tableaux: empty. Buses, cars, shops, homes. Everything empty. Dallas pulled into an old wharf converted to upscale boutiques and cut the engine. Blown glass glinted from windows, their jewel tones intense against the island's sun-drenched pastels.

"Once," Dallas said, "Marlin brought a souvenir back with him. A glass fish—a marlin, naturally. At least, he tried to. It was gone by the time we got back to Fort Lauderdale."

The wind shifted, and the smell of nutmeg and caramelized sugar washed over them. Beside the glass shop, a manufacturer of rum cakes had a sign in its window advertising tours twice a day, at noon and again at five. "Is that why you told me not to eat anything?" Paul hadn't eaten since he'd grabbed a quick egg-and-bagel sandwich before he grounded his morning's flight. His stomach clenched with equal parts nausea and hunger. Maybe the baked goods in the window didn't even exist, at least not as they might define existence.

Dallas glanced back over his shoulder. "You'd seriously consider it?"

Paul peered at the stack of bundt-shaped rum cakes glistening with sugar glaze. They looked delicious, at least until Paul envisioned the semi-digested food disappearing from his system when he hit the return turbulence, and maybe taking something important into the void with it. Not just stomach acids, either. Something on a molecular level. Mitochondria. Cells.

He gazed out over the parking lot. Gulls clustered around a dented dumpster that poked out from behind the building, helping themselves to stale cake. They had no qualms about eating it. And why should they? It was unlikely they'd fly high enough to hit that pocket of turbulence, so they might as well indulge.

"I suppose I'd *consider* a taste…but I doubt I could go through with it. Especially since we don't know what happened to Marlin. Maybe he did eat something, and it caught up with him later."

Dallas turned back and started the engine again, and Paul braced himself against for the scooter's acceleration…only Dallas stayed right where he was. And then Paul realized he was breathing strangely. That, in fact, his chest was heaving with stifled sobs.

"Hey…" Paul said. He never knew what to do when someone cried. Especially when it was over something he'd said. Damn, he could be such a creep when he thought he was right. "I, um…I'm sorry. That really didn't come out very well."

Dallas gave a whuff that was part sniffle, part rueful laugh. "It's true, though. I need to find out what happened to Marlin. We were friends, you know." No—Paul didn't. He hadn't even considered the fact that if he felt closer to Dallas after a quick spin around the island, the crew of Flight 511 must consider each other family now that they'd survived repeated trips to the empty Bermuda. "Marlin would be stuffing his mouth with cake by now if he took it in his mind that he wanted some. Stupid, or brave? Hell if I know. That man knew how to have himself some fun. The world was his playground." Typical straight guy. It fit Paul's perception of most of the guys he'd known in aviation. "Once we'd done a few trips and he realized we would eventually make it back home, he had fun with it, treated it all like a great big game—and all he needed to do was figure out the rules."

And how was that different from the Marlin who'd been trying out his racy standup comedy routine over Flight 511's PA system? Paul could see it wasn't the time to ask, and he kept the question to himself, filing it away for later, when the sting of Marlin's death was no longer fresh. People didn't refer to Paul as "fun." He was "smart." Or "meticulous." Or, if he was currently standing out of earshot, "tightly wound." One thing was for sure, if Marlin was a free spirit, the pilot who'd now assumed his vacant seat was his polar opposite.

They pulled up to the rental kiosk once more and replaced the scooter, the helmets, the key and even the landscaping pebbles where they'd found them. As they headed back toward the aircraft, walking side by side, Paul desperately missed the physical closeness they'd shared on the scooter. When he extended his hand, the brush of his fingertips over Dallas' was gentle, tentative enough to be ignored.

It wasn't.

Dallas slid his hand into Paul's. He clasped it firmly, with no apologies, and Paul squeezed back—too emotional suddenly to turn, to meet Dallas' eyes. Hopefully the squeeze communicated enough.

They paused beneath the aircraft and looked up at it, because looking there rather than into each other's eyes seemed infinitely easier. The door was still open, stairs down, as if the Captain was one hundred percent certain no one would sneak up on her while her crewmen were gone—as if there was absolutely no way another living soul besides the three of them could have been transported to this alternate Bermuda. And even so, with no one to judge her, and no one to threaten her, and no one to stop her, was she off indulging herself? Raiding the kitchens, for instance, or trying on rich women's jewelry, or skinny dipping in hotel pools?

"*Dove siamo?* Dove siamo."

No. She was working on her Italian.

What was it that made the flight crew different from their body doubles, anyway? The Captain went from straightlaced to carefree. Marlin, frankly, didn't sound much different without his super-ego riding along…just a lot less inhibited. Paul finally found the courage to say, "I take it this isn't your first time on this side of the cockpit."

"It's not. But I normally stay in the cabin so I can wrangle Kaye and Marlin during the overnight. Keep her from spending all her money and him from…."

From what? Getting himself killed? Paul quickly added, "And what about you? How do you act when you're on autopilot?"

Dallas was looking at him now—Paul could tell, in his peripheral vision. He could also tell that Dallas wasn't about to answer him without eye contact. Once he steeled himself inside, Paul turned. Dallas locked eyes with him and said, "The Dallas Turner who's out there showing you a good time in Bermuda is the most selfish bastard you'll ever have the pleasure of knowing."

Paul swallowed so hard he heard his dry throat click. Surely any moment Dallas would crack a smile and tell Paul he was just kidding, and everything was fine, and really, none of this was actually happening.

Unfortunately, what he did say was, "What remains to be seen is how that little taste of freedom's going to affect you."

CHAPTER 8

Half a pot of tepid coffee. Over a hundred tiny packets of pretzels. A partially-thawed bag of ice. A few individually wrapped chocolate chip cookies, which were the emergency bribes for overtired children on the verge of meltdown. Practically every type of soda you could think of, but only a few cans of each. The commuter jet's galley didn't hold much; it was a small aircraft. It was, however, more than enough food to keep the three-person flight crew from starving overnight.

Especially since Paul refused to swallow so much as a drop of ginger ale or a crumb of pretzel.

Dallas popped open a can of room-temperature bloody mary mix and drank deeply. Once he lowered the can, he swallowed pointedly, then fixed his eyes on Paul. "This food came through the turbulence with us. It's fine to eat. I promise."

Yes, Paul was hungry (as well as parched) but he could certainly survive a single night without eating or drinking. Maybe Dallas and the Captain were willing to dig in to the airplane snacks, and maybe they'd been doing so for over a year. But he would no more take their word for its safety without firsthand knowledge than he would clear an aircraft for takeoff without inspecting it with his own eyes. "How do I know? Maybe it's fine for you...because you're not even here. Maybe we're each in our own little dimensional bubble with facsimiles of one another. Maybe you can both indulge, but if I do—"

"You're making this more complicated than it needs to be." The Captain stood and served herself from the beverage cart, diet cola over ice in a tiny airline-sized plastic tumbler. "None of us has ever had a problem with something we ate."

Dallas raised an eyebrow. His expression spoke volumes.

"You know that's not what I mean," the Captain muttered, then shook her head. "The rest of me is probably off pounding down a platter of shrimp and a half-dozen Dark & Stormy cocktails. But here, now, inside the plane...you can eat. It's fine."

Maybe. But Paul hadn't tested anything himself. He didn't understand how the turbulence would have affected only the cockpit and not the cabin. Only the people but not the objects. And without knowing whether food would be considered an object or a part of a person, it was clearly not advisable to take any chances. "Frankly, I don't see how you two ever started eating the airplane food, either. It's freaking me out."

"That would be my big discovery." The Captain sat back down with a long, drawn-out sigh and kicked off her shoes. She flexed her toes as she tore open a bag of pretzels. "Once we all decided we should probably keep doing the flight—because, hey, better us than some new crew who's going to get blindsided by the turbulence—Marlin and I started bringing extra supplies with us, just in case. Extra drinking water, extra bandages, extra aspirin, you get the drill. It was a Thursday afternoon, our second-last flight of the week. I'd made myself comfortable out here with my soda and my rice cakes. I was about halfway through the bag when I thought, wait a minute. I brought the white cheddar flavor, not the nacho."

Paul's jaw protested. He'd been clenching his teeth so hard his head hurt now. He forced himself to relax—his jaw, at least.

The Captain said, "It belonged to one of the passengers. It was out here in the cabin all along."

In his heart of hearts, what he wanted to do at that very moment was grab the Captain by the shoulders, give her a good, solid shake, and yell, "You are nowhere near observant enough to deal with this situation, lady—not even close!" But since any coup against the Captain would leave him in charge, and since he was under no illusions that he knew what was going on, he simply said, "Uh-huh," as neutrally as he could.

"I didn't start foraging through the cabin right away or anything," she said. A bit defensively, Paul thought. "But when Monday rolled around and I felt perfectly fine, Marlin decided that we could get a lot more use out of our weight limits if we didn't need to haul our own water. I let him test that theory himself, and yeah, it did spook me, initially. But he drank the bottled water from the beverage cart, it didn't bother him any, and finally I gave in and tried it. Once we were drinking the water, it seemed pretty arbitrary to say the soda was off-limits. And then the pretzels."

Paul's head was spinning…probably from dehydration. "So the airline food is fair game, but the rum cakes back on the wharf weren't?"

Dallas sat beside him in 1C, pressing their arms together more than he absolutely had to—which was saying a lot, given the cramped seating. "They were probably fine. But I was worried about you doing something you might regret, once you had a chance to think about what you'd done. I wanted to be sure you'd be going into this with your eyes open—from here on out, anyhow. The way I see it," he leaned across Paul toward his beverage cart and ran his fingers over the tops of the cans, "this is mine. It feels right. Whereas, this…" he stretched back over his seat and snagged a slouchy denim purse from seat 2B, stirred its contents around a bit, and came up with a pack of gum. "I wouldn't even think about chewing this."

"How is it any different?" Paul asked.

"It just is."

"No. It isn't. It was loaded onto the plane this morning. The only difference is that the ground crew loaded the food, and the passengers carried on these other things."

"First of all, it belongs to someone else."

"Does it? Since that person disappeared, isn't her purse fair game?"

"I'll pretend I didn't hear you say stealing is an option." Dallas replaced the gum. "In my heart," he said patiently, "and in my gut, it feels different. And that's what I trust. Look, it's easy to do the right thing when the right thing is obvious. But when you don't know which end is up, that's when you got to dig deep. For me, that's when I listen to that still, small voice inside me, and I let my faith be my guide."

Faith? Paul put as much trust in faith as he did in those computer generated penis enhancement emails.

If Paul really wanted to know what was going on, he'd need to come up with an explanation himself. Figuring out what exactly happened during the turbulence must be the key. Were they really in two places at once? Or was this some sort of dream? And did anything they did here affect "real" Bermuda, or not? "So how does chewing this passenger's gum amount to stealing? Did the owner of the tacky denim purse show up in Bermuda without it?"

Dallas rifled through the bag a bit more and pulled out a passport. "Don't think so. I see ten other purses and briefcases from here, and that's with the overhead bins still locked. We'd hear about it if a couple dozen people were held up by Customs and flown back to Florida in the morning—if not in an AVA report, at least a bunch of really angry travelers on Twitter."

"So this bag isn't really her bag. How can it be? She's got it with her in Bermuda. And when we fly back to Florida, this one disappears, right? So that particular gum you just showed me ceases to exist whether we chew it or not." That didn't seem quite as scary as what might happen with the potentially disappearing rum cake creeping through someone's digestive system. Then again, there was probably a minute part of the gum that was absorbed, a chemical, a flavoring agent of some kind. What about that? Plus… "What happens to the other gum—the gum that stayed with the passenger? If we chew some here, does a piece of the other gum just disappear?" And why did people's carry-ons stay behind, but not their *clothes?*

And their glasses? And fillings? And pacemakers?

"What about the air?" Paul said, low and urgent. "What about the oxygen? Does it disappear from our bloodstream when we hit the turbulence? Can a person even survive something like that?" Paul clamped his mouth shut and concentrated on taking only the smallest sips of air.

"You're getting yourself all worked up," Dallas said.

"The air is fine," the Captain said.

Was it even possible to breathe less air…just in case? Paul supposed that was a question a person would never pose to themselves until it was too late, and they were trapped under an avalanche waiting for a rescue team to find them.

Or trapped on an empty Bermuda with no idea what actually happened when the turbulence hit.

The Captain topped off her diet cola and took a sip. "Sometimes I wonder if the air is even a little better. A few engines are still idling out there, but most of them have shut down by now, and no flights have landed or taken off since we touched down. Imagine what that does for the air quality. Lately I feel like I sleep better here than I do in my own bed."

Paul imagined his eyes drifting shut. What typically happened to his body while it slept? Hormones were secreted. Digestion limped along. Crud gathered in the corners of his eyes.

Plus he breathed. A lot.

And then there were all the neurological things that happened while the body was in its nightly stasis. What about those things—brain things? Electrical, neurochemical…what happened to all those changed biological compounds when they hit the return pocket of turbulence? Did the synapses un-fire and the glands un-secrete their hormonal load?

All these things that made up the brain—that made up the personality as they knew it—what about those? Did the personhood just cease to exist?

Paul forced his breathing to slow. He may have had a white-knuckle grip on the seat rest as he did so, but he managed. Everything would be fine. He'd stay in control. He'd get through this.

But there was no way whatsoever he planned on *sleeping* there.

CHAPTER 9

Dallas double-checked to make sure the gum was right back where he'd found it before he tucked the blue denim purse beneath the seat of 1B. Then he stowed away the laptop case in 5C, and the mini-backpack on 8A. He tucked the magazines into the seat pockets, and one by one, raised each seat back to its upright position.

No, he didn't have to do it. He doubted that Kaye and Marlin straightened the cabin when they were the only two who'd ridden through the turbulence. As far as Dallas knew, none of the passengers had ever suddenly discovered a stranger's handbag up their butt on the return trip. Even so, he considered it his duty to ensure that fateful call for assistance never came. Not on his watch.

"If you walked into a crowd and lobbed three water balloons at random," Marlin had once said, "you couldn't nail three people more different than you, me and Kaye."

It was painful to think he'd never see Marlin again, so awful it physically hurt. But it was impossible to switch those thoughts off as if Marlin had never existed. Seeing Paul there in his First Officer's stripes...that was like the time in third grade when Dallas found a substitute in the chair where his favorite teacher, Mrs. White (who'd never seen fit to explain to a bunch of third-graders that she was not actually fat, but pregnant) should have been sitting. If Dallas had known Mrs. White was not fixing to pursue her career in education but rather bear five more daughters one after the other, he wouldn't have got himself nearly as attached to the woman.

Yet he could hardly hold the situation against Paul. For all he knew, handing Paul a phone number had been the thing that sucked him into the shorthanded crew of Flight 511.

Maybe it was.

Had Marlin been there, he would have disagreed. "You seem to think everyone's well-being is your personal responsibility," he'd told Dallas. "Kaye is reliable, you're nurturing, and I'm bold—practically fearless."

"And so modest, too."

"Think about it: we're archetypes. The Leader, the Keeper, and the Guide."

"The Keeper? You trippin'. Who says I want to be the Keeper? I think I'm the charming one, that's what I think. Not to mention the only one here who can carry a tune."

Dallas stared down at the tray table in 12C he'd been folding up…for the past two or three minutes, easily. If he were anywhere else, he would have started digging up phone numbers and making calls, getting himself some answers as to exactly what had happened to Marlin. Hearing that he was dead with no explanation at all made the painful news even worse. Was there anything unnatural involved? Had he suffered?

Had some small action on Dallas' part inadvertently done him in?

Maybe Dallas did feel that in some way, big or small, he really was responsible for everyone else. And maybe the reason he felt that way was because he *was*.

Take Paul, for instance.

Dallas could have simply admired the view and moved along. But he hadn't. He'd chatted. No, he'd flirted. He'd *engaged* the man in conversation—really, he'd fallen for him. As if he was in a position do something normal, like go out and get a little tipsy…then go home and get a little nasty. Honestly, how would he have handled anything beyond a one night stand? Just pretend Flight 511 was a completely normal assignment and go about his weekends as if nothing about his work week was out of the ordinary—all the while, fooling around with a pilot? Not just any pilot, but an AVA pilot who would've jumped at the chance to grab the first empty seat to Bermuda on Flight 511 as soon as he had a day off? No matter how Dallas looked at it, no way he could have kept the turbulence a secret forever.

Maybe the role of "The Keeper" wasn't so far-fetched after all, since he could never aspire to being a Leader or a Guide. If he had a strong suit, it was dealing with the situation at hand, not planning ahead. His thought process at the time had been more along the lines of, "What a shame those fine legs aren't wrapped around my hips. I want me some of that."

He wanted Paul? He got him, all right.

"What we need to do is shut the door," Paul was telling Kaye.

"We're not shutting the door. The air is perfectly safe. I've been breathing it for a year."

"Maybe you have, and maybe you haven't. Maybe you're not even you. Maybe each of us fragmented off into some kind of quantum bubble where we're interacting with our projections of each other. So everything you're telling me isn't factual at all. It's just something I'm inventing to lull myself into a false sense of security."

Kaye groaned. "Do you always think this much?"

Paul was already up out of his seat and messing with the actuator, despite Kaye telling him explicitly that the door would be kept open. Kaye might have been the Leader, but for now she didn't repeat herself, and didn't argue. She just watched Paul's anxiety play out.

The stairs raised up and the door sealed. Dallas felt his eardrums flex, and though there was probably enough air in the cabin to last three people a good long while, his lungs began to subtly ache as if the oxygen was already getting scarce.

Paul turned back to Kaye and Dallas and said, "If the two of you sleep in shifts, you can make sure I don't nod off."

When Dallas tried to imagine Marlin saying something like that, he came up blank. Marlin *had* been fearless—and maybe that wasn't actually such a good thing. After all, Marlin wasn't there with them now. And Paul was.

"Thirteen hours to takeoff," Paul calculated. "If I breathed through the CPR mask outside, the oxygen tank should last through my pre-flight check—"

"Enough." Kaye spoke quietly, but her implacable confidence silenced Paul immediately. "Let's get a few things straight. If you're stressing yourself out too much to manage sleeping, if you need evidence that we're real, that this isn't all some crazy dream and we're not all sock puppets of your subconscious, then fine. I'll allow it. Even though I'd prefer you at least try to get in a few hours before the return flight tomorrow, I'll allow it. But with that door shut, it's going to get hot in here fast—and we're not wasting fuel by powering on anything other than the auxiliary lights. This is non-negotiable."

Paul stared at Kaye for such a long, drawn-out pause, Dallas had plenty of time to fret about who he'd need to side with, should it come right down to it: Kaye, who he'd entrusted with his life, his reality, for the past year? Or Paul, the innocent bystander who he'd just managed to suck into the turbulence with him?

Fortunately for Dallas, once Paul considered Kaye's decision, he nodded. "That makes sense. We can't waste anything. Even if I figured out how to work the fuel truck, it'd be stupid to take off with fuel in our tanks that could just disappear."

Dallas made his way back up the aisle and rested a hand on Paul's shoulder. He could simply reach around Paul and flip the actuator himself, but it seemed to him that the two of them would be better off in the long run if he convinced Paul they were all on the same side. "You done breathed the air already, from one end of the island to the other. Kaye's right. Open the door."

Paul searched his eyes hard, then some tension went out of his shoulders, and he nodded and hit the switch. The stairs folded down, and cool, sweet late-afternoon island air rushed in.

"I appreciate that you want to test all the limits for yourself," Kaye said. "I can totally relate to a cautious approach, and I agree there's really no substitute for firsthand experience. Putting in your hours on a simulator is not the same as taking your first solo flight. But that doesn't mean a sim is useless. You're not going to go into a sudden nosedive in a real aircraft just to get the feel for the best way to recover."

"What does that have to do with…this?"

"I'm trying to say, yes, trust your own eyes. And your own thoughts, and observations, and conclusions. But don't dismiss second-hand evidence out of hand. Not until you've seen it."

"Is that your roundabout way of telling me to shut up and let you and Dallas run the show?"

Captain Lehr responded to Paul's snitty remark with a raised eyebrow that warned him that even she had her limits. She ducked into the cockpit and came out with her flight bag. When she reached in, she produced not a chart, or a flight plan, or even a laptop, but a well-worn spiral bound notebook bursting with scraps of paper and scrawled-on napkins. "What I'm saying is that you might find it useful to stop yourself from going off half-cocked before you take a look at Marlin's research."

CHAPTER 10

-ONE YEAR AGO-

Dallas snapped open the handle on his rollerbag, turned toward the door and said, "If y'all need me, I'll be down by the pool."

Marlin, the only member of the crew who'd stayed behind in the cabin this time around, hadn't thought much past trying to keep Captain Kaye out of trouble. Dallas had ridden the turbulence in Marlin's place this trip, so the FA in front of him wasn't entirely Dallas. Even so, if he was willing to survey their surroundings and report back, they would have the puzzle unraveled in no time. "Cool—what's your plan?"

Dallas turned and looked Marlin up and down deliberately, then said, "Change into my trunks. Park my fine ass in a lounge chair."

"Okay, then what?"

"I'll sit." They stared at one another for an extended pause, and finally Dallas said, "I've been on my feet all week long, and I am ex-haus-ted. So I'm putting my feet up, and I'm sitting. And that's all I'm doing. If I'm feeling really ambitious, maybe I'll try one of those twelve dollar mojitos."

Marlin looked from Kaye to Dallas and back again. While his current crewmates weren't exactly themselves, they didn't seem completely alien. Then again, neither did he when the lights were on but the real Marlin wasn't home. And Dallas had video to prove it.

"Before you go anywhere, hear me out." In a voice hushed with enough melodramatic flair to tell one hell of a ghost story around a campfire, Marlin said to his team, "What if I told you...I've got a *plan*." He brandished a notebook and paused long enough for one of them to congratulate him on his sharp thinking. Except Dallas just raised a challenging eyebrow and pursed his lips. And Captain Kaye was looking at the room service menu.

"I spent all day on it yesterday," Marlin added.

Dallas turned to the mirror and checked his hair.

"The *whole* day."

Kaye shrugged and reached for the phone, frowning when she put the handset to her ear. The first thing Marlin had done—per her earlier request—was unplug the phone and stash the cord in his luggage. "Do you still have my cell?" she asked.

Marlin patted his pockets. "I must have left it on the plane," he lied.

Kaye clucked her tongue. "Fine. I'll go downstairs, then. Give me my credit card."

"You gained four pounds last week—"

"Oh, who gives a flying fuck?"

Dallas sniggered.

Definitely not themselves.

"Maybe you should try stepping up your workout," Marlin suggested. "Then you could up your calorie intake without—"

"Do you have firsthand experience with the metabolism of a perimenopausal woman?"

"Well…no."

"Then don't tell me what to do."

"Relax," Marlin said. "Chill. Everything's cool. We're all frien—"

Kaye thrust her hand in his face palm-up. "Card. Now."

"Oh, come on," Dallas said. "Just let the woman eat."

"Sorry." Instead of a credit card, Marlin presented Kaye with a Bermudan ten dollar bill—enough for a *very* small meal at the island's outrageous prices, and zero glasses of wine. "I have my orders."

"This is so stupid," Kaye fumed.

Marlin considered pointing out that she also had rice cakes in her bag, but decided it would probably just piss her off. Better to try one more time to wow her with his stunningly analytical bent of mind. "Never mind the food. You're in two places at once by now—if they can even be called places. Tell me that's not totally far out."

Captain Kaye narrowed her eyes. The regular day-to-day Kaye would probably feel baffled, frustrated, anxious. This Kaye felt mostly hungry. But some small part of her did seem to wonder about what was going on…if only Marlin could keep it engaged. "Yesterday, when I rode the turbulence, I wasn't out exploring the empty island. I was measuring the aircraft. Every square inch of it. Not just surface area, either. I checked the temperature of the hull and the tarmac at one hundred distinct points. I took dozens of snapshots. I smelled the jet fuel—I even *tasted* the fucking fuselage. We go out and do it all again, this time from here, wherever we really are—we're bound to spot something, some minor inconsistency, that'll let us unravel this whole thing."

Dallas turned back from the mirror, brushed some imperceptible lint from his sleeve, and said, "Fine, I'm curious about your little diary. So dazzle me. Show me what you got."

Marlin opened the notebook to a page at random, confident that any single page of carefully recorded facts and figures would be sure to impress. Captain Kaye's eyebrows drew down. Dallas' eyes went wide. Marlin felt satisfaction swell within him, because surely now they were on the cusp of a major discovery.

"Is that a codpiece?" Kaye said.

Dallas stifled a laugh.

How the two of them could interpret a string of figures as a codpiece was beyond—

Marlin flipped the notebook around and found not a neat column of numbers, but a drawing in ballpoint pen. Of a barechested man. On a bike. A sweet midnight pearl Harley Nightster, with the road he'd just traveled unfurling behind him, and his hair whipping in the wind.

And a codpiece. A studded codpiece.

"Is that supposed to be you?" Kaye guffawed.

"Let me see that." Dallas snatched the notebook from Marlin's stunned hands. "Bitch, I know you ain't hiding pecs like that under your uniform."

Kaye said, "The proportion's all out of whack. If the motorcycle is facing us, the hands should look larger. But there's no foreshortening. So it looks like you drew yourself with tiny little hands."

"And you know what they say about small hands," Dallas added.

Kaye turned the notebook sideways and scrutinized it hard. "Do you actually own a codpiece?" Snort. "You can tell us. We won't judge."

"Hold on." Marlin grabbed the notebook back from Kaye. Maybe Dallas (*this* Dallas) had gotten hold of it and added an artistic flourish while Marlin wasn't looking. Or maybe it was a different notebook entirely. Except the cover was the same, a bright solid red. With a price sticker in the corner that read $2.59, and some light scuffing on the bottom edge. And he couldn't imagine when Dallas would've found the time to rifle through all his stuff, and then draw something this elaborate in it. Not to mention...he'd never told Dallas about his Nightster, or his tribal armband. Not that he remembered, anyway. Though, if he thought about it, he didn't have a clue what all he'd told Dallas while most of him was riding the turbulence and Dallas had been the one to stay behind in the cabin.

He flipped through the book. Rocking out in a packed stadium surrounded by Marshall stacks. Cliff diving in Maui. Giving a high five to Jerry Garcia. Drawings, all drawings in the same ballpoint pen, and yes, probably all by his hand—none of them particularly good, though they definitely had energy to them, and lots and lots of heart.

"Who's that?" Kaye said. "Santa Claus? Smoking a doobie?"

Lots of heart.

But facts, figures, all the data he'd so painstakingly collected on the other side of the turbulence? Nothing.

Marlin didn't try to stop Dallas when the FA grabbed the notebook again to put it through the wringer with Captain Kaye. "Ooh, look. Here he is swimmin' with the dolphins. Check out the size of his head. You know your hair don't do that, right?"

"Ohmigod! In a Speedo!"

All the work, all the scrutiny, all the planning and thinking and recording, all of it for nothing.

"You won't catch me swimming with no dolphins," Dallas said. "Always smiling, like they know something you don't."

Not only did Marlin have the loss of all his work weighing on his mind, he also needed to deal with the totally unfiltered remarks of his crewmates. He couldn't really blame them, though. And in a way, maybe the world would be a more honest place if everybody just said what they meant and did what they wanted. Maybe there would be more opportunities to scale Mount Everest and swim with the dolphins.

"That's it," Marlin said.

Kaye and Dallas both looked up from the notebook and regarded him skeptically.

"The me that rode the turbulence, the person shaped by society's expectations, who pays his taxes and renews his license plate and flosses almost every night—the guy you're talking to right now—he *did* measure the crap outta that plane, and he did record each and every little ding and blip. But that was in *his* notebook, not this one. This notebook was the one I brought with me from Florida, but what if it wasn't the same one that went through the turbulence with me. Two Marlins…and two notebooks. My personality made it back through the return turbulence, but my notes didn't. And the Marlin who drew in *this* notebook was the raw, unvarnished Marlin who doesn't give a rat's ass what's going on, just as long as he's having a good time."

What did it all mean? Marlin wasn't exactly sure. Whatever it was, though, it was huge.

"Unless you got any more hilarious pictures to show me," Dallas said, "I'mma be out by the pool."

One thing was for sure. From now on, he'd need to jot down his notes *after* he rode the return turbulence.

CHAPTER 11

-PRESENT DAY-

Paul blinked. The light that touched the edge of the college-ruled notebook paper was tinged pinkish orange. He tore his eyes from the page and looked out the aircraft window. A brilliant sunrise aflame with oranges and reds peeked through the hangars. True to his word, Paul had indeed stayed up all night. Not because he was convinced any longer that sleeping in empty Bermuda would do some sort of damage to his mind. He'd broken the moratorium on drinking around ten, and eating, just after midnight. He would have been willing to succumb to the urge to doze off. However, sleep never came. He'd been up all night reading that damn notebook from cover to cover at least half a dozen times.

It was like watching a train wreck—a train wreck that came with a remote control that allowed him to back up and pause during any point in the catastrophe. There'd been a few pages torn out somewhere along the way. Even so, the notebook did seem to follow an internal pattern. A downward spiral, yes. But it was consistent in its decline.

Measurements filled the first few pages: size, temperature, distance. Marlin had even brought a litmus test from his fish tank to see if the evaporation dripping from the coils was the same pH on "either side of the turbulence," as he put it. The aircraft appeared to land in the same spot at the same time in both Bermudas. It took off at the same time, too—which was at first a source of great concern for Marlin and the Captain. What if the two return flights somehow missed each other in the turbulence? What if they failed to be put back together? Eventually, though, it seemed that whether the pilots timed their departure down to the last second, or whether they "winged it," their return trip managed to reassemble the crew's consciousness with its counterparts on a populated vessel, in an inhabited world.

None of them knew what to make of the situation, but they did all agree: if they didn't run this flight, Scheduling wasn't about to cancel it, and someone else would end up in their shoes. None of them were comfortable bowing out and putting someone else through that sort of ordeal, not even a perfect stranger. And so they persevered.

Marlin performed more tests. Every day, something new. Small objects left behind reappeared on the aircraft after the return turbulence—usually. On the first test run, Auto-Kaye flung her cell phone into the hotel pool when Marlin left its counterpart in the empty Bermuda. It was sucked into the filter and never seen again. After that, not only did they pick small, disposable items, but they pre-arranged for Dallas to keep an eye on them. Those objects—a comb, a pencil, a child's barrette—all reappeared in the cockpit after the return turbulence, no worse for wear.

And then they started experimenting on living creatures.

I never thought I'd *find myself feeling sorry for a cockroach—but the little guy took one for the team so that none of us needed to. And he's returned to his full vibrational alignment with Source, so it can't be all that bad. Roach in the cockpit (in a margarine tub) was duplicated when he rode the turbulence, just like Kaye and me. I flattened the post-turbulence roach and left his carcass in the container. After the return turbulence, his counterpart was not flattened, but he was legs-up. So we'd better take it easy with any risky business, on either side of the bump.*

To be absolutely positive it was the same roach, Kaye put a dot of nail polish on the next volunteer's shell. Both roaches had the dot—and neither roach made it back to Fort Lauderdale alive.

The next test was more disturbing.

I removed the left rear leg of Roach 3 inside the turbulence. Not only was he still alive when we embarked on the return flight, but when we came back through the turbulence, HIS LEG WAS STILL INTACT.

They ran the test three more times to be sure they were seeing what they thought they'd seen. One of the roaches did die on the return trip, but even so, it possessed all six of its bristly little legs. Kaye then suggested they perform the test on a mouse, but was overruled by Marlin and Dallas, who both insisted that a life was a life was a life, and they would learn nothing new by snipping off a poor rodent's tail tip.

Kaye adapted the experiment by instead trimming her fingernails down to the quick in empty Bermuda. After the return turbulence, they were their normal practical length.

Paul's head spun with possibilities. Could he lose an arm here, and if he didn't bleed out and die, find himself whole again upon his return? What would it feel like—both to lose a limb, and then to find it back again as if it was never gone? And how did the mechanics of it all work? Was the Autopilot body the "real" body, and this post-turbulence existence some mental construct? Maybe so. Maybe it was an elaborate, shared dream. And just like in dreams, when you have one of those falling nightmares and you hit the ground, you die. Even as the thought occurred to Paul, he was mortified by it. What sort of intelligent modern human would even think something like that?

One who'd been morbidly fascinated by Marlin Fritsch's whacked out, new age ramblings. That's who.

It's so easy to get caught up in our everyday lives and forget that we are all Source energy, and we create our own reality. This experience of an alternate Bermuda is something that Kaye and Dallas and I have Co-Created. Kaye periodically challenges AVA Scheduling about the flight, but whenever she mentions 511, the people in charge go into a kind of trance. She suggests they cancel it and they act like they haven't heard her. She doubles up on fuel? No problem. She decreases the weight limit? No one cares. She even got them to load us up with first-class meals, and no one blinked an eye. Whatever she wants, she gets—just so long as Flight 511 leaves on time. None of us has the balls to take off late anyway, in case we end up going the same route of everyone else who's disappeared in the Bermuda Triangle.

This experience is in our Vortex (all of us!) We're a vibrational match, and we are all in a state of Allowing. We can't help but Receive it. And so it is.

At least he was courteous enough to capitalize all the words Paul needed to read past and dismiss, though apparently Paul was too over-tired to do all that good a job of shielding himself from the crazy. Not if he was giving serious thought to dream physics.

Auto-Kaye and Auto-Marlin are more than capable of handling the takeoff of Flight 511. They have the towers, and they have ground crew to fall back on if anything goes wrong. But if I ever dodged the turbulence and something happened to Kaye while she was in solitary, the second Flight 511 would be grounded. So from now on, the two of us ride the turbulence together, while Dallas stays whole and does his best to wrangle the Autopilots. It's the only way.

Okay, that much did seem logical. But then….

These are the roles we've been waiting to play all our lives. Maybe they're even roles we've played in previous lives. Kaye the Leader, Dallas the Keeper, and me the Guide. Maybe we slogged through the fields at Normandy together. Or stormed the Alamo. Or lopped off heads in the Crusades.

The smell of coffee jerked him out of his ever deepening dismay and back to reality—his present reality (which apparently was nowhere near as creative as Marlin's). It smelled better than the typical AVA in-flight coffee. Maybe better coffee had been another one of the Captain's blandly-honored requests. Paul looked up as Dallas creased the empty coffee packet, slid it neatly into the garbage, and said, "I'm going to go stretch my legs." Or probably he was going to pee. Though according to the notebook, it didn't make any apparent difference if they used the chemical toilet in the aircraft or went and urinated off the control tower.

Since they'd managed to convince Paul that breathing more air wouldn't make a bit of difference, the door had been open all night, and a mild, pleasant chill had settled in the cabin. The Captain stretched and cracked her neck, one side, then the other. "I hadn't realized it was…" Paul began. Gratitude flooded him. For his crewmates' patience. For their calm. For their willingness to allow him to acclimate and get his bearings. "Thank you."

The Captain raked her fingers through her hair, then caught it back in a clip. "For what?"

"For staying out here. In the cabin. With me."

"Don't thank me. That's where I always stay."

"But the hotels...." Not just any hotels, but luxury hotels, with spas and fountains and cushy king-sized beds. Within walking distance of the airport.

"No one's been able to convince me that we don't all disappear the minute I step off the plane."

Paul stared. "And so you're never...?"

Kaye stood, cracked her neck yet again, then hovered by the brewing coffee, fiddling with a paper cup. "The way I see it, my job, my only job, is to be sure Flight 511 comes back home. No matter what."

And so while Marlin was out measuring and tasting and touching everything, poking through the island and tearing legs off roaches, Kaye was here. In the aircraft. The very small aircraft. Four nights a week...for the past year.

Learning Italian. Or was it French?

"You get used to the seats," she said simply.

Paul sat back in *his* seat and took off his glasses. He pinched the bridge of his nose, and sighed.

"You've already been outside," she said, "so obviously it's fine for you to go wherever you want to go—hit the beach, check out the sunrise, reassure yourself that we're still the only ones here—just so long as you don't hurt yourself, and you're back by nine for the pre-flight inspection. I'm counting on you for that."

"Why? What difference does it even make? If I saw a problem, there's no mechanic to page."

"No. But we brought a bunch of duct tape." The Captain cracked an odd smile then, though Paul suspected she was actually serious. He didn't smile back; he didn't have it in him to appreciate the absurdity of the situation. She handed him a coffee, black. It was very hot—and, yes, much smoother than the usual cheap AVA blend. She sat beside him and echoed his sigh. "The one you should be thanking is Dallas. Riding the turbulence spooks him even more than babysitting the Autopilots." She blew on her coffee, then studied Paul and said, "He must care about you."

Paul felt his cheeks grow hot, and not from the coffee. "We only just met."

"You meet a lot of people on an airline." The Captain faced forward and drank her coffee methodically, one sip at a time, until it was gone. "Your personal life is none of my business, Paul. I can call you Paul, can't I?"

Paul nodded uneasily.

"Stress makes people do all kinds of things. People come together who'd normally sail right on by without even a passing glance. We're not solitary creatures. We need each other. For validation. For comfort."

Paul could have informed her that he'd actually scored Dallas' phone number in the safety of the Fort Lauderdale crew lounge before any of this happened, but he decided he wanted to keep that information for himself. At least until he figured out where she was going with her current thought.

"Dallas Turner...is the most decent human being I've ever met. That's all. As one person to another person, and not a Captain to a First Officer, I'm asking you to remember that. I know there are no guarantees in life. But keep it in mind: he's a good man."

Paul tried to think of a reply and came up blank. He cleared his throat, stood, and said, "Uh, thanks. I'm just gonna, uh, get some air." By which he did not actually mean that he had to pee, only that the interior of the aircraft suddenly felt phenomenally close.

Wade International didn't even feel like an airport to Paul when he stepped onto the tarmac. The still, the quiet, was striking. Paul wanted to think of it as eerie, but it really wasn't. It was peaceful.

Dallas wasn't around, but since the Captain hadn't seemed concerned, Paul did his best to keep his worry-meter running at its lowest setting. There he was, in Bermuda, in paradise, with no cars, no exhaust fumes, no bustling crew or frantic tourists. Just him and his ERJ-135 with its white paint job tinted rosy pearl by the last wisps of sunrise.

It turned out to be the most transcendent pre-flight inspection he'd ever done.

With no one watching him, no one salivating at the thought that he might screw up—really, *hoping* that he would, so it might teach his pansy ass a lesson—Paul lovingly scrutinized every last dip and curve of the aircraft from cockpit to tail. Every bolt. Every valve. Every antenna. And every last inch of the craft was perfect.

He brushed his fingertips over the hull one more time, for no reason other than to appreciate the beauty of the little Embraer, then looked up. Dallas stood watching him from the shade of a set of rolling stairs meant to service a much larger jet. His neat goatee was trimmed and his shirt was freshly pressed. Paul wondered if showering, shaving, any of that even mattered. If a cockroach could re-grow its leg, surely it was possible the three of them could ride the return turbulence and find themselves physically clean. Mentally, though, it was this Bermuda they'd remember. So maybe a shower was more than just a shower.

When he saw Paul was done with his inspection, Dallas strolled over and stood with him. "I should have told you about the turbulence," Dallas said. "Somehow. Not knowing what to say—that's no kind of excuse."

A decent man. "I guess you could have dragged me into the cabin..." Paul tried to imagine that scenario playing out—and somehow it seemed even more bizarre than what had actually unfolded. "But I'm glad you didn't. I need to see things for myself to get a handle on them. Always have."

"When we get back, Scheduling's going to ask you if you want Flight 511 Monday morning. You don't have to say yes."

Of course he did. Not because he didn't possess free will—but because he had to know what was going on. He needed to know—to figure it all out. Not with tea leaves and numerology and tarot cards, but with observation and rational thought.

"This weekend," Paul began, and he realized his heart was now beating wildly. He tried to will it to slow, not that it seemed to help. "I can't stay in Fort Lauderdale. I'm going back to DC."

Dallas' gaze fell to the tarmac. "I understand."

"It's not that I don't want to see you," Paul rushed on. "But I can't pretend the turbulence doesn't change anything. Because it does."

When he grabbed Dallas and turned him so they faced each other, Dallas didn't protest. But he didn't meet Paul's eyes, either. Paul gave his arms a squeeze. "I need time to get my stuff in order." More accurately, to get his *head* in order. Because what kind of man was he? He wasn't sure. But he was ready to find out.

***

Had the jet engine always been that loud? Was that its usual pitch? In the silence of the empty airport, it was impossible to tell. Paul looked to Captain Kaye. She nodded, and spoke through her headset. "Everything sounds good."

Paul nodded back, and activated the electrical systems. They powered on. One by one, every cockpit check cleared. Yes, the pneumatics sounded just as strange in the eerie silence as the jet engines had. But all the gauges read normal…until a voice from the radio made Paul leap out of his seat suddenly enough to rap his head on the windshield.

…winds from the east-southeast at twelve knots…

"Paul," Captain Kaye was saying. "Paul—calm down. It's the automated loop."

As Paul took a few deep, steadying breaths, the flight advisory droned on. "Right. Yeah. Of course."

"Paul," the Captain repeated. He looked at her and swallowed nervously. "You'll do fine."

Fine was not the word he would have chosen himself…but he'd manage.

Dallas sealed himself in the cockpit and folded out the jump seat, and before Paul knew it Captain Kaye was taxiing to the runway, murmuring a steady stream of commentary on every move she made, probably to keep Paul from freaking out over the absence of the tower, the huge void where clearance and instructions should have been. *We can't hit anybody.*

There's nobody to hit. Even so, Paul's stomach heaved when Captain Kaye advanced the throttle, drew back on the yoke, and the landing gear left the runway with a gentle shudder.

When they finally reached cruising altitude, Paul finally began to unclench. His fists. His jaw. Even his sphincter. The flight plan had been scrutinized just as thoroughly—obsessively—as Paul's pre-flight check, and the return flight held no surprises.

Even the return turbulence was entirely expected.

Nonetheless, its approach washed over Paul like the calm in the eye of a tornado. Captain Kaye had just said, "Here it comes," he realized, as if his peaking anxiety had inserted a delay between her warning and his comprehension. And then it hit them—a massive jolt. The electrical gauges spun, or swung back and forth. According to the attitude indicator they were flying sideways. The fuel gauge leapt from half-empty to full. And the pneumatics all bottomed out as if all the air had been sucked out of the system.

Everything went white, only for a fraction of a second, but long enough for Paul to decide that he was actually dead. And then the aircraft shuddered, and leveled, and the gauges all settled back to normal.

Paul squeezed the yoke—but only with one hand. Captain Kaye began chatting with the tower in Fort Lauderdale as if everything was status quo, and for her, it likely was. But Paul was too busy wondering how the tumbler in his hand had gotten there.

Kaye finished confirming weather conditions in Fort Lauderdale, then switched her microphone to the cabin's channel. "We made it. Are you okay?"

Paul tried to remember how to breathe. Inhale. Exhale. Yes. That's how it worked.

A hand dropped onto his shoulder and he flinched. Dallas' hand, he realized. It gave a reassuring squeeze. "I got to get back to the cabin now. You did good."

Paul stared at the drink, then raised it and gave it a sniff.

Orange juice—and champagne. Mostly champagne.

"What the—?"

Captain Kaye said, "You'll want to dump that in the toilet before we touch down."

"I'm so sorry. I can't believe—I'd never—oh, man."

"I know." Completely unfazed. "That's how it goes when Dallas doesn't stay behind to keep us in line. I'll probably throw up once we land." She sighed. "That's probably for the best."

They did another scan of all the instruments. Everything checked out. Dallas buzzed, and Kaye let him in. The smell of coffee filled the cockpit. "Twenty-six passengers, two of them over ninety, bless their hearts. Everyone lookin' *real* happy. Seems like the mimosas were on us." He took the drink from Paul's unprotesting hand and replaced it with a cup of black coffee. Then he leaned in close and mouthed the words, "You okay?"

Paul clasped his forearm briefly, squeezed, and nodded.

Dallas held his gaze one more moment, then turned and went back to his passengers.

Captain Kaye did most of the flying on Flight 511's return trip. When she did give Paul a task to perform, it was obviously busywork. Checking the flight plan, verifying the weather. Paul appreciated it, though. The decision he'd been circling in on, back there in the empty airport as he'd crept through the pre-flight check, had seemed so easy at the time. So obvious. But it hadn't taken into account the sheer terror of the turbulence.

Paul checked the flight plan yet again, and then all the completely normal gauges, and then did a visual check of the airspace. The sky yawned before him, wide open hazy blue, clouds stretched beneath him like a field of froth. What was flying, anyway, if not a journey?

And, more importantly, what kind of man was he?

"If Scheduling offers me Flight 511 Monday," he told Captain Kaye, "I'm taking it."

"You do what you need to do," she said. But Paul would have liked to think that she sounded pleased.

Paul checked all the systems again—normal—and then he listened to the tower in Fort Lauderdale as they neared. His adrenaline ebbed, and while he wouldn't call himself comfortable by any stretch of the imagination, he would allow that the flight was manageable. And as he rode the turbulence more, eventually he might be able to take it in stride, like Captain Kaye, like Dallas.

His gaze fell on the red notebook protruding from his flight bag.

Like Marlin?

CHAPTER 12

The flight from Fort Lauderdale to DC was surreal. Since there were empty seats in the 737, Paul caught a ride home in the cabin rather than a jump seat. Normally he would doze while he was deadheading, especially at the end of a week-long trip, but on this commute he'd felt overtired, too punchy and ill to let sleep overtake him.

He knew the Reagan Airport as well as he knew his own neighborhood, but once he'd emerged from the skyway, his imagination ran away with him. In his mind's eye, the terminal yawned with emptiness, baggage carousels rotating endlessly with no passengers to scoop up their bags, big pretzels crisping dry under the heat lamps of unmanned concession stands. It was actually a relief to be jostled by the travel-worn crowd.

When he stumbled out to the cab stands it was nearly five, just in time for the thick of Friday evening rush hour. He was beyond calculating how long he'd been awake. Thirty hours? Forty? Math was usually his strong suit—the only one in his clique faster at figuring a tip was Richard, the accountant—but at the moment he didn't even bother tallying up what taking a cab home instead of the Metro would mean for his budget in terms of how many lattes he'd need to forgo. He just hailed it, climbed in, and nodded into a fitful doze as soon as he gave the cabbie his address.

Every lurching stop on the short drive to Georgetown, every pothole and ding, felt like turbulence. Except it didn't. Even sort-of-asleep, Paul could tell the difference between being rattled around in a cab and lurching into an empty Bermuda. A divot in the pavement might rap his head against the car window, but there was no flash of light, no spinning of gauges, no hair raising sensation of utter *wrongness* that would indicate that his body was going in one direction and his consciousness in another.

Even so, when the cab pulled over, he snorted awake with the thought that it was Dallas in the driver seat chauffeuring him to an empty pink-stuccoed hotel…until the driver turned and said in his Nigerian accent that Paul owed him seventeen dollars.

Hopefully giving him a twenty and telling him to keep the change was adequate. The credit card reader wasn't accepting Paul's card, and he was too wrecked to figure even that simple of a tip.

Setting foot in his building felt somewhat more real, as did emptying his mailbox. He received very little mail, as his bills were all direct debit and he was fastidious about bumping back unwanted junk mail with "return to sender" and "remove me from your list" penned on the offending correspondence in assertive block letters. The only things that greeted him after five days' absence were a sample of carpet freshener and three letters from his condo association.

They'd been a little too hands-on lately for Paul's taste, but three communiques in five days seemed a bit much. Even for them.

He schlepped upstairs, let himself in and dumped the mail on the sideboard. His condo smelled of whatever green biodegradable cleaning agents his hippie housekeeper used—slightly sour, but not too unpleasant. Not musty, at least, which was how the place had smelled before he hired her. A bit like pickles, actually. It should have seemed familiar, but even that slight whiff of vinegar felt surreal.

Paul's normal routine, upon returning home, involved getting together his dry cleaning, defrosting whatever he might want to eat over the weekend, and laying out his clothes for Friday night with the clique. Instead he found himself staring out his living room window at The Gap across the street, and the pedestrians roaming the sidewalk, and the traffic. And he wondered why his life suddenly felt like a dramatization.

He went to his bedroom. There it was: neat and sparse, just like he liked it. Plaid duvet in cocoas and tans. White noise generating clock-radio with dimmable numbers. Modern furniture, wood with a hint of chrome. He planted himself in front of his dresser and looked in his plain mirror. There *he* was. Same as always, just like his home. It seemed as if the change he felt deep down in his gut should have been more apparent. Visible. Tangible.

He'd only intended to lie down for a moment, to reorient himself, to rest his eyes. But he woke with a lurch to the sound of someone knocking, and the awareness that a large-ish amount of time had probably just passed. His window was dark. The muted bedside clock read 10:15. And the knock sounded very insistent.

Due to the security on the first floor, the only people able to "drop in" on Paul were the other condo owners from his building. And the only people likely to do it were Mrs. Dresch, who occasionally needed her furniture moved and couldn't wait for her sons to come and do it, and Dennis, one of Paul's drinking friends. And it was way too late for Mrs. Dresch to pop by.

Paul opened the door and found Denny in the hallway, jeans expensively distressed, eyebrows manicured, thinning blond hair exactingly tousled. Paul wondered when, exactly, he'd begun to consider Denny a "drinking friend" rather than simply a friend.

Denny shouldered by Paul and took a pointed look at the rollerbag in the middle of Paul's entryway, and then at the short-sleeved uniform shirt with its triple-striped epaulets that Paul was still wearing. "So, did you have a delay—or were you thinking it was Village People night at the bar?"

"It was, uh..." Paul restrained himself from saying, *Shut up, everyone thinks pilots are a hell of a lot hotter than dentists.* He'd caught himself before anything that couldn't be unsaid had escaped. Barely. "My schedule got juggled. Extended. Look, I don't think I'm up for—"

"Oh, right. It's your turn to buy the first round, and now you're trying to weasel out of it because you worked late. My office was fully booked today, you know, and we even had to squeeze in an emergency crown cement. You don't see me complaining."

Paul glanced at his living room clock. The math came easier now. He'd had a four-hour nap, and was unlikely to fall back asleep even if he could convince Denny to leave. And a martini really would hit the spot. "Right. I just need to shower."

Denny sighed dramatically and wandered into Paul's kitchen to roll his eyes at the sight of the sparse contents of the fridge. He helped himself to a Perrier while he waited.

Although Paul shaved quickly and opted to wear the first outfit he pulled out of his closet, they still got a later start than normal. The cab pulled up after eleven. The club teemed with men, who spilled through the door and onto the outdoor sidewalk seating. It was muggy outside, but it would be even more humid inside. Still, they'd come all this way. They might as well have that drink.

Richard was standing at the end of the bar, shoulder to shoulder with a cluster of boys twenty years younger and twenty pounds thinner. He was practically invisible in his middle-aged plainness, but Paul spotted him eagerly. Thanks to some American Medical Association shindig in town—and the fact that doctors dominated the clique—there would only be the three of them tonight. Richard's muted presence was an unexpected relief. Yes, he was the epitome of boring. But if it weren't for him, showing up with Denny would've felt uncomfortably like a date.

Paul worked his way up to the bar and ordered three Gray Goose martinis (two with olives, one with a twist) and repeated the shoehorning process in reverse to get back to the evening's sparse company. Since he had drinks in his hand, Denny and Richard were particularly attentive. There were no free tables, so they found a spot on the wall, and they leaned.

Denny had a story about some new trainer at his gym who clearly had the hots for him even though the guy was supposedly straight, but the effects of too much stress and too little sleep washed over Paul as soon as the vodka hit his system, and the narrative faded as he let the pulse of the music drown it out. His eyes wandered. So many people, so many gay men, all of them searching for something. Friendship. Community. Or a little company for the night. There: happiness—sort of. Down the bar a bit, intensity. By the dance floor, desperation? Sadly, yes. And over there...most of the black guys were over there, by the DJ. This group was definitely younger than Paul, probably twenties. Close-clipped hair, dark skin gleaming in the humid atmosphere with the reflection of the strobing dance floor lights—red, blue, red, green. They moved differently than white guys. Even held themselves differently while they were standing still. Well, not the chubby one. He stood kind of like Richard, a bit hunched, like he wished he was smaller. But in general…how had Paul never considered the difference? The self-possession. The cocky grace.

"What's wrong?" Denny said in Paul's ear. "Is your wallet missing?" He took the empty glass from Paul's hand and began working his way up to the bar again. Luckily, there were a few rows of sweaty gay men between them by the time Paul registered what he'd just said.

Richard, oblivious to the whole exchange, began telling Paul about his new ergonomic keyboard. With time now to consider his reaction, Paul mentally rehearsed telling Denny he was an arrogant, over-privileged, self-righteous racist. Denny might only catch a word or two over the backbeat of the current song, but any part of that exclamation would do.

Then again, it would feel better to throw a drink in his face—but those sort of theatrics only worked when they were spontaneous. Paul's outrage wasn't a spontaneous, well-placed spike. More of a churning seethe. Fine. It would be a waste of good vodka, anyway.

When Denny made his way back and handed out the drinks, the response that came out of Paul's mouth wasn't one that he'd planned. "So you wouldn't date any of those guys?"

Denny scanned the club. He'd already forgotten the last thing he'd said. "Which guys?"

"Over there. By the DJ."

Denny searched.

Paul cleared his throat a few times, gathered his courage, and said, "The black guys."

Richard's eyebrows shot up toward his hairline. Denny laughed as he sipped his martini. A ripple danced over the vodka's surface.

"Why not?" Paul tried his best to make it sound curious rather than defensive, though the nuance was probably lost with the question shouted over the throbbing bass.

"You're serious, huh?" Denny scrutinized the men more carefully now, *very* carefully, and Paul began to wish he hadn't said anything. "Maybe... for a quickie. It's not like you'd have anything to say to each other once the clothes went back on."

Paul turned away from the black guys, as if they might feel the shame radiating from him even from the far end of the dance floor, and he buried his face in his drink. His mood had tanked. The martini tasted like rubbing alcohol now.

Or maybe his mortification wasn't the only reason. "You ordered the house brand vodka?" Richard cried. It was the most animated he'd been all night. "What the hell?"

Denny hid the hint of a smirk behind his glass. "The bartender must not have heard me."

"Oh, right, and you didn't notice the tab was twelve dollars less? Unless the only rail drinks you got are the ones you handed Paul and me. Give me your—"

"Don't touch my—they're all the same!"

While Richard and Denny girl-fighted, Paul backed up before the awful martini really did find itself on anyone's shirt. An unexpected pocket of free space opened up behind him, and he took a few more steps than he'd actually intended. And then a few more. And soon he was walking with purpose and the exit was there in front of him, the outside world beckoning just beyond it. He almost wandered onto the sidewalk carrying his cheap drink, and at the last moment, pressed it into the hand of a willowy twentyish guy in a baseball cap and a skintight tank top. "Gee, thanks, Mr. Glasses," the kid called out behind him. "Hey, you're kinda cute—what's your name?"

The young ones never spared Paul a second glance unless someone within earshot mentioned he was a pilot—probably the only thing that'd piqued this one's interest was the fact that company was the last thing Paul wanted at the moment. He ignored the invitation and kept on walking. One block. Two. Several. And finally hailing a cab was no longer necessary, because he'd be back home soon. In his pickled condo. With his sparse bedroom. And his empty refrigerator.

No, his empty life.

Calling the clique "drinking friends" seemed a bit generous. Paul was beginning to suspect he didn't even like them. Maybe it was mutual. They got their top-shelf round out of him. Now neither of them had even bothered to check where he'd—*wait a minute.*

Paul pulled out his phone. Flight 511 had thrown him for such a loop, he'd been so wiped out from lack of sleep, that he'd never turned his cell back on when he landed. He strode over to the nearest bus shelter, sat on the bench and powered on. Several messages lit the phone, from as far back as Thursday afternoon. He hadn't seen any of them since Scheduling had assigned him to Flight 511, though. A shudder coursed through him at the idea that some of them—in particular, the messages from the condo association—had come through while he was in Bermuda. Empty Bermuda.

Which was different from his condominium how, exactly?

Paul scrolled directly to the end of the list. There—good old reliable Richard had indeed called him not ten minutes after he'd stormed out of the club. He felt a bit guilty for blanketing Richard with the same distaste he currently felt for Denny. It wasn't Richard's fault Denny was being such a jerk about...Paul gasped.

Dallas.

There was a message from Dallas that would have happened when Paul was deplaning from his commute to DC in a haze of exhaustion and disbelief.

He pushed the play button, then abruptly stopped the message before it even began, thinking that he should save it and listen to it somewhere better than a bus stop bench—but he was still several blocks from home. There was no way he could wait that long. But maybe, if he ran? He stood, considered running, then decided against it and sat down again. Once he navigated to the message, he waffled a few more times (*Listen? No. But maybe...no, not yet, save it. Wait, yes...*) and then finally, holding his breath, put the phone to his ear.

"Hi, Paul, it's Dallas. I guess I thought you'd be home by now...."

A pause. Did he think Paul had deliberately let the message go to voicemail, that Paul was avoiding him? No, wait, it wouldn't have rung, it would have gone straight there, so he wouldn't have taken it personally. Right?

"Anyway...I just wanted you to know...."

He sounded so serious. What? *What?*

"Seems like we had ourselves a little shopping spree—and whatever's still got tags on it is getting returned Monday. Whatever I can't take back... well, I'll reimburse you."

Shopping? Really? That seemed awfully tame.

"It wouldn't have happened if I'd stayed in the cabin. But...I think you needed me more in the cockpit, and if we had to do it over, I would play it the same way again. Money's only money, you know? Listen, I just wanted to make sure you're okay. If you're not up to talking, at least text me, all right?" A long pause in which Paul was sure Dallas had hung up, and then, "I don't *think* anything else happened. But...let me know."

Paul clenched his ass. Hard. If anyone had been getting busy down there, he certainly would have noticed—even without the subtle hint that he should check. Still, the thought of what might have occurred while the cognizant part of him was sitting on an empty commuter jet reading a weirdo's notebook left him feeling...what? He wasn't sure. Part of him was profoundly relieved he hadn't come home to find the hotel soap, a remote control and a few used condoms rammed up his rectum, but part of him couldn't help but wonder.

Why not?

CHAPTER 13

While Dallas could appreciate a fine undergarment just as much as the next man…nearly sixty dollars for the tiny handful of red silk he was holding did seem a bit extreme. Even for inflated Bermuda prices. He held the underwear up in front of himself, right over his jeans, and considered his reflection in the mirrored closet door. Was he curious how his ass would look with that whisper of a thong slipped between his cheeks? Who wouldn't be? He was only human. But—he gave them a sniff—this particular pair hadn't been manhandled, and it still had its tags on. Monday morning, it was going right back to the store.

They'd better not balk about doing a chargeback, either. All those charge slips piled on his nightstand, the scraps of paper (some thin yellow, others slick white, all of them with a certain Paul Cronin's signature splayed boldly across the bottom) added up to one hell of a good time. Pilots didn't live as large as most people thought, not unless they were Captains who'd been flying with the same airline since the seventies. Besides, Dallas wouldn't dream of letting Paul foot this bill.

Dallas pulled another shopping bag from his luggage. Neckties in this one. Dallas had never considered a daffodil-colored tie, so it must have been Paul who'd picked it. He held it up to his chest and checked himself out. Not bad taste for a white boy. But, tags? Yes. Receipt? Yes. Good.

Return pile.

Yet another pair of underwear—though this one, on closer inspection, had a hole in it, a split where two fabric panels met just alongside the basket. Dallas caught a whiff of tell-tale muskiness from them. They'd been worn, but not for long. He poked his thumb through the hole. Manufacturing issue? Doubtful, at the prices they'd paid for everything so far. Maybe the briefs had been torn off him. Or...maybe that ratty edge was actually toothmarks. They hadn't tapped into his condom stash—he'd counted—and his body didn't feel like it had done a booty call while they were on autopilot. Still, he supposed it was possible they hadn't been entirely chaste.

His heart sank. It wasn't that the thought of Paul tearing through his underwear wasn't a good one—and it wasn't that he was disturbed that he couldn't say for sure if it had actually happened. What truly bothered him was the idea he'd been playing Paul like a gold digger.

And he couldn't even claim he would never dream of doing such a thing. Because apparently, he had.

The urge to call again and at least try to explain himself was hard to resist. If Paul had been in another time zone, just an hour earlier, maybe Dallas would have picked up that phone and dialed. It was after midnight now, though, and Paul needed to catch up on his sleep. Yes, that was it. He wasn't avoiding Dallas. Or so freaked out that Dallas would never see him again. He was just asleep. Out cold. Without even checking his messages.

Not that Dallas believed it. But it felt better than dwelling on the thought where some other First Officer, some stranger, met up with them in the crew lounge come Monday morning.

At least there were no more guilt-inducing shopping bags left in his luggage. He took out a uniform shirt and lobbed it to the hamper. Paul still had his spare slacks: at $29.95 new, hardly a fair trade. Nothing left but a pair of socks...although they felt awfully heavy. When Dallas allowed them to unfurl, a small, heavy box dropped onto his coverlet. A jewelry box.

Dread filling his chest, he opened it. A pair of huge diamond-stud earrings winked back at him. He closed his eyes and turned his head away, worried he might throw up on them. And then he felt his ear. The piercing, which hadn't held an earring for months and should have felt like a little mostly-shut lump, was tender and slightly crusted. Dallas had no idea what the diamonds would cost, only that they'd probably run twice as much on Bermuda. And receipt or not, worn or not, these earrings were about to get a very thorough cleaning—and then they were going right back where they came from.

***

Instant oatmeal tasted like wallpaper paste, and it wouldn't really compliment the lingering hint of olives and cheap vodka that coated the back of Paul's tongue. However, those pre-measured packets did have a very good shelf life. The microwave beeped. He removed the bowl, stirred, and proceeded to swallow it down, too hot and not fully coagulated. His nausea abated with something other than liquor in his stomach. Even so, everything around him still felt just as surreal as it had when he'd landed Flight 511. The bowl burning his hand. The countertop digging into his hip. The land line giving off its familiar digital ring.

At one o'clock in the morning?

He was about to let the built-in machine get it when he realized it might be Dallas calling, and he skidded across the hardwood floors in his socks and nearly doused the phone in fake apples and cinnamon in his eagerness to pick up. He overshot, wobbled, got his bearings, and grabbed. But when he saw *D Armstrong DDS* on the caller ID, he snatched his hand back from the phone, clutching his sad oatmeal to his chest. Denny was the last person he wanted to talk to.

-beep-

"You're so offended by a rail drink you storm out like Scarlett O'Hara? *Come on, Paul, I was just having some fun with you two. Wanted to see who'd notice first. That's all. You didn't even taste it,* I'll *bet."*

His voice sounded hollow, like he was in the stairwell. And then a door clicked. A hallway door on Paul's level. Not Denny's.

Paul's eyes cut to his front door.

"So Richard turns out be the one with the refined palate? Who'd a thunk

it? It's always the quiet ones who surprise you."

Just go away, Denny.

"Don't tell me you're asleep already. Your lights are on."

That's right. And my phone remains unanswered. Now, please take a hint.

"Or maybe it wasn't the drink that sent you packing. Maybe you scored... and you're not actually alone in there."

As if it was any of his business.

"But you, picking up a guy in the two seconds my back was turned? Well, you and I both know the chances of you working that fast are slim to none."

That kid by the door actually might have...damn it, that wasn't the point.

"Come on, Paul. I know you're in there."

Seriously, Denny was starting to sound like one of those bad seventies slasher flicks. The ones that ended with, "We traced the call...and it's coming from your own house!" Paul hugged his oatmeal bowl harder and made sure he was breathing very, very quietly.

And then he saw motion beneath his front door. The strip of dim illumination now showed two dark gaps where a pair of feet blocked the ambient glow from the recessed hall lighting.

"How about a little nightcap?" Denny's voice was very low, too low to hear through the door, but terribly distinct on the machine. *"I'll leave when we're done—I promise. I know how you hate it when I untuck your hospital corners."*

Paul's gorge rose at the thought of Denny kicking around in his carefully-made bed. And the chemical smell his hair products left behind on the pillowcase. And that weird face he made when he...ugh.

"Offer's going once...going twice...."

Then *go* already.

The answering machine beeped off and spared Paul from Denny's final desperate attempt at a blasé, half-hearted seduction, the results of which neither of them would particularly enjoy—that Paul would have likely avoided entirely if the doctor posse hadn't been at that conference tonight. But with only Paul and Richard to choose from, Denny's sights had landed on Paul. The twin dark patches remained under his door for nearly a minute, a minute during which Paul breathed so shallowly his head started to throb, but then finally they moved along, and receding footsteps sounded in the hallway, a door opened and closed, and blessed silence remained.

Paul waited a long moment just in case Denny resurrected himself, just like one of those hockey-masked killers who sat back up again, bristling with knives, fireplace pokers and ice picks the minute you thought everyone was safe and the end credits were about to roll. But no. It seemed Paul had dodged his friends-with-benefits duties.

For now.

Paul tiptoed over to his kitchen and scraped the congealed remnants of the oatmeal down the garbage disposal, though he didn't dare run it. Not with a horny dentist skulking through the hallways and stairwells searching for evidence that he was awake.

Maybe in the morning he could find a greeting card to deliver the message "Let's just be drinking friends!" If Hallmark didn't already make one, they damn well should. His phone message light blinked at him, taunting him with the possibility that Denny might get bored with masturbating and come back downstairs and urge Paul to take over wherever he'd left off. Unplugging the power cord took care of that. The light went dark.

Paul did his best to put Denny out of his mind as he changed into his pajamas and brushed his teeth. In the grand scheme of things, he decided, a few awkward advances really shouldn't merit more than a passing thought. He'd finally gotten the evening's events firmly compartmentalized into his "boring night out" category when his cell phone chirped out its text message signal from the slacks he'd worn to the club, which were now draped over the vanity chair, waiting to be evaluated and relegated either to the closet or the dry cleaning pile.

Evidently Denny couldn't resist getting in a parting jab. Paul considered not looking. But he couldn't leave a new text unread any more than he could leave his bed unmade. He was already running through the gamut of "leave me alone already!" responses he might reply with when it registered that the text was not from Denny at all. It was an automated notice from AVA informing him that next week's proposed schedule was waiting in his inbox.

Paul powered on his computer. It seemed to take forever to load, to get online, to bring up his email. And then, there it was in his inbox. A link to his schedule.

He hadn't been this anxious to see it since he was a reserve pilot on call. He gathered his courage, and he clicked.

Monday - depart FLL 14:04 - arrive BDA 16:40....

There it was, Monday through Friday, fly to Bermuda, overnight, and back again in the morning. Never, in all his years of flying, had he seen a flight pairing so utterly simple. Paul's weeks normally began and ended in Boston, and hit another eight to twelve cities in between—whenever possible keeping him off the clock, wandering the local AVA crew lounge and dozing in a recliner, or spending the night watching boring TV in a strange motel. He kept hoping that with two airports, he could manage to end up on a DC hub eventually and no longer need to commute and keep a residence in both cities. But to fly somewhere and then turn around in the same jet and come back again? Five days a week, as if he was just driving a car to a regular job? It was ludicrous.

And the way the overnights were structured, all of them counting toward his flight time, it actually netted more money, too, with less time flying. A schedule like that was a pilot's dream.

A dream...if you overlooked the turbulence. The schedule failed to mention that little blip, maybe as an asterisk between his departure and arrival, but Paul had no doubt he could count on its occurrence.

He took off his glasses and knuckled his dry eyes. He may have told Captain Kaye he intended to take Scheduling up on its request if he was given the chance—but it wasn't duty that was driving his hand toward the mouse, and his cursor toward the "accept" button. It was the fact that even though the Bermuda memories were slightly older, tarnished with panic and disbelief, the single night he'd spent on the island felt more vivid, more real, than the existence that, until this point, he'd spent his entire life creating.

CHAPTER 14

It was early when Dallas pulled up in front of Marlin's house. The paperboy (not even a kid, but a guy hardly younger than Dallas in a rusty pickup truck) was slinging Sunday papers out on walkways and lawns. That didn't happen on Dallas' street. In Oakland Park, the inner-city neighborhood Dallas called home, most people were renters in tract houses—and if a Sunday paper managed to appear in the vicinity of your doorstep, unless you were right there waiting for it on the other side, it would be gone by the time you eventually came out to get it.

People with money lived in these big ol' two-story suburban homes. Maybe not the type of CEOs you'd find on the covers of in-flight magazines, but the kind of folks with six-figure incomes, four-car garages, and boats or RVs in their driveways. Marlin only owned the two vehicles: his motorcycle and his all-wheel drive Subaru. But he liked to tinker with things, and he'd filled the rest of his garage with tools and toys and whatever else he'd picked up on his travels. "Mortgaged to the hilt," he used to say. (*Used* to say? The thought brought a lump to Dallas' throat.) It wasn't a complaint, exactly—Marlin wasn't a complainer. He always insisted that he created his own reality, which Dallas took to mean that if he had a problem with his massive mortgage, he should either move to a cheaper place or find a better paying job.

If Dallas tried hard enough, if he blanked out the memory of Kaye's voice saying the two awful words, "Marlin's dead," he could almost see that garage door opening up and Marlin striding out, with no shirt, hair all crazy, sunglasses on his forehead and a pair of those godawful martial arts pants he liked so much, some ridiculous snakeskin pattern that wouldn't look decent on nobody. And somehow, he'd be pulling that look off. He'd beckon and say, "C'mon out back, man, the water's fine." No, wait, that wasn't it. He'd say it was *awesome.* And he'd be working on a cookout that was more of a science project, with a whole turkey smoking over hickory in an aluminum trash can, and some homebrew he'd been saving for the occasion that would taste so nasty they'd end up running out to the Publix for an emergency twelve-pack of Miller instead....

And now that would never happen again.

Dallas had spent all day Saturday on and off the phone with Kaye, with AVA, with every hospital he could find in the phone book, scouring for some indication of what might have happened to Marlin and coming up blank. The house didn't offer up any clues as to what had happened. There were no broken windows, no fire-blackened stucco, no tatters of black and yellow crime scene tape fluttering from the cypress. The place looked empty, though. Felt that way, too.

Dallas was peering at the living room window, searching for movement inside that might negate what his eyes were telling him—that the house was empty, that Marlin was well and truly gone—when a vehicle he'd thought was just passing him by pulled up beside him, far too close. A cop car, driver side window down.

They hadn't told him to step out of the vehicle at least. Yet.

Dallas hadn't had a run-in with the law since he'd been hauled out of a seedy club as a teenager for underage drinking. He schooled his features to be calm, unflappable, and no doubt slightly arrogant, and then he waited for the cops to talk first so they couldn't infer anything from his tone and use it as an excuse to give him the business end of their magnum flashlights. "You've been parked here for nearly half an hour," the cop in the driver seat said. He was a white guy, stocky, middle-aged. The other one was the same, but leaner. Both wore mirrored shades. Neither had an expression Dallas could read.

"It's my friend's house." Sure—they believed that. Their expressions didn't change. Their faces were so immobile they could've just come from a Botox treatment. Obviously what they thought was that Dallas was casing the place. Because that's what happened when people who lived alone died. Brothers from the 'hood came around to see what sorts of goods might be liberated while nobody was home.

When people died.

The who's-less-flappable standoff was over before it began as Dallas' expression slipped. When he spoke, his voice wobbled. "Marlin and me, we worked together. And nobody at AVA is sayin'...." If someone had broken in and popped a cap in Marlin while he was listening to one of those meditation tapes of his, these cops would know—it was their beat. Of course they'd know. "What happened?"

Their expressions didn't shift, exactly, but something in Dallas' delivery, either his tone, his intensity, or the details he'd just given, must have reached them. Their body language changed. He hadn't realized they'd been sitting assertively, on high alert, until the driver settled back into his seat, looking uneasy now. "I don't have that information, sir."

Maybe they just didn't want to tell him, or maybe it was true. Maybe Marlin—rock climber, bungee jumper, jiu-jitsu black belt—had actually slipped in the shower and split his head on the edge of the tub, and that death had been too routine to constitute noteworthy gossip at the Sheriff's Office. "Who has it, then?"

"You'll need to contact the family."

Dallas looked at the house again, as if it should have been able to answer him itself. No doubt Marlin had a family. He hadn't sprung into the world from nothing, after all. But in the entire year in which Dallas had known him, he'd never once mentioned so much as a picnic or a phone call. Even on Christmas, when Dallas had earned Auntie Esther's eternal wrath by leaving to prep Flight 511 before the rib roast was brown—December 25th was just another day for Marlin Fritsch.

"What about the urgent care clinic?" Dallas asked. "Would they know something?"

"The family," the cop repeated flatly. "There's nothing here to see."

Checking the urge to glance one more time at Marlin's house (as if it might back him up by offering some kind of new insight) Dallas wordlessly started his engine, made sure he signaled properly and did his head and mirror checks, pulled away from the curb, and pointed himself toward Oakland Park. He did glance at the rearview one last time, just in case. But the house hadn't changed. Neither had the pair of cops waiting in front of it to make sure he was actually leaving.

How was he supposed to find Marlin's family? He turned the thought over as he made his way back home, noticing not only that the lawns were more unkempt in the neighborhood where he lived (his, included) but that the driveways were cracked and shot through with weeds. He'd shared so much with the rest of the flight crew over the past year, it was easy to forget their differences until they stared him in the face…or crept up through the blacktop. He snagged a tangle of chickweed on his way up the driveway and tore it loose, then stared at his hand, wondering what, exactly, he'd planned to do with it. He dropped it into the rock mulch beside his front steps, let himself in, and wondered where on earth to begin searching for this family he wasn't even sure existed.

The phone book was the obvious choice. There'd be fewer Fritsches than Turners, anyway. But because it was probable that Marlin's family wasn't even in Fort Lauderdale since he'd never once mentioned visiting them, Dallas wasn't expecting much. And even if he did locate a relative, what would he say? *Can you tell me what happened to Marlin? Oh, you* weren't *even aware that anything was wrong? Let me burden you with the terrible news….*

Maybe there'd be some answers online by now. Combing the web might be time-consuming and ineffective, but it was safer than blundering into a phone call Dallas might end up regretting. He'd just stumbled upon a series of online articles on juicing and enzymes Marlin had written several years before—accompanied by a tiny Marlin photo in the sidebar, with dark, windswept hair, smiling with an intensity that bordered on manic—when his phone chimed to alert him to an incoming text.

Maybe Kaye had found something. His heart sank, because maybe he really didn't want to know…then again, maybe it was Chantal checking in.

Or maybe it was just Scheduling, who really should have texted by now to let him know his usual itinerary was ready to be approved.

He was so sure the message would be something in the spectrum of mundane to terrible that he needed to stare at the readout for a moment before he realized the text was from Paul.

OK if I come to FL today?

In other words...could he spend the night? Dallas read the text again and tried to figure out how to say it was more than okay. That he was so lonely, that his house felt so empty, he'd turned the TV up way too loud (on a *golf tournament*, no less) to make it feel like there were people around. That every time he realized he'd never see Marlin again, he felt like a piece of him had been ripped out. That the thought of being with Paul was the single bright spot in the most dismal weekend he could remember.

As he stared at the message, another implication struck him. Paul was not only asking to spend the night, he was confirming that when Flight 511 taxied to the runway tomorrow, he'd be at the yoke.

It took him five tries, deleting more flubbed characters than he actually typed, but finally Dallas managed to send, *Come on over*. He was following up with his address when the doorbell rang. He picked up his remote and muted the golf announcer. Hopefully whoever was on his stoop would be quick about telling him whatever they needed to say or selling him whatever they wanted to unload. He didn't have time to waste—he needed to get himself presentable. And change the sheets. And see to all that chickweed in the driveway. But when he opened the door, the impulse to ditch the person on his doorstep vanished when he saw who it was.

CHAPTER 15

"Surprise," Paul said, smiling anxiously. He pressed a bottle of wine into Dallas' hand. "I hope this isn't awful. The card reader at the liquor store wouldn't take my card, so I had to pay cash. It was either this, or a box of chablis. And I figured the one bottle wouldn't lead us down the road to headache-ville, even if I've never actually heard of the vineyard before… and it was on sale for nine bucks."

The card reader? Oh, no. Shame welled up inside Dallas, but his manners took over where his confidence left off, and he stepped aside and invited Paul into the air-conditioned shade of his living room.

"So," Paul said, "Scheduling gave me your address. Which is kind of disturbing. Because I'm sure we've both flown with plenty of people we were just as happy to never see again."

Dallas carried the bottle toward the fridge, realized it was a shiraz, and set it on the countertop instead. And then he wished he hadn't, because holding it had given him something to do with himself. It was tempting to say that he'd wondered if he would ever see Paul again either, but since that would sound pretty desperate, Dallas kept it to himself.

"Good thing your invitation still stood, since I'd be spending the night in the crew lounge if you didn't—"

"Paul." The nervous chatter stopped. "We've got to be real with each other. You don't know me, and I don't know you."

Paul reeled back a step, and then recovered. "Not yet."

"Not yet," Dallas agreed, softening his tone. "But being where we've been, and seeing what we've seen…we can't afford to play games."

Paul considered Dallas' words, then said, "Okay."

"Then I'm going to be plain. And if you can't handle that, you should back out now."

"No. Go ahead."

Dallas took a deep breath, and said, "Ever since I can remember, I have relied on one person, and one person only: me. This place ain't nothing to look at, but I can afford it. And my car's not new, and it's not fancy, but it's paid for, and it runs."

"I don't get what—"

"Let me finish. I didn't set my sights on you because you're a pilot, and I'm sure as hell not after your money. You caught my eye. That's all."

Paul toyed with the hem of his shirt for a few seconds, then said, "And here I thought you were gearing up to tell me something scary."

"There was no problem with the credit card reader. It was our fault. We spent us some money in Bermuda."

"Okay."

He sounded awfully matter-of-fact. Obviously he hadn't been online to check his account. "Paul, you threw away over eight thousand dollars on me—and that was just on the stuff I found the receipts for. We probably blew another grand on dinner and drinks."

"Okay."

"Once we return everything that we can, I think we can get it down to half that, and hopefully—"

Paul crossed the room and ran his hand down Dallas' arm, pausing to circle the crook of the elbow with his thumb. His touch sang through Dallas' nerves like adrenaline. "Don't worry about it. It's nothing. I mean, it's not *nothing*—it'll take me some time to pay it off."

"I will be the one to pay—"

Paul leaned in and cut off Dallas' intended tirade about how he fully intended to make good on every last cent before it even started, easing up against him lover-close, and speaking so softly that no one in the world but Dallas could hear. "It's not important." He paused, then, with his lips poised just shy of Dallas' mouth. Either of them could have initiated the kiss, yet both held back. Dallas, because he'd convinced himself that Paul clearly didn't know what he was getting himself into. But Paul, so close he was a blur of pale skin and black glasses frames...Dallas really couldn't say what he was waiting for.

"I can't stop thinking about you," Paul said. He moved, maybe only a hint of a movement, as if he would pull away now that he'd finally voiced what was on his mind. But Dallas caught him around the waist and held him, until he gave in and pressed their bodies together, instead. All the tension Dallas had been holding, all the uncertainty and the shame, all the ugliness drained away as he figured out how he and Paul fit together. Now, up close, Paul felt slighter than him, but only a bit. Wiry and firm, maybe a shade taller, or maybe it was only the difference in their shoes. Paul didn't seem like a forward kind of guy, but there was a firmness in the way he held himself now that said he didn't plan on going anywhere, and when Dallas nudged him closer still, walking his fingers across Paul's back, Paul was the one to finally seal their fragile connection with a kiss.

Paul fell into the kiss like a gambler playing his last card. He parted his lips, breath stuttering as Dallas slid his tongue in. It turned deep, and then rough, and then eager, as the need in each one of them spiked, need calling to need, whipping itself into a frenzy. They sagged, grappled, then spilled onto the floor, heads on the worn living room carpet, legs sprawled over the kitchen linoleum, and the rounded metal strip that divided the flooring pressed into Dallas' shoulder blades.

Paul straddled Dallas and shoved his shirt up. The situation was out of Dallas' hands now, as this unexpected intensity from Paul—this determination—swept him up and carried him toward the point of intimacy, the moment he'd been approaching gingerly in his mind, convinced that it might not come at all, but if it did, he'd need to be careful so as not to spook Paul and chase him off. All that fussing and fretting turned out to be for nothing. Paul already had Dallas' shirt off. He could have tossed it aside, but he didn't. He rolled it up and slipped it beneath Dallas' head, looking him square in the eye the whole time. Dallas reached for Paul's shirt, but Paul brushed his hands away. He pushed against Dallas' chest, pinning him there, and said with total seriousness, "No, let me."

It had been a long time since Dallas had been with anyone, and even longer since he *remembered* being with someone. Lying back and enjoying the ride while his partner did all the heavy lifting wasn't exactly his style. If he shifted his focus to Paul, though—seeing the way Paul looked at him—the watching and the waiting took on an entirely different feel. Paul began by caressing his chest, fingers splayed wide, spanning Dallas' body. It felt good, but the pleasure seemed incidental. It was more as if Paul thought he needed to learn his way around.

The parts might be a different color, but it took the same thing to wind them up and set them off. Dallas was tempted to say it, but he held back. Maybe he was reading things all wrong. Maybe Paul was always careful. No doubt he was. But this level of focus could also mean that Paul was heading into uncharted territory, and he didn't quite trust his own footing. Pointing it out would only make him self-conscious. And with his hands already at Dallas' waistband, he was building his momentum plenty fast without any need for encouragement.

Paul yanked Dallas' shorts, underwear and all, down around his thighs. Dallas' freed cock fell onto his leg, already fat and willing, stiffening fast as Paul's gasp tickled his balls like a playful breeze. Was Paul itching for him to talk nasty, give a few orders and tell him how to suck that big black dick? Maybe.

Paul took off his glasses and set them up on the countertop.

Maybe he was beyond words, because now that there was one less thing between them, he'd already planted his sweet mouth on Dallas' stomach, kissing, licking, savoring his way down, and the low noises coming from his throat—eager and horny—were hotter than any sex-talk that would only sound like a line from a bad skin flick. Dallas couldn't hold back anymore. He reached down and got hold of Paul's hair—thick and straight, slick between his fingers like satin sheets—and he squeezed. Paul grunted and went deeper, tongue-first, into Dallas' crotch. His tongue was everywhere, balls and shaft and taint, and then finally, higher, until delicious wetness of his mouth plunged down.

It may not have been what Dallas set out to do, but every time he nudged Paul, every time he encouraged him to take more, Paul squirmed like he was getting off on the idea. And pretty soon Dallas had Paul by the head, forcing himself deep, and hard, and Paul's fingertips were digging into his hips and he was humping the floor, and the heady funk of sex welled up around them, sweat and musk and man. Dallas would have wanted it to last, to be tender, even kind. But there was no way. Their needs had taken over, as unstoppable as the turbulence—only with both of them present now to bear witness to what their bodies were doing.

Dallas' spine arched up off the carpet, and his lower back peeled off the linoleum. He would have been a gentleman and pulled out before he came, but he wasn't the one on top, and all he could do was hold on tight while Paul sucked and sucked and sucked until he thought he'd turn inside out. He came hard, a shock so sudden it almost wasn't pleasure anymore. Except that once he'd gone beyond that brink and it was almost too much, Paul gentled his mouth, easing Dallas back down to earth with the finesse he'd use to touch down his landing gear on the tarmac.

Dallas caught his breath, dazed, shirtless, shorts around his knees, staring up at the textured ceiling while his pulse pounded in his temples and groin. Paul crawled up beside him and settled into the crook of his arm. The only thing Paul had taken off were his glasses. He looked different without them. Vulnerable. "I can't help but wonder," he said, "why all we did while we were on autopilot was go shopping. Doesn't that seem weird?"

"I never know why the autopilots do what they do."

"You talk about it like they're separate people. They're us, right? Sort of?"

"Sort of." It was the type of distinction Marlin would have enjoyed theorizing about. Realizing that he hadn't thought about Marlin for the past few minutes—that he'd actually gone and enjoyed himself while the news was still fresh—allowed the heavy coldness of guilt to seep in, where before there'd been only optimism and joy.

Paul said, "Maybe your autopilot wasn't into mine."

"Now you talkin' crazy."

Paul cracked a shy grin. "Okay, maybe it was liberating to say, 'To hell with the money, we're gonna have fun.' Maybe I should try it sometime. Within reason."

Dallas smiled into Paul's hair. A shopping spree with a budget wasn't exactly a spree. You couldn't be a moderate version of an autopilot—they were entities unto themselves. But if rationalizing things could help Paul make peace with his other self, Dallas was all for it. Better than poor Kaye, always at odds with her counterpart.

Just stop thinking about it. The autopilots. Bermuda. Marlin. You're with Paul now, and you've finally found someone you can really connect with. Enjoy it. Dallas rolled to face him, to brush their lips together. He ran his hand up Paul's thigh. "Your turn."

Paul nudged Dallas' hand away. "Later. I think I just needed to get that out of my system."

"You sure?"

Paul traced Dallas' knuckles with his fingertip. "We've got plenty of time. I mean…since I'm spending the night." It wasn't what he'd meant at all, though Dallas didn't call him on it. It was enough that he'd agreed to pilot Flight 511. He didn't need to analyze his reasons.

At Dallas' knee, his phone chimed an incoming text. He would have ignored it, but when Paul rolled into a sitting position, it did seem like a pretty good opportunity to get them both off the floor. He stood and gave Paul a hand up. Paul brushed himself off, put his glasses back on, and said, "Could I use your bathroom?"

Dallas pointed him toward the hall, pulled up his shorts, and then took a glance at his phone.

Scheduling.

AVA didn't usually wait until Sunday afternoon to send him his Monday morning assignment. He hadn't really read anything into it… until now. What if that meant something was wrong? What if it wasn't his usual assignment? What if he'd open up his email and find out he was flying out to Newark in the morning instead of Bermuda?

He opened the laptop on his coffee table, hopped online and hit his AVA bookmark. The login page seemed to take forever to load—a forever during which he imagined himself kissing Paul goodbye at the airport, and then leaving him to the tender mercies of the turbulence in the hands of some other flight attendant, some *stranger*. No. There was no way he'd allow that to happen. He glanced back at his text to try and determine if it was different in any way, but no, it looked the same as it always did. Same all-caps. Same message. Same…wait, what was that? That square thing, off to the side?

Dallas squinted. The white square was a little camera icon he'd somehow managed to overlook all weekend. He'd taken a photo—or, since he didn't remember taking any pictures lately, his autopilot had. He navigated away from the text and called it up.

Even on the tiny screen, it was quite an eyeful.

Paul, without his glasses, looking anything but vulnerable. Apparently this afternoon hadn't been his first time with a big black dick in his mouth after all. Given that the picture had been snapped with Dallas' phone and the torn underwear were in view, the dick in the photo likely belonged to him (or technically his autopilot). It lay there on Paul's tongue, hard, massive and shiny-brown, while Paul tipped a bottle of bubbly over it, capturing some of the champagne with his cupped tongue while most of it ran down his neck and shoulders. Not just any champagne: Dom Perignon. A hundred-fifty a bottle here—three or four in Bermuda. And not just one bottle. Through the extreme perspective, Dallas saw a few empties that lay at their feet, tiny, as if they were a mile away. With Paul jerking off on them.

No wonder this afternoon he was content to wait. He'd probably milked his balls dry in Bermuda. Carefully, so as not to chafe.

If he didn't know any better, Dallas would have suspected his autopilot had snapped the picture to secure bragging rights. Except he did know better. The autopilots never saw themselves as separate entities, they didn't plan ahead, and they showed no interest in communicating with their more rational selves. The other Dallas probably just thought Paul looked mighty fine on his knees and decided to save the view for posterity.

The computer monitor lit up with his schedule, tearing him away from the sight of those pale, naked thighs, the ruddy dick in Paul's fist...those gleaming rivulets on his flushed chest that could've been more than just champagne.

Dallas tucked his phone away, turned to his computer and found the airport code, heart pounding. Not Newark. Bermuda.

Relief flooded him, with guilt right on its tail. He had no right to feel relieved. This was not a normal assignment. This was not a normal anything. It would be wrong to get all swept up in Paul—given Marlin, given the autopilots. Given, especially, the turbulence.

Then why did it feel so right?

He accepted his schedule with a deliberate click, then went into the kitchen and dug a pair of wine glasses from the back of his cabinet while water ran in the bathroom—a sound a hell of a lot more companionable than a golf announcer. He'd been alone ever since Chantal went off to USF, and yet having another person in his house felt like the most natural thing in the world. It made Dallas feel downright domestic. Were these the right kind of glasses for a shiraz? It'd be a better treatment than they'd given the Dom P—once he rinsed off the dust.

Paul came up from behind and wrapped his arms around Dallas' waist, palms gliding over his stomach. Close. Familiar. Easy. When he spoke, the words tickled the back of Dallas' neck. "So, the text you got—everything okay?"

Dallas would be on Flight 511 tomorrow, same as Paul. And when Paul hit the turbulence and came out the other side on autopilot, who'd be right there to keep him out of mischief and see him through the night? Dallas, that's who. He slid his phone from his pocket as if to verify the contents of the message, though he knew full well what it said—and he quietly deleted the photo that would cause Paul "within reason" Cronin to die of embarrassment if he ever saw it. "It's all good, baby." He pocketed the phone and unscrewed the metal cap of the nine-dollar shiraz. "It's perfect."

CHAPTER 16

-ONE YEAR AGO-

Barbecue. Marlin cruised up to the house. Pink balloons that read "Congratulations" were tied to the mailbox, the lamp post and even the wax myrtles, but the smell of hot dogs blistering on the grill would have drawn him to the correct address as sure as a line of runway lights. After a week on Flight 511, he wasn't taking anything for granted—and since it was quite possible that nothing was what it seemed, he now noticed absolutely everything. He parked his Harley, slung his helmet under his arm, gave his sweaty hair a quick tousle and headed toward the sound of music and laughter in the back yard.

Tiki torches and patio lights were twinkling, margaritas were flowing, and a pair of middle-aged women were attempting to use the boom box as a spontaneous makeshift karaoke machine. He paused at the fringe of the crowd and soaked up the atmosphere, then took a deep breath. Charcoal, citronella and fresh-cut lawn. It didn't get much better than that.

"Oh my God!"

Marlin turned. The host of the party, his buddy Ralph, stood framed in the screen door with a pitcher of fresh margaritas on a tray and a tiara on his head. He looked a bit pudgier than he had the last time Marlin had seen him, with bigger bags under his eyes and a shinier bald spot—a student's schedule will do that to you, especially at forty-five. But his smile was still bright, maybe even a little cocky. Marlin was relieved that Ralph's big achievement hadn't changed him any. And then he wondered why he'd ever thought it might. People are who they are. The things that happen to them only accentuate their uniqueness.

Marlin smiled. Ever since the turbulence, it seemed there was an epiphany around every corner.

He dumped his helmet in a weed-choked planter and jogged up to the deck. "So...are we gonna have to start calling you 'Doc' now?"

"Oh, go on." Ralph tossed his head, but the tiara managed to stay put, though it slid a bit to one side. He probably had a drink (or five) in him by now. "That does have a catchy ring, doesn't it? Everyone knows me as Rev. Ralph, though. And Reverend Doctor is such a mouthful. Pity."

They stopped walking as an older woman wove her way off the deck, barely avoiding impact with a card table full of chips, dip and salsa. They fell into step behind her, since she seemed so sure of her wobbly trajectory, when she spun around to face Marlin so suddenly he needed to back up a step to avoid colliding with her.

"You're the pilot," she said brightly, "aren't you?"

He took in her frizzy perm, then glanced down at her *World's Best Grandma* T-shirt. She didn't strike him as the type of person to have an aviation fascination. But Marlin wasn't one to judge by external appearances. People owned bodies. They weren't owned by them. "Yep, that's me."

"It's such an important job...but such a dangerous one."

The glib response would be that you're more likely to die in a traffic accident on the way to the airport than you are in the cockpit, but something about the way the World's Best Grandma was searching his eyes made the shallow response fall away. "I don't worry about fear," he said. "In my book, it's not an emotion. It's more like...a choice."

"And you're happy with your choices?"

Marlin considered the bizarre turn his life had recently taken, and realized that if he had been given a choice between embracing the turbulence or charting a course around it, he would definitely have taken the more interesting option. No doubt in his mind. "Totally."

One of the other guests snagged the World's Best Grandma for their bocce ball team and dragged her toward the far end of the lawn while

Marlin snagged a handful of Doritos. "Who was that?"

Ralph shrugged. "Must be from the Center—though I can't put a name to the face. I'll ask around."

As they meandered toward one of many picnic tables covered in pink plastic tablecloths Marlin remarked, "Awesome balloons, by the way."

"Aren't they a stitch?" Ralph set down the tray. One of his guests immediately made off with the margarita pitcher. "A few of the neighbors swung by to ask if I was expecting a little girl. Is it that obvious I've put on nearly twenty pounds?"

"Maybe they thought you were adopting."

"Have you seen what it costs to adopt? There's no way I'd be able to afford it unless I found a sugar daddy. I'll be paying off my student loans until I'm sixty."

"You must be due for a salary hike, now that you've got all those fancy letters after your name."

"Puh-lease. I've tried having jobs just for the money. I was the most miserable insurance adjustor you ever laid eyes on." No big surprise. Marlin couldn't even picture him in a suit. "There are jobs, even careers. And then there are vocations. Things you do because you're in Alignment with them and doing anything else feels plain wrong. And the prestige, the money, none of it really matters. When you're living your Alignment, you're free to be you."

Vocation. Alignment. Yes. Bermuda should have felt wrong—entirely, freakishly, straitjacket-and-padded-room wrong. But when the assignment appeared on Marlin's online schedule that morning, five simple flights to the island and back, didn't signing on for another week feel like the most natural thing in the world?

Marlin paused halfway to picking up a carrot stick from the veggie platter and lost himself in reverie. Ralph's hand closed gently over his wrist. "You seem distracted," Ralph said. "What is it?"

Nothing I could explain to you in this mob of happy, tipsy middle-aged partiers. "Work has been a little, uh…weird lately. Interesting. But still weird. I'm not really sure what to make of it."

"You're at that age—thirty-four? Thirty-five? You don't even look it with that gorgeous head of hair. That's when I started to wonder if I was on the right track or not. Whether that was all there was to life. And then I found Unity, and I took a good, hard look at myself, started paying attention to my Alignment...and here I am now. Happy. In debt, but happy."

"I'm in Alignment," Marlin said quickly, surprised at what a knee-jerk reaction that assertion was. Because maybe the Bermuda situation was total weirdness...but since when did being weird ever make anything wrong? In fact, wasn't exploring this bizarre, unsettling, empty destination a heck of a lot more interesting than ordering room service and staring at the institutional wallpaper inside a lame hotel room? When Marlin was in flight school, he'd envisioned himself soaring over the Alaskan wilderness on rescue missions, or dropping care packages over drought-ravaged sub-Saharan countries. Not flying commercial jets. Bermuda would have been a better destination than any of the boring commuter hubs he'd flown into and out of over the past five years. But extra-dimensional Bermuda was even cooler. "I'm happy, too," he said, testing the word.

"Are you?"

Marlin mulled over the concept, then spoke with more certainty. "Yeah...I am. I'm just a little confused."

"Color me intrigued. What's got you wondering?"

"My purpose, I guess. What's my purpose?"

"That's quite the question to ask, especially when the ink on my diploma's barely dry. Speaking of which, wanna see?" Marlin nodded. Ralph steered him across the deck and through the back door. "I just can't stop showing it off. At this rate I'm gonna wear a rut across the carpet."

It was a small, plain document, but it was displayed with pride. Ralph Kemp, D. D. "What's that stand for?"

Ralph beamed. "Doctor of Divinity."

"Nice."

Marlin put his arm around Ralph, and together they gazed at Ralph's massive accomplishment. And then, as he turned to see who the latest arrival was to the margarita bash, the newly titled Reverend Dr. Ralph

Kemp spied something on the opposite wall that caught his bleary eye. "Maybe no one else can tell you what your purpose is but you...but I do have a suggestion to help you find a bit of clarity."

"I'm all ears."

Ralph crossed the room and spread his arms wide to present a poster-sized collage. Marlin hadn't paid it much mind, figuring it was something the Center's youth group had put together. On closer inspection, Marlin saw newspaper and magazine cutouts of dozens of unrelated images: gay men with bright white smiles holding hands; white stucco houses with Spanish tile roofs; an iPad; a yacht. "It works," Ralph said. "See?" He pointed to the words *Follow Your Calling - Masters and Doctors of Divinity Program* printed in happy blue letters that had been cut from a brochure. "I made this two years ago—no, wait, three. I've already begun to manifest."

"Can I touch it?" Marlin asked. Ralph gestured for him to go ahead. He ran his fingers over the densely packed images. Lots and lots of smiling men. Ralph hadn't manifested himself a man quite yet, at least not a steady one. But now that he was Reverend *Doctor* Ralph, serving a spiritually, racially and sexually diverse congregation, the sky was the limit. "I like it. Is this a technique you made up, or has it got a name?"

"I can't take credit," Ralph said warmly, as if he wished he could. "It's called a vision board."

"Right on."

"You don't need to say so just to be polite. If it's too soccer mom scrapbooky for you, maybe you could try journaling a question to your higher self, or—"

"No way." Marlin ran his fingertips across a red tiled roof, imagining the collage populated with images of Bermuda as clearly as if it were already manifest in physical reality. "This is perfect."

-PRESENT DAY-

"Finally." Kaye elbowed Dallas out of the way and sprinted toward the pool, shedding her towel and flip flops as she ran. The lifeguard called out that there was no diving—a fact that was painted in large, obvious letters all along the rim of the pool—but he was too late. Kaye was already in midair. Just like always.

Kaye, or rather her autopilot, didn't know that she disregarded both the lettering and the lifeguard four days a week. For her, every dive was a first. The lifeguard, though? Dallas thought he should be used to it by now.

Kaye executed her dive flawlessly: shallow, yet purposeful, and somehow still graceful. Dallas supposed the angle of approach was probably a lot like a plane heading for a runway.

Discovering Kaye's autopilot's affinity with the hotel pool had been a blessed relief for Dallas—who typically rode through the turbulence in the cabin, and thus disappeared with all the passengers so he kept his wits about him in Bermuda. This distinction left him responsible for his crewmate's bodies while their personalities roamed the empty Bermuda, and it was no simple task. The claim that they had no money didn't usually work, and the explanation that the credit card readers were on the fritz wasn't very convincing either. Kaye might not be operating at full capacity when she was on autopilot—but even so, she was capable of seeing all the other travelers swiping their cards left and right.

Luckily, she didn't tire of the pool: floating effortlessly, supported by the warm, chlorine-crisp waters, nearly weightless. She was a good swimmer too, although she didn't bother with anything so mundane as swimming laps. Once the initial dive was out of the way, all Kaye's autopilot wanted to do was float.

Paul's autopilot, on the other hand, seemed nowhere near as impressed with the swimming pool. "Where are the hot cabana boys?"

"The waitstaff here ain't much to look at," Dallas said. Not true. A few of the staff members were easy on the eyes, and although Bermuda was fairly conservative, the hospitality industry was what it was, so it seemed like they might be gay. Not that he planned on pointing them out to Paul. He wasn't in the habit of lying, but since anything he told an autopilot would be forgotten in a few hours anyhow, a few harmless fibs seemed preferable to letting the autopilots have their way with his friends' bodies.

Dallas took Paul by the elbow and guided him to a deck chair. "You've got a stressful job. Might as well take advantage of the opportunity to relax on the clock." He would have felt better if Paul simply sprawled in the first chair he saw. Unfortunately, Paul's autopilot was shrewd. He positioned himself so he could keep an eye on Kaye, both doors, and the staff area adjacent to the counter. Dallas dutifully spread his own towel on the adjacent chair, hoping Paul was only angling to appreciate the "cabana boys" with his eyes. If he was looking to actually start an orgy, it probably would have happened already that first night in Bermuda, when Dallas' conscience had ridden through the turbulence in the cockpit—sometime between spending five figures and taking a load to the face for the camera.

Dallas glanced at Paul's autopilot, who gave him a lazy, sultry smile. He supposed it would have been pushing his luck to hope for this version of Paul to be tractable. At least he was pleasant.

A young family with small children splashed and squealed by the shallow end of the pool, and Kaye swam a few gentle strokes, providing just enough momentum to glide toward a more deserted part of the water. A pair of businessmen paused in their conversation to watch her drift by. Maybe they were Kaye's age, maybe a handful of years younger. Although she wasn't "pretty" per say, her confident autopilot got a lot of lingering glances from men. As far as Dallas knew, those men were shit outta luck. Kaye Lehr's ex-husband had left her picking up the pieces after he crashed and burned their twenty-five year marriage, and while Kaye claimed she hardly gave it a second thought anymore, Kaye's autopilot would probably enjoy watching the man take a softball to the groin. For her, dessert was preferable to men. And in the absence of sweets, a float in the pool would do.

Dallas passed Paul a bottled water. Paul cracked the seal, took a sip, then rolled the sweating bottle across his bare chest. He didn't insist on a ten-dollar drink, which was a relief. It was difficult enough to keep Kaye from exceeding her paycheck and her calorie count without worrying about Paul's spending too.

Although if it were true that Paul's autopilot wasn't itching to spend money, the most likely reason for Paul's diamond earring shopping spree was the encouragement of Dallas. Or his autopilot. Which was really him. Sort of.

Paul perked up when a hotel staffer appeared at the counter, but once he saw it was a woman, he shrugged, rolled up his towel and planted it under his neck, cranked his chair back a few notches, and settled in. He seemed content to just lie there, unlike the Paul Cronin who'd filled the previous evening with careful, slightly nervous small talk.

They sat, side by side, watching the children splash while Kaye floated. And eventually Dallas felt the dread of herding the autopilots begin to loosen. Because Kaye was content to be in the water, and Paul was content to lounge in that chair. And maybe, of the three of them, Dallas had ended up with the easiest task after all.

He hadn't even realized he'd allowed his eyelids to drift shut until his eyes snapped open at the sound of Paul's voice. "So, do you date many white guys?"

Immediately, Dallas' heart started racing. Paul's autopilot wanted to *talk*?

Great.

"Some." Normally, Dallas would be eager to dig a little deeper. Take the conversation a little farther. But not when he'd be the only one to remember it.

"How many Caucasians are we talking? Every other guy? Every third guy? Or once in a blue moon?" Paul rolled onto his side to face Dallas and wait for his answer. It couldn't have been comfortable, considering the angle of the deck chair, but he just flowed himself into the gentle V shape as if comfort was entirely irrelevant to him, since his comfort emanated from within.

It was hard to keep from staring. From ogling. "A few."

"So that's what we're doing? Dating?"

Dallas shook his head and tried to quell a smile. "We shouldn't talk about this now."

"Why not? I know Bermuda's a straight-laced little island, but no one's paying any attention to us."

"That's not it." Reasoning with him would be futile, but what else was there to do but explain? "You won't remember—so it's not fair."

"Fair, schmair." The autopilots seemed to know, on some level, that they existed. They must be aware of it, given how adeptly they would avoid discussing their state of being. "Are we officially an item, or is it too early to say?"

Dallas didn't answer.

Paul said, "We could both be cautious—piddle around and skirt the issue—but why bother? I know what I want. If you do too...."

Dallas allowed his head to loll toward Paul, and to get a good eyeful of him. Shirtless. Relaxed. Crazy hot. "Then, yeah. We're an item."

"Sweet." Paul re-positioned his towel roll and flipped onto his back with a contented sigh. "Caution is totally overrated."

Luckily Paul's eyes were closed, so Dallas was able to allow himself to chafe away the gooseflesh that sprang up on his thighs. For a minute there, Paul's autopilot sounded uncannily like Marlin.

Paul dozed. The night before had been a late Sunday night, filled with shy kisses, timid conversation, and tentative jockeying for the more comfortable side of the bed. Good thing Paul had slept. He was flying the plane—he needed his rest. Now, though, Dallas didn't drift off. He felt as though he couldn't afford to. What he could do was conserve his strength. And watch. And wait.

CHAPTER 17

Paul winced. The coffee tasted better when Dallas made it. Since it was a totally automatic procedure—tear open a pre-measured packet, dump it into the filter and add water—it should have made no difference which one of them hit the on-button. But somehow it did.

Captain Kaye stretched and rubbed sleep from her eyes. "You didn't have to stay with me." Her voice in the small cabin gave Paul a start after so many hours with nothing but the breeze stirring branches and the drone of insects to punctuate the silence. Paul poured her a cup and handed it over. "I'm not just saying that," she insisted. "Marlin used to comb the island 'til all hours of the night. I don't know if he ever slept in the same place twice."

"Well…I'm not Marlin."

"No one's expecting you to be."

Paul settled himself into 1B and 1C where he'd flipped up the armrest and molded a half-dozen airline blankets into the shape of a chaise, and set his coffee aside where it wouldn't, by some fluke, end up in contact with the precious red notebook. Marlin's notebook.

If only I could establish some line of communication with Dallas while both of us are at our stations. I've been working my way through the library, but it would be so much easier if I could take the stuff with me. Sometimes the research is there when I send Dallas back for it. Sometimes it's not. He's been pretty good about grabbing things for the black box. Flyers, brochures, business cards. Stuff like that. But it's starting to seem like it might be impossible to sort out the static from the signal.

Oh, the irony.

"You didn't stay up all night again," Kaye said, "did you?"

"No. Mostly not." Maybe he'd dozed. Some. "That doesn't matter much anyway, does it? Once we go through the turbulence, my other body will take over." As he was about to add, *a body that got a full night of sleep*, he caught himself. There was no guarantee he had simply put on his pajamas and climbed obediently into his own bed. He felt his cheeks grow hot, and turned to his window as if he found the reflection of the rising sun off the terminal windows absolutely riveting. "So once Marlin checked out the aircraft in every way he could think of, he moved on to the island."

"It seemed like the next logical step."

"Logical" was probably the last word Paul would use to describe Marlin. "What was he looking for?"

"He wasn't sure. You never know which small piece of information might turn out to be the key to this whole thing."

"What makes you think there even is a key?" He sounded testy. Likely, it was the lack of sleep talking. Or maybe it was the frustration over the notebook that looked completely logical, at least until it devolved into la-la land. "What if there is no puzzle to solve, and no riddle to answer, and no problem to work through? Just this aircraft flying back and forth through an electrical field."

When Paul looked up, Kaye was staring down into her coffee. Finally she said, "I suppose that's always a possibility."

"Look, I'm not trying to be a jerk...but I'm also not going to go around assigning meaning to a bunch of corollaries and coincidences. I refuse to create meaning where it doesn't exist just because it makes us feel all warm and secure."

"Maybe what you need is a nap," Kaye said, deadpan. Paul didn't know her well enough to tell if she was teasing him or not.

Sleep was the least of his worries, anyway. He could always catch up on sleep in Fort Lauderdale. Figuring out *where* he was supposed to spend his afternoon break would be the tricky part. If Flight 511 was definitely a regular gig, he should end the lease on his crash pad in Boston and find one in Florida so he could grab a few hours of rest between arrival and departure. He could grab a motel room, but it seemed like a waste of money when he just needed it for a few hours…and not for the same reason most people grab a motel room in the middle of the afternoon, either. He could hardly presume Dallas' invitation to spend the night would extend through the week. That would be like moving in together after one date. If a nine dollar bottle of wine and a frozen pizza constituted a date.

Paul lived alone (Denny, his friend-with-occasional-benefits who lived in the same condo building, most definitely did not count) so he was sketchy on the etiquette of ensuring one didn't wear out his welcome. Plus there was the very likely possibility that people on either side of the color divide had their own ideas as to what constituted a relationship, and when the actual boyfriend status had been earned. As far as he could surmise, the polite thing to do would be to shower in Bermuda and cool his heels in the Fort Lauderdale crew lounge until he received a very specific invitation to return to Dallas' place.

Until? That was uncharacteristically…optimistic. After all, Paul's doppleganger was doing who-knows-what in Bermuda. So it was a real possibility there could be a "let's keep this relationship purely professional" speech waiting for him once he touched down in the states.

His eyes dropped to the scuffed red notebook, seeking Dallas' name written in Marlin's odd, back-slanted block letters. *Sometimes the stuff is there when I send Dallas back for it. Sometimes it's not. He's been pretty good about grabbing things for the black box. Flyers, brochures, business cards.*

Paul read it again, blinked, and then ran through it a fourth time.

Things for the *black box?*

He riffled back to the front of the notebook and thumbed through it rapidly. All the measurements, the temperatures, the litmus test…all of it done on the fuselage. "Kaye…I don't see anything here about Marlin checking out the inside of the craft."

"I'm the Captain—the cockpit is my responsibility."

"But what about the rest of the interior?"

"I practically live in the cabin. I would have noticed something—"

"The flight recorder. What about that?"

"I filed a reportable incident and requested the data—several times. AVA either acted like they didn't even hear me, or they shut me down by telling me I had no right to waste time and resources on a 'normal' flight. *Blind spots*, I call 'em. Some of them I can work around, some of them are a lost cause."

"But did you open it yourself?"

"Paul...."

"Do you even know where it is?"

Kaye glanced over her shoulder toward the tail—the part of the aircraft most likely to survive a crash intact. "Even if we knew specifically, the data records over itself. And those devices that actually read the data—you can't exactly pick them up at corner hardware store with your furnace filters and your nail guns."

"Then what does this mean?" Paul leaned across the aisle, slid the notebook onto her lap and pointed.

Kaye read, brow furrowed. "Black box? I don't think Marlin would have called the flight recorder a black box. He might have been casual, but he was still a pilot."

The way Paul saw it, Marlin might have been a pilot, but he was still a crackpot.

-ONE YEAR AGO-

Marlin watched the altimeter as the gauge inched closer to the critical height. Closer. Closer. In his peripheral vision, Captain Kaye took a deep breath. Marlin noted that his body's reaction was the same. But he was ultimately responsible for his own reality. And while he wasn't about to beat himself up for being afraid, there was nothing that said he had to wallow in that fear. Fear was a choice. Yes, Kaye Lehr was holding her breath. But when the turbulence hit, Marlin chose, instead, to breathe.

Two small bumps, and then the massive slam where everything went white.

Marlin had just filled his lungs when his vision cleared, the pneumatic systems came back online, and the electrical gauges stopped pitching and yawing. Attitude was level. Directional gyro was pointing directly at Fort Lauderdale. He let his breath out calmly.

There. That wasn't so hard.

Dallas' voice greeted them through their headsets. "Everything okay in there?"

Captain Kaye gave the cockpit a once-over. "I'm not hungover and my pants still fit. That's reassuring." Marlin flipped open his notebook and scribbled down the series of memorized measurements he'd been repeating for the last ten minutes while it was still reasonably likely to be accurate. While he wrote, Kaye checked in with the tower and re-checked the weather, allowing him to scour his mind for more impressions and ideas, to commit as many details as he could remember to paper until it was time for the "Fasten Seatbelt" sign to herald their descent.

Once they'd touched down in Fort Lauderdale and begun shutting down the systems, Kaye said, "So have you figured out what's happening yet?"

"It's right around the corner…so close. You know when you have an awesome curry, and you think you know what that one spice is, but it's not cardamom, and it's not coriander…." Marlin turned his palms up and gave a shrug. "I can almost taste it."

Kaye nodded grimly and opened the cockpit door.

There was a gap in the stream of exiting passengers when a businessman blocked the aisle to wrestle his huge bag out of the overhead bin, and both Kaye and Marlin took the opportunity to step onto the skybridge platform and stretch their legs. Kaye turned to the window—she was too rattled to lavish a fake smile and a mandatory "thank you" on the passengers as they squeezed off the plane. But Marlin didn't mind. Sure, the turbulence was weird. But they'd come through it these past couple of weeks no worse for wear. He smiled and nodded and thank-you'd, and those passengers who weren't too travel-frazzled to make eye contact smiled back.

Especially the women.

And especially the very attractive blonde woman with the sparkle tank top and the pink carry-on. Her eye contact was so heavy, in fact, that she tripped over the joint in the carpeting. It wasn't a dainty trip, either. It was a full-on sprawl. Her carry-on went one way and her shoulder bag the other. Her sunglasses even cartwheeled off the top of her head and hit the accordioned wall of the skybridge with a loud plastic smack.

Every man within three yards of her rushed to help, but Marlin was the closest. He sank down to one knee and tried to help her up, but she waved him off, red-faced and mortified, muttering something semi-coherent about her "stupid shoes."

Someone handed over her sunglasses and someone else helped her to her feet. Marlin gathered a few things that had scattered out of her purse—a lipstick, a travel toothbrush, a paperback book…a familiar paperback book. *The Secret.* She reassembled herself as quickly as she could, clearly eager to put her less-than-glamorous return to Fort Lauderdale behind her, and refused to make eye contact when Marlin gave back her things.

He handed her the lipstick and the travel toothbrush. But when she took hold of the book, he held on. She tugged once, twice, and then finally looked up. "Have you read it yet?" Marlin asked.

"I'm halfway through."

"What do you think?"

As the woman stammered out that she wasn't really sure, the men who'd helped her up were still lingering as if they might be of more service. Maybe she'd need a wheelchair. And maybe they could be the hero to go get it. But Dallas gently herded them off the skybridge to allow the last few passengers off the plane.

Marlin said, "It's not a bad introduction to metaphysics. But it oversimplifies a lot of things."

"Oh, I, uh…does it?" She tucked her long flat-ironed hair behind her ear and her high flush receded a bit.

Marlin searched her eyes, wondering if it was possible to tell whether she really was ready to take on some new concepts, or if she just thought he was coming on to her. Not that she wasn't attractive—she totally was. But his experience had taught him that hooking up with women who weren't even inclined to look at the metaphysical side of things didn't turn out well in the long run. She smiled nervously, and he released the book. She shifted her weight as if she was going to scurry away, but then she paused and gave him one more searching look. He decided he might as well leave the channel open, just in case there was anything worthwhile there.

"If you ever want to know more..." he couldn't exactly invite her to *church*, could he? Thanks to two thousand years of patriarchal despotism, that word was incredibly loaded. "There's a group where we study these kinds of things." The pretty woman blinked her eyes rapidly. No doubt if she'd been expecting a pickup line, it wasn't this one. He flipped open his notebook and scrawled the URL of East Shore Unity Center on a page, tore it out, folded it one-handed and slipped it into her purse. If she was a kindred spirit, one of Ralph's sermons would pique her curiosity. And if not...then it was never meant to be.

-PRESENT DAY-

Thankfully, Kaye had enough composure to stand in the cockpit door, smiling and nodding at the passengers as they deplaned in Fort Lauderdale. It was only Paul's second return trip through the turbulence, and even with Dallas there on the intercom once he'd hurtled through it reassuring him everything was "just fine," he still felt like he might hurl from anxiety at even the slightest provocation. And even if he did end up spewing on the passengers, maybe they wouldn't have noticed. Just like Kaye's requests for flight data that didn't register with AVA.

"All right," Kaye said over her shoulder. "That's the last of them."

For now. Paul took a few bracing breaths, squared his shoulders, and went into the cabin to see if Dallas knew anything about the "black box."

Dallas' face lit up when he saw Paul...but then he dropped his gaze and began picking up the things the passengers had left behind on purpose: napkins and empty cups, folded and re-folded newspapers, mangled magazines and half-eaten bags of pretzels.

"I'll see you this afternoon?" Kaye said.

Paul turned back toward her. "That's what the schedule says."

"And I'm asking you." She scrutinized him for a long moment, then said, "You're sure?"

"I'm sure."

She nodded once, then pulled her rollerbag onto the skybridge and strode away. And then it was just Paul and Dallas on the tiny, cramped commuter jet...and Paul realized the black box was the last thing on his mind. The words came rushing out before he could stop them. "I did something in Bermuda." He watched Dallas holding his face still. "I did, didn't I?" He sagged against 1A, draped sideways against the seat back. "How bad was it?"

Dallas smiled faintly to himself. "You had several interesting recommendations on how we could be spending our time."

Paul took off his glasses, mashed his face into the top of the headrest and groaned. "I'm so sorry."

"Nothing to be ashamed of." Dallas gave the overhead bins one final check, then hauled his bag of airline trash to the front of the aisle and looked Paul up and down. "Nothing at all."

All around them, the airport was giving off typical airport sounds and smells—warning beeps, engines and machinery clangs, jet fuel and hot rubber. But with the two of them alone together at the door of cockpit, Paul felt as if he could shift his focus and pretend they were entirely alone. Him and Dallas. He cleared his throat awkwardly. "So long as I didn't say anything...weird."

"Well, you didn't want to take no for an answer."

"I'm *so* sor—"

"Shh." Dallas stroked Paul's forearm. "You were just persistent. That's all." He leaned in close, and said, "You talked me into kissing you. But that's as far as it went. I'm not gonna let anything happen when you won't remember. I can even use the same tired excuses every damn night...and you won't be any the wiser."

"Okay," Paul said in a husky voice. Did his mouth feel different, having kissed Dallas in his absence? He ran his tongue over his lower lip. He didn't think so. They stood for a moment, just looking, until contemplating the sheer amount of trust he was putting in Dallas made Paul break the connection and reach for his flight bag. "So I was hoping you'd give me a lift to the hardware store, and then I'll just hang around the crew lounge 'til it's time to fly out again."

"You'll what?"

"Or I can get a cab to the store."

Paul made to step onto the skybridge, but Dallas wheeled neatly around him and gave him a "don't you dare" look. "Aside from the offers it damn near killed me to refuse, you asked me to be your man."

He *what*?

"Ain't no man of mine living at the airport. Got it?"

Paul stared, heart pounding, ears whooshing, attempting to picture himself asking anyone to be his *man*. "I...said that?"

Dallas pivoted and began walking, and Paul caught up with him on numb feet. "Specifically?" Dallas sounded casual. "You asked if we were an item. And we decided we were." His gaze slid sidelong in Paul's direction.

"Okay, then," Paul said quickly, and Dallas raised his eyebrows, pursed his lips, and planted his eyes straight ahead. Paul could have pressed for more details—and oh, he wanted to. Badly. Especially since it seemed there was some pretty liberal paraphrasing going on. But when it came right down to it, as long as he was getting what he wanted, maybe he could let go of the specifics.

For now.

CHAPTER 18

Though Paul was the pilot, it was Dallas who took the helm of the bright orange shopping cart. Paul wasn't much of a do-it-yourselfer, and one look at the imposing racks of hand tools and power tools made him realize that he had no idea which one of them could be used to crack open a flight data recorder. Unfortunately, researching the device on a smartphone as he was walking down the mega-hardware store's aisles and trying not to wander into the very macho plumber-type guys wasn't much help.

"These things are indestructible," Dallas said, "right? We should talk to a mechanic and find out more about it before we go spending any more of your money on things we don't need."

"You're sure Marlin never showed it to you."

"Could have, but my brain wasn't home when he did."

But that didn't make sense. Wouldn't Dallas have remembered? He was usually in the regular Bermuda with Marlin's autopilot, not in empty Bermuda where they could have been rummaging around in the hold, though he supposed anything was possible on the rare occasions Dallas joined the others in the cockpit. Thinking through the logistics was enough to give Paul an ulcer. "His notebook said you were gathering things for the black box."

"I picked up research for him all the time. Newspaper articles, that kind of thing. Printed things that were too long to memorize. But he never said nothing about messing with the black box."

Paul veered around a burly man in paint-splattered coveralls. "It probably meant something completely different, anyway."

Dallas paused the cart. "Like what?"

"Who knows? I never have any idea what he's talking about. Alignment... there's all kinds of talk in there about Alignment. With a capital A."

"Oh, that. It's new age, like Oprah's always talking about."

Paul didn't get the reference. His daytime TV consisted of CNN news feeds and weather forecasts. "I don't think 'black box' was capitalized like all the other space cadet talk, anyway. But I'd have to double check to be sure."

Once Dallas managed to convince Paul that buying tools wouldn't help if they didn't know which tools to buy, they went home empty handed, except for a couple of drive-through burger combo meals they ate on the way back.

"Just rest." Dallas steered Paul to the bedroom, sat him on the edge of the bed, and plumped up a few pillows. "I'll Google it and make a few phone calls."

"Just rest" extended far beyond clearing his head for a few moments while his lower back unkinked. When Paul opened his eyes, the digital clock read 3:30 p.m., and his thigh was hot where Dallas' leg was thrown over his. He hadn't meant to groan, but the noise escaped him before he was fully lucid. Beside him, Dallas inhaled deeply, rolled onto his back, and mumbled, "Hey, sleepyhead."

"I can't believe I...why didn't you wake me up?"

Dallas nuzzled his shoulder blade. "It's my experience that when a pilot nods off after lunch, it's a good idea to let him get a couple hours of sleep."

When Dallas climbed over Paul to get out of bed, the brushes of his arms and thighs were incidental, but easy and welcome. It seemed Paul's new "man" had slept well. Dallas managed to stroll out to the kitchen and put the coffee on without the kind of limping shamble Paul felt like he'd be doing without a few more minutes of rousing and a good stretch, though the update Dallas had in store woke him up plenty. The flight recorder could potentially be buried anywhere in the tail section, but between the search engines and a quick call to a flight attendant married to an aviation mechanic, Dallas had managed to determine that Flight 511's data recorder was tucked up in the baggage compartment. According to the mechanic, they should be able to pop off the casing with a simple Phillips-head screwdriver.

"Thing is," Dallas said, "not much you can really do with it once you do get it open. You can't just stick a USB drive up in there and copy the files. He said they got a special machine that plugs into the front of it to pull the data, big ol' connections like you never seen before, and special software to read it all, too. Without any of that, ain't nothing for you to find in there but a bunch of wires."

"That's fine." Paul was surprised he felt so calm. "It's been recording over itself on a continuous loop anyway. The only people talking on it now—other than the towers who never seem to know anything's wrong—would be me and Kaye."

"So why bother cracking in?"

"Well, Kaye knows every inch of the cockpit and the cabin, and Marlin documented everything that was possible to measure on the exterior of the hull. But what about the cargo hold? Since the cabin and the cockpit are affected differently in the turbulence, there could be something else entirely going on in the baggage compartment. Something we should look into."

Marlin must have stashed those papers and notes from Dallas somewhere, after all. Not to mention, judging by the little tabs of paper stuck around the red notebook's spiral spine, the sheets he'd torn out. Once Paul found those, he was certain, everything else would fall right into place.

***

"You want to start taking things apart?" Kaye gasped.

In retrospect, Paul realized, it might have been a better idea to test his black box theory first, and then run it by Kaye once he'd actually found something. After all, if Marlin had indeed been stashing key notes to himself inside the casing, he would have done it while Kaye thought he was off exploring the island. All he would've needed to do was wait until she'd plugged in to her Italian lessons to climb in the luggage area and poke around without her being any the wiser.

Still, Kaye was the Captain. And Paul wouldn't feel right going behind her back on anything that might affect the flight. "It's not like I'm disassembling a crucial part," he explained. "I'll just unplug it, open it up and look inside."

Kaye squinted at him across the cockpit console.

"Even if something went wrong with it," he went on, "it's not as if we couldn't take off without a flight recorder, not without anyone here to stop us. Plus, once we went through the turbulence, everything would be fixed. Right?"

Kaye raised an eyebrow.

He probably shouldn't have introduced the idea that anything might go wrong to begin with. "It's built to withstand a crash," he said. "How delicate can it be?"

Kaye gathered herself and took a deep, steadying breath. "Promise me this—you won't force anything. If a screw won't unscrew, if a latch won't open, if anything, anywhere is stuck, you abort. And then you put it all back the way it was."

"Sure."

"Because we can always have it checked out in Fort Lauderdale."

"Right."

"And you know how easy it is to strip a screw."

"I hear you—we're on the same page."

"Promise me."

Paul widened his eyes in a way he hoped would come off as sincere. "I promise."

"All right." Kaye loosened her neckerchief, took off her hair clip and shook out her hair. "Take a couple of flashlights with you…and a blanket to catch any small parts."

Paul gathered the equipment while Kaye scoped out the cabin, planting herself toward the tail section to better hear what was going on down in cargo. He paused at the top of the stairs and met her eyes across the cabin, doing his best to project reassurance. "Thank you for trusting me with this."

"Marlin would have looked first and told me later."

Maybe. Or maybe Marlin had been tinkering with it all along, and never told her at all.

ERJ-135 aircraft are small, by jet standards. Small enough for Paul to walk up to the baggage door, reach up, undo the latch and slide the door into the fuselage. Probably small enough for him to haul himself up into the compartment unassisted, since the bottom edge of the hatch was about shoulder-high.

But then there was getting back down again. And the thought that if he ended up shattering a knee or splitting his head open on the tarmac during his dismount, Kaye Lehr wouldn't be willing to exit the craft to come and drag him back to safety for fear of everything disappearing the moment she stepped off those stairs. Paul commandeered a rolling ramp designed for a much larger craft and finessed it into position without even scuffing his airplane's paint finish. He was sweating by the time it was all in place.

The inside of the baggage hold felt very dark. And claustrophobic, and cold. The luggage had all slid to the aft side of the enclosure from the force of landing, which was where Paul needed to be to retrieve the flight recorder. By the time he got the luggage shifted to the fore he was drenched, despite the fact that the baggage was still chilled from its recent proximity to high altitudes in a minimally-heated hold.

Once the cargo was out of the way, the panel in the ceiling was hard to miss. He blotted his palms on his slacks, unrolled the blanket, fixed a flashlight into position in the handle of a rollerbag, and unhitched the latch.

It wasn't even locked.

The flash of orange he saw as he opened the hatch flooded him with relief—because he wouldn't have been surprised if the flight recorder was missing, or mangled, or replaced with a bag of live scorpions. Thankfully it was there, and it seemed to be intact. The device was roughly the size of a small desktop computer CPU. The deep orange casing was crossed by a couple of diagonal reflective stripes. Plain black lettering on the side warned: FLIGHT RECORDER DO NOT OPEN.

If only everything in life were so clearly labeled.

The ports in the front of the device were just as Dallas had described, riddled with huge connectors that looked like the type of plug that might have been on a mouse back in 1990, only triple its normal size. No simple USB ports there. Paul couldn't imagine the type of instrument that would hook up to it. It didn't matter, he reminded himself. All that mattered was finding Marlin's missing notes.

Paul worked carefully, setting the cables that fed in to the recorder aside in the order in which he'd found them once he eased them from their sockets. The connectors came out easily. The brackets released without a hitch. And soon, there it was in his lap, a good twenty pounds of circuitry and bright orange steel. With each screw, he tensed, wondering which would be the one to refuse to turn. Which would be the one to put a stop to his mission until ground crew back in Fort Lauderdale got involved. But then he gave the final screw a twist, and nothing more stood between him and the truth.

He braced himself and slid off the casing.

Inside, more ports and wires. No paper.

But there must be. Paul clicked on a second flashlight and shone it into every nook of the device. As he aimed the beam, combing every inch of the machine, and then searching through the cavity in which the whole recorder was housed to no avail, he realized that the likelihood of Marlin going through all this effort without alerting Kaye to what he was doing was pretty slim.

And finally he had to concede that whatever notes were missing from Marlin's notebook were simply not there. If they even existed at all.

-ONE YEAR AGO-

Technically, Marlin understood, his vision board didn't need to be anything fancy. An empty wall, a roll of cellophane tape and a few pushpins would be enough to get started. Even so, he felt drawn to the idea of dusting off the mitre saw in his garage workshop and really doing this thing right. Rev. Ralph was always telling him to follow the thoughts and impulses that felt better, and now, detail sander in hand, Marlin was certain that framing out his new idea bank was the best possible use of his mental energy and free time, an investment that would pay off in a major way.

Once the massive frame was tack-ragged and primed, he eased it down onto some spread newspapers and took up a can of black spray enamel. Spray paint dried to a great brushmark-free finish if you were careful not to let it pool anywhere, and patient enough to build it up in several fine layers rather than attempting to blast on the color all in one pass. To avoid spatter, special care needed to be taken at the beginning and end of each stroke, aiming the stream beyond the edge of the target on either side, resisting the urge to swing in an arc and moving the arm instead in a steady motion parallel to the ground. Marlin was engrossed in his task, so when the kitchen door opened with a bang, it didn't startle him. He was so deeply in Alignment he was beyond jumping or flinching.

"When are you coming to bed?"

Three more passes, and there. The first coat was done. He looked up and found Caitlin in the doorway, bare-legged and sleepy, hugging one of his button-down shirts around herself. She tucked her flat-ironed blonde hair behind her ear and scowled.

She'd been scowling a lot lately.

"I'll need to spray on another coat," he explained.

"Now?"

"Best time to do it is when the paint is dry to the touch, but not cured."

"Marlin, it's two o'clock in the morning."

He glanced at his watch. That's what time it was—but he didn't see why it might matter. He felt clear-headed and alert. No reason to quit what he was doing just because of an arbitrary number on a clock. "It could streak or peel if I don't." He crossed to the opposite corner of the deep frame where he'd started the first coat, crouched down and touched the paint gently. Yep. Just about ready. When he shook the spray can, the sound of the mixer-ball rattling inside filled the garage like samba percussion.

"You're gone all week," Caitlin said, "and even when you are around, it's like you're not even here."

"I'm totally here." The frame with its single coat of paint looked black until Marlin began spraying on the second coat, and then the blackness went from "so-so" to "wow." He moved his arm steadily, aiming the strokes so the wet edges barely overlapped, consistent, even, and watched his creation take shape.

"Sometimes I think you don't even like me."

"Your happiness shouldn't depend on what other people think."

"Do you even hear yourself? A normal guy would say, 'You're amazing, Caitlin, of course I like you.' But not you—you won't even look me in the eye." Her voice wavered. "You care more about that stupid black box on the floor than you do about me."

As Marlin laid down the final pass of paint on the right side of the frame, he considered telling Caitlin that black boxes were actually orange. Given how upset she was, he doubted she would appreciate the trivia. Although he didn't think he should have to censor himself, he didn't see any need to escalate her distress.

Who could say why people rendezvoused with one another the way they did? No one really knew anyone else, only the version of that person they'd hooked up with in their own reality—but why would anyone Align themselves with a version of someone who upset them? He pondered the tumultuous three weeks they'd been together as he repositioned himself to start across the top of the "black box," and he wondered why he'd rendezvoused with the version of Caitlin who found him so disappointing.

Life could be such a curious thing.

-PRESENT DAY-

The rumble of the return turbulence stilled, and Dallas' voice came through Paul's headset. "Y'all okay in there?"

As Paul was currently crushed by his disappointment at finding the flight recorder casing empty, it was Kaye who answered. "Just fine."

A pause, and then, "Paul?"

"Yeah," he said, not very convincingly at all. "Fine."

Landing was uneventful. Kaye seemed as if she might be about to offer more of her low-key, pragmatic words of encouragement, but she'd said all that could truthfully be said about the situation—that none of them had figured out what was going on in the past year, so Paul couldn't let the first roadblock get him down.

But how could he not? He'd been so damn sure.

Once the final passenger had exited the cabin and Dallas was through picking up newspapers and empty cups, he spied Paul gazing in the direction of the crew lounge. As if he could hear Paul wondering whether, in the face of his failure, it would be time to camp out in a recliner for the afternoon, he said, "Don't even think about it."

Paul sighed.

"I take it you didn't find what you were looking for," Dallas said gently.

Paul shook his head. "Nothing."

"You been at it less than a week—you barely got the lay of the land." Dallas indicated the skybridge with a nod, and they stepped onto it, striding side by side, dragging their wheeled bags behind them. "Give yourself some time to figure out what's what."

They walked toward the parking garage with the purposeful gait of professionals, though inside, Paul felt anything but confident. What if the only thing Paul brought to the table was a fresh set of eyes? And what if he failed to find anything with them?

What then?

"Say something," Dallas prompted.

"I can't believe I…how am I going to…?" He paused, slipped his fingers beneath his glasses frames, and pinched the bridge of his nose. "The longer it takes me to figure this out, the longer you're spending all these nights with me in Bermuda that I can't even remember."

"And?"

"That doesn't strike me as a very good way for you to get to know me. I'll probably say something obnoxious, do something stupid—"

"Well, for the record, you're not the first white man I've dated."

"What's that supposed to—I didn't come right out and ask you that, did I?"

"You did. And it's fine."

If Dallas thought it was something he needed to know, chances were he hadn't just asked...but he'd asked more than once. Paul wished he could slink away through an emergency exit without setting off an alarm.

Dallas said, "I've dealt with Kaye in Bermuda for the past year, and I don't hold anything she says or does there against her. Same will go for Bermuda Paul."

It was hard enough getting a handle on this whole relationship thing, which Paul had never been any good at to begin with. Now he had the additional disadvantage of all the outrageously stupid things he might say to Dallas when he wasn't around to stop himself. "I feel like you'll be spending more time with him than with me."

"That was one fine-looking man back there in the hotel." Dallas watched Paul until he raised his eyes and locked gazes, while all around them, passengers streamed toward their gates or their baggage—embarking on adventures, or arriving safely home. "But you're the one I want to be with. You."

CHAPTER 19

The neighborhood seemed surprisingly normal to Paul.

Dallas coasted to a stop at the curb in front of Marlin's house. Given what Paul knew of his predecessor, he wouldn't have been surprised to find that Marlin had lived in a geodesic dome. Or a commune. Or a tree house. But the Fritsch residence was only remarkable in its unremarkableness. Spanish style architecture built in the mid seventies, clay-tiled roof, broad lawn, now slightly overgrown, jaunty red mail box.

And the front door a few inches ajar.

"If that's the police," Dallas said, "then you'd better be the one to go in. 'Cos they think I'm casing the place, and they already sent me home once."

And if Marlin was being posthumously robbed, Paul was probably the last person equipped to confront the criminals. But one of them had to get in there and find out what was what. Paul steeled himself and got out of the car, leaving Dallas behind the wheel. He punched in 911 on his cell, paused, and made his way up the walk with his thumb poised over the send-key.

Was that motion he detected in the picture window, or just a reflection of a gull landing on the porch roof across the street? He couldn't tell. It seemed awfully quiet, though, if there were either cops or robbers inside. He'd expect cops to be talking in loud, entitled, macho voices while the two-way radios on their hips squalled and squawked. And robbers would be turning over furniture and emptying drawers, and randomly shooting anything that moved—although, robbers probably wouldn't hit a vacant house at noon, would they? Wouldn't they wait until the wee hours of the morning? If Paul called in a break-in and he was wrong, no doubt he'd find himself in no better standing with the local police than Dallas currently was. So he crept forward in an attempt to determine what, exactly, he was dealing with, and he heard a single distinct word.

"Bastard."

A woman's voice. Paul crept closer. He heard footsteps and rustling, but nothing threatening like breaking furniture or gunfire. He pocketed his phone without finishing the emergency call and rapped on the doorframe, calling out, "Hello?"

A single figure standing at a tall filing cabinet spun to look toward the doorway, papers fluttering around her as if a whirlwind had picked them up and scattered them. The woman was somewhere around Paul's age, conventionally attractive, he supposed. Her carefully-highlighted hair was so exactingly styled in its manicured flip that it didn't move whatsoever when the rest of her did, and she swayed a moment as if attempting that twirl in such high heels might not have been the world's best idea. Paul held up his hands to show he meant no harm and said, "Sorry—didn't mean to startle you."

The woman squinted as she took in Paul's uniform. "You worked together."

"Right, I'm an AVA pilot," Paul said, hoping to come off as if he belonged in Marlin's house just as much as she did without actually claiming he knew the guy. "I'm sorry, I don't think we've met. I'm Paul."

"Bernadette. You couldn't have met me—I live in Miami. I haven't seen Marlin since he moved here, what, five years ago?" She looked down at the paper in her hand, shook her head, and repeated, "Bastard."

Paul wasn't sure how to reply to that—although given what he did know of Marlin, he was quite inclined to agree. But he opted to go the safe route and simply say, "I'm sorry for your loss."

"Now the Coroner wants to know where to release the…." She pressed her lips together and squeezed her eyes shut rather than give voice to the word *body*. "I don't know where he keeps his insurance paperwork. I don't know if he's got any retirement accounts I can tap to pay for the expenses." She glanced at the filing cabinet. "You wouldn't have any idea. Would you?"

"Personnel might be able to help you with some of that." Maybe. "If you're immediate family, I mean."

She huffed in annoyance. "I'm his ex-wife. Does that count?"

Paul was out of his league. "Listen, my..." how should he refer to Dallas—his friend? His partner? His *man*? "...my co-worker might be able to help us out. He was a lot closer to Marlin than I was." *Co-worker* was not a very satisfying description of their relationship, but the term did seem like it would inspire the most trust in a total stranger. He leaned out the front door and gestured for Dallas to come inside.

Since they'd swung by Marlin's house straight from the airport, they were both still in uniform. While they hadn't engineered the visit that way, Paul wondered if their reception would have been quite as welcoming if they'd come in their off-duty clothes. At the very least, fewer explanations were necessary to gain a stranger's trust. He introduced Dallas to Bernadette, who was eager to meet anyone who might help her determine how to pick up the pieces Marlin had left behind. "I've never had to arrange a funeral." Bernadette sounded angry, but a tiny tremble in her voice made Paul suspect that beneath the anger, there was plenty of helplessness, maybe even grief. "And his filing system is useless. I'm not putting this thing on my own credit cards—do you know what it costs to have someone cremated? It'll max them right out."

Paul's initial impulse was to offer to handle it—then he'd have a perfect excuse to rifle through Marlin's house and find the black box research. But even though he'd returned the bulk of the expensive purchases, his own bank now had him under the microscope from his shopping spree in Bermuda. No doubt if he put a stranger's funeral on his card, they'd peg it as identity theft and clamp down on his credit line so hard he'd be lucky to be able to rent a movie. Fortunately, Dallas saved him from offering to do anything he'd regret later. "You don't have to do it alone," he told Bernadette, taking her hand. "I'll help, anything you need. But first, call his church. They'll handle things."

"His church?" Bernadette coughed out. Initially Paul presumed it was a sob, but then he realized she'd actually choked on the word. "Marlin's not religious."

Dallas corrected her gently. "Actually, he is. His favorite thing about his schedule was that it gave him time for Sunday service."

"But he's an atheist," Bernadette insisted.

Paul had to stop himself from making a scoffing sound. Weirdos like Marlin gave atheists like Paul a bad name.

"No," Dallas said, "maybe he didn't use the word 'God.' But he prayed and tithed and went to mass, all the same. Come on, I think there's a magnet on the fridge with the church's name on it."

Dallas led Bernadette into the kitchen and Paul followed. He wasn't sure what he'd been expecting—nothing in particular—but the sight of Marlin's countertop with a box of Ritz crackers front and center, still open as if he expected to stroll by and grab a handful any moment, gave Paul a chill. "What I don't get," Bernadette said, "is how so much of his stuff is just like I remember. His dirty clothes all over the bedroom floor. His motorcycle. His stupid guitar and his Pearl Jam posters. Even the blanket over the back of his couch is the same, and it's so linty I should have thrown it out five years ago when I had the chance. Since when did he start going to church?" She stared at the front of the refrigerator as if it might answer her. "Since when was he suicidal?"

She made another coughing sound, but judging by the way her shoulders hitched, this one actually was a sob. Paul hovered awkwardly behind her, but Dallas didn't hesitate to put his arms around her. After just a moment of trying to hold it together, she sagged against Dallas and allowed herself to cry. It was only a matter of moments until she cried herself out, like a sudden gale sweeping across the wings, there and gone in moments. "How long had he been depressed?"

"He wasn't," Dallas said. He sounded very sure.

She pulled away from him. "Nobody kills themselves for no reason at all!"

"Maybe it was an accident," Dallas suggested.

She began sobbing again—no, wait, this was laughter. Sharp, brittle laughter. "He drowned in four feet of water—with forty pounds of iron weights strapped to his waist. *Forty* pounds? He could curl forty pounds in one hand. He could hang off a cliffside by his fingertips with a forty pound pack on his back. All he needed to do to stop drowning was *stand up*. Does that sound like an accident to you?"

"Was there a note?" Paul asked. She shook her head. He glanced out the back window at the small in-ground pool with leaves and dead beetles floating on its surface, and he clenched himself against a shudder he couldn't manage to suppress. Was that the very spot? The depth was right; it must have been. "Maybe someone drugged him, or hit him over the head to make it look like—"

"The Coroner said he was clean. No sign of struggle. No injuries, either. Just…drowned."

"He wasn't depressed," Dallas insisted. "I worked with him every day. I would have known."

"Did he have trouble with a woman?" Bernadette asked. "You can tell me, I won't freak out. I re-married, you know. I'm not carrying a torch."

Right. Women never carried torches for pilots who rode motorcycles, bungee jumped off bridges and played electric guitars.

Dallas said, "There was no woman—and I think he liked it that way. He'd rather be alone to do all his things. He never mentioned a woman."

"Really? Then who's that?" Bernadette pointed to a photo on the refrigerator door. It was a group shot, and even though they'd never met, Paul spotted Marlin right away. It was a marina scene, bright sun, blue water, a handful of people posed loosely in front of a speedboat. One dark-haired man front and center stole the show. He looked so easy in his own skin he didn't need to be handsome—but of course, he was. He held up a massive kingfish he'd vanquished, like a cave man who'd just secured dinner for his tribe and would now have his pick of the women.

It was mostly a guy-outing, the type of event Paul wouldn't touch with a ten-foot pole. Of the two women present in the tribe, one was of the same generation as Paul's parents, with a perm shown off to poor advantage in a lime green visor and a Tampa Yankees fanny pack cinching her waist. Paul guessed the other one was more Marlin's type. She was fragile, and blonde, and very pretty. She looked about half his age.

"Caitlin, you mean?" Dallas said. "This was last summer. They haven't been together since then."

"So why does he still have her picture up?"

"For the fish," Paul said, without intending to speak it aloud. No, he'd never met Marlin Fritsch. But he knew the type.

Dallas, who never had a catty word to say about anyone, deflected the conversation from the photograph by peeling a cheap magnet off the fridge and handing it to Marlin's ex-wife. "Call his church and tell them what happened. They'll help you make the arrangements."

"I guess it couldn't hurt to ask." She was scowling as if she didn't quite believe him—but she wanted to.

"I'll give you my number, too." Dallas handed her a business card. "Any way I can help, you tell me. I'm overnighting, international, but my weekend is free. And you can always text me."

She shuffled the magnet and the business card as if she was about to perform a very simple magic trick, and in a thick voice, said, "Thanks."

Dallas' offer to help didn't sound suspicious at all—not like it would have been if Paul had tried to pay with his iffy credit card. If Paul and Dallas could arrange to be the ones to clean out the house, then they could get a really good look at Marlin's things without anyone finding it unusual. It was anybody's guess where Marlin would keep his stash. There was probably no basement, not in Fort Lauderdale, but there might be an attic, plus whatever closets were in the house, plus that big garage. Paul glanced around the room to begin cataloging potential hiding places and his eyes lit on the computer hulking on the corner desk, a massive beast of a setup that had been top of the line when it came out, but was painfully obsolete now. Nowadays everything was slim and compact, chrome and white. Not Marlin's computer. The huge monitor was black. The massive printer was black. The oversized CPU was also black. A big…black…box.

Paul's heart hammered against his sternum. "Y'know," he said as casually as he could, "it's possible he kept some benefits records on his computer, if he signed up for AVA's paperless statements." There was no such thing. Every year, Paul got so many documents from personnel it required three or four file folders to contain all that paper. Hopefully, if Bernadette remembered the paperwork, she'd think the airline had gone green sometime in the last five years. "I could take a peek for you. I'd have a better idea what to look for."

Bernadette stared at the computer, dazed, overwhelmed by the task of settling Marlin's affairs. "Yeah, okay, that's a good idea."

Dallas ushered her out of the kitchen, saying, "Come on, we can make the phone calls together." Hard to say if he was trying to swing it so Paul could work in private, or if he truly was just being helpful. Paul supposed it didn't matter either way, as long as he got access to Marlin's computer for as long as possible. He booted it up and waited for the system to start. It was slow going, and when the desktop finally came up, it was filled from one side to the other with folders and documents Marlin had never organized or filed. Paul looked for a folder called *Bermuda*, or *research*, or anything at all that sounded helpful. Hopefully Marlin hadn't hidden it somehow. Given that there was a file in the middle of the desktop labeled *PORN*, Paul hoped that he'd put the black box research somewhere obvious.

It wasn't.

Paul skimmed files and folders as best he could, but the computer ran logy from age and poor housekeeping, and especially from an insanely big MP3 collection, which he was tempted to delete to make some room on the hard drive, but figured he'd better leave just in case there was a clue buried there. Eventually he even peeked at the porn folder. He wasn't well-versed in hetero porn, but the folder's contents seemed pretty standard to him, naked women with long hair, fake fingernails and waxed labia. He wasn't sure what he'd expected. Something freakish, or at least subtly disturbing.

He was out of ideas when he decided to check Marlin's email. Not that he thought Marlin would be chatting with anyone about the turbulence (who on earth would believe him?) but maybe he'd been e-mailing notes or ideas to himself. For a moment Paul thought it was his lucky day–the password helpfully filled itself right in. But then the inbox scrolled higher and higher as it pulled dozens upon dozens of unread messages from the server. Over 500 new messages. Important? Junk? Hard to say, judging by the subject lines. And the sound of Dallas and Bernadette speaking in low murmurs was coming closer now. Rather than shutting down the email as if he'd been snooping anywhere he shouldn't have been, Paul took a steadying breath and typed "insurance" into the search bar.

"Find anything?" Bernadette asked.

Paul scanned the monitor. Most of the emails promised that with a simple fifteen minute investment of his time, Marlin could save up to fifty percent on car insurance...and some of those stunning offers were over three years old. No emails about benefits. No emails from AVA. "No, sorry. Nothing."

Since Paul was considering renting a place in Fort Lauderdale, it might not seem strange for him to offer to buy the computer from Bernadette and take it off her hands. But this behemoth—could he even ask for it with a straight face? "Turns out I'm in the market for a computer. You wouldn't be looking to sell this, would you?"

"Oh...I suppose I'll need to do something with it eventually, won't I?" Her eyes darted around the room, and sheer enormity of all the stuff she'd now have to deal with made her blanch. "What do you think, fifty bucks? It's pretty old. Just as soon as I get a chance to wipe the hard drive."

"You don't need to bother." Paul was surprised at how utterly calm he sounded. "I can take care of that for you when I upgrade the memory."

"Thanks, that's sweet. But I've done so many at my office the last time we swapped out equipment I can practically erase them in my sleep. Besides, it'll give me something to do to take my mind off...anyway, first I want to have a look through his files myself to make sure I've got all his important records."

Paul couldn't argue with that. Not without coming off like a freak.

Dallas came up beside Paul, pointed at his watch and said, "We gotta go."

Already? The hours in the real world seemed to slip away twice as fast as the time in empty Bermuda. And there would be no calling in sick, no holding up Flight 511—because if they did, who knew what might happen? Other flight crew might get sucked into the turbulence in their place, and innocent people could very well die.

They said goodbye to Bernadette and made their way to the car. As they reached the curb, Dallas tossed Paul the keys. "Drive?"

"Sure." Funny, how natural it felt to slip into Dallas' driver seat. To sleep in his bed, for that matter, or shower in his bathroom. Yes, Paul spent most of his time in his impersonal Boston crash pad and even less personal motel rooms, in rental cars and crew lounges, so if he was accustomed to anything, it should be a lack of familiarity. But Dallas Turner's things were different. They were broken-in and used—well cared for, but worn and patinaed. They had history. Resonance. Dallas' things were familiar. Not to Paul, not yet…though it seemed that they would be, soon.

Paul started the car, but paused before he pulled away. Dallas was squeezing his temples. He looked like he'd just about had it. "Hey," Paul said, rubbing his knee. "You okay?"

"Marlin wasn't depressed."

"No, doesn't sound like it."

"Then how could he…?" Dallas shook his head, searched for a word, and came up with nothing. "How *could* he?"

If only the Sterile Cockpit Rule applied to new relationships. Takeoff was just as critical in dating as it was in aviation, and just as fraught with potential hazards. Was it possible for Paul to say something even remotely truthful without coming off as an insensitive ass? "We'll never know what he was thinking." Understatement of the year. "But chances are, he had a really good reason for what he did."

Dallas turned to Paul and cupped his jaw tenderly. "What did I ever do to deserve somebody as sweet as you?" Together, they leaned over the armrest toward one another, lips meeting in a kiss. Yes, it was the middle of a weekday afternoon, and yes, they were in a conservative, white, middle-class neighborhood that only saw two men kissing when their TVs were on and Glee was airing. It didn't matter. Because although Paul felt awkwardly exposed, at least it was better than looking Dallas in the eye and trying to sustain the fantasy that he was, in any way, "sweet."

Paul held Dallas' hand all the way back to his house, and didn't release it until he pulled into the driveway and put the car in park. What had possessed Marlin to kill himself? Maybe he was hearing voices. Maybe he'd convinced himself he could breathe underwater. Maybe he thought he was in Alignment with the bottom of his swimming pool. Paul didn't particularly care, not until he saw how devastated Marlin's final act had left Dallas. Unfortunately, there wasn't much he could do but chalk it up to the inexplicable things about Marlin that ended up leaving them all in the lurch.

Paul retrieved the rollerbags from the trunk while Dallas unlocked the kitchen door, and they rushed in to change into fresh uniforms and try to make it back to the airport on time. Once Paul pulled his undershirt over his head, Dallas came up behind him, grasped him just above the elbows, and pressed a kiss to the back of his neck. "Make yourself a couple sandwiches for the trip," he said, then slipped into the bathroom to wash up.

Figuring it was best to avoid getting mustard on a clean shirt, Paul headed out half-dressed to prepare his dinner, marveling at the ease with which the two of them seemed to operate. No haranguing, no fussing, no one-upmanship or second-guessing. A true team in every sense of the word. Strange, how different he'd presumed they would be, judging solely by the color of their skin. He pulled out the bread, the mustard, the baloney and cheese. There were differences, sure. But the two of them complimented each other when it counted, especially—

The phone rang, startling Paul. Mustard spurted out of the bottle and overshot the bread, splattering the countertop with yellow.

"Who is that?" Dallas called.

Paul checked the caller I.D. "It's the Captain."

"Pick it up!"

And now Dallas was having Paul answer his phone? Paul would have thought this much togetherness would be suffocating. Instead, he felt elated. He picked up the handset. "Hello?"

"Paul?"

So Captain Kaye recognized his voice. Paul did his best to sound like he didn't have a big dopey smile on his face. "Yes."

"You're not going to believe this. Is Dallas there?"

Dallas strolled into the kitchen in his underwear, barefoot. Paul hit the speakerphone. "He's here. What is it?"

"I just got an email," she told them both. Paul felt his smile drain away even before she finished her thought. "From Marlin."

CHAPTER 20

Dallas walked up the aisle and told the gentleman in the Hawaiian shirt to turn off his electronic device…for the third time. When he received a surly look in return, he stood in the aisle and loomed over the man until the passenger looked away. It would serve that fool right if Dallas tossed the damn thing down the trash chute, but he restrained himself. Smooth and steady was the name of the game, bringing everyone back and forth through the turbulence unscathed. There wasn't time for pettiness. Regardless of how satisfying it might feel to deliver the smackdown to the man in 5B.

He strapped himself into the cabin's jump seat and waited out the final moment before the bumpy ride began, and though he tried to clear his mind, he couldn't help but come back to the email.

Marlin's email.

Kaye hadn't been the only one to receive it—she'd just been the first one to fire up her computer. There'd been time for Dallas and Paul, barely, to print up a copy on their way out the door to their afternoon flight.

```
To: CaptainK, cc. Dallas.Turner
From: Atlantic_Marlin
Subject: Flight 511

travelers in dark,
when the blazing sun is gone
find the tiny light
```

The receipt of that email had sent a rage of shivers down Dallas' spine—despite the fact that he knew damn well it hadn't come from the great beyond. The message was launched when Paul turned on the computer in Marlin's kitchen. That was all. The date was the previous Thursday. Normally you'd take that kind of thing for granted, but nowadays Dallas didn't count on anything to work in a logical way. And while it was comforting to be assured that Marlin had written the email while he was still alive, the thought that it might have been the last thing he did was pretty damn depressing.

A bump, another bump, and then, the doozy. Passengers murmured in concern. A moment later, Captain Kaye's autopilot announced over the PA, "That'll be the worst of the weather, but since we'll be approaching Bermuda in just a few minutes, I'll go ahead and leave the fasten seatbelt sign on. Dallas, prepare for landing."

Flight 511 was down to such a predictable routine, he already had. But he walked up the aisle and double-checked all the overhead bins just the same. Because you never knew when the foolishness was getting ready to throw you another curve ball.

Someone landed the plane—someone who was the spitting image of either Kaye or Paul—and Dallas shuttled twenty-two passengers to the door where ground crew, lacking skybridges, manually helped them descend the aircraft steps and cross the tarmac toward baggage claim and customs. For one brief moment, Dallas was alone with his thoughts, anxious thoughts filled with apprehension and dread. And then the cockpit door banged open, and sort-of-Paul darted out and made a beeline right for Dallas. He backed Dallas into the side of 8A and gave him a very thorough (and very wet) greeting.

Rather than telling them to get hold of themselves, at least while they were in uniform, in public, Kaye's autopilot snickered. "Get a room. Oh yeah, you already have one."

Before the Captain could exit the plane and end up God-knows-where, Dallas turned his mouth away from Paul's and called out, "Kaye, could you bring that tequila I left in the galley?" There was no tequila. But it worked like a charm—every single time. She was still rifling through the compartments once Dallas had finally coaxed Paul off him and finished picking up the papers and trash.

"I must have left it in my car," he told her, once he was ready to hand the plane over to ground crew.

As always, Kaye believed him. But that didn't mean she was above complaining about it. "How can you *forget* a bottle of tequila?"

Dallas kept a pair of swim trunks in his bag, and yesterday he'd added a spare in case Paul was up for a dip in the pool. But given what they'd just learned about Marlin's death (Dallas refused to think of it as a suicide) the hotel pool no longer held any appeal. They trooped up to their rooms, Kaye's single and the double Dallas shared with Paul where only one bed saw any use, and Dallas racked his brain for some other way to distract Kaye when she came around looking for her credit cards. The real Kaye knew her autopilot swam, since she could smell the chlorine on her skin. But Dallas never confessed that he left her in the pool for hours as a healthy alternative to watching her gorge herself and then drink herself to sleep. But now that she knew about Marlin—Paul, thankfully, had spared Dallas from telling her—would they need to come up with a new distraction?

Paul's double was in the midst of treating Dallas to a naughty-pilot striptease, though he'd only gone so far as to remove his tie and unbutton his uniform shirt, when Kaye banged on their door. "Did you see today's special at the restaurant downstairs?" she called through it. "Swordfish. I love swordfish."

Dallas tossed Paul a polo shirt. Paul shucked his uniform and pulled it on, smirking as if he fully intended to continue his little performance later. "I got an idea," Dallas called back to Kaye. "Why don't we hit the pool first? Work up an appetite?"

He steeled himself to hear that after the news about Marlin, Kaye had no intention of going anywhere near the pool. But after a moment's consideration, she said, "Sounds good, I'll meet you boys down there."

What a relief. Dallas turned to see what Paul's twin had got himself up to, only to find he'd crept right up, quiet as a mouse. He gave Dallas a long, lingering look, then said, "You're going swimming? After what we found out this afternoon?"

It was easy to forget that the autopilots didn't exist only in Bermuda. Yes, they'd forget everything that happened on the trip when they reintegrated with their main consciousness—but they still carried all the knowledge of their other selves up until the moment of the very last turbulence that fragmented them off. "I don't feel like swimming," Dallas admitted, "but I'd like to sit and rest a while." Maybe this Paul could be enticed into relaxing. It was easy enough the last time. "It's been stressful."

"No kidding," Paul said. Dallas turned to dress for the poolside, figuring the conversation was played out, but Paul caught him by the arm and pulled him close. "You worry so much about everyone else it's a wonder you can function at all."

It was such an un-autopilot thing to say, Dallas found himself laughing awkwardly in surprise.

"It's true," Paul insisted, sliding his hands around Dallas' waist, cupping his ass. It might have seemed gropy from someone else, but he did it with such matter-of-fact purpose that Dallas allowed himself to be manhandled. Found comfort in it, in fact. "Who takes care of Dallas?"

"Why? You angling for the job?"

Paul watched Dallas' lips as he spoke, as if at any moment he'd get bored with talking and dive in to taste them. "I thought I already had it. Isn't that what being your *man* entails? Or is there someone else in the running?"

"Ain't no one else." Which was obvious, given the amount of time they spent together. But sometimes these things just needed saying…though it would be better to say it when Paul would remember.

When Paul kissed him, Dallas allowed it. Regretfully—because it really wasn't fair to the real Paul. And yet this facsimile was so sweet in his own way, Dallas would feel like one cold-hearted bastard dodging him at every turn. Paul's tongue eased into his mouth, gentle, but needy. The key was in figuring out where to draw the line, but without trampling on anyone's feelings. A kiss was only a kiss. It wouldn't hurt to indulge in that much. But anything more….

Paul's fingertip stroked the cleft of Dallas' ass, and Dallas broke the kiss and pulled away. Paul looked confused. "Just a quickie," he said reasonably. "Captain Kaye didn't say *when* we'd have to meet her at the pool."

"I can't," Dallas said, heart racing. "Not right now." Funny, even after all this time using the same lines, the same excuses on the autopilots trip after trip, he still felt like he was one lie away from being caught. Even now. "It's…embarrassing."

Paul's double was all concern, though he was still just as touchy, rubbing Dallas' upper arms, staring so earnestly into his eyes. "You can tell me."

"I.B.S." Dallas said succinctly. He'd actually been more blatant the last time he'd claimed the affliction and said "irritable bowel syndrome," but it hadn't been necessary to spell it all out. Paul knew exactly what it was.

And he still did—in fact, he reacted exactly as he had the first time Dallas used the excuse. With concern so heartfelt it was almost comical. "I'm *so* sorry. I knew this pilot, right out of flight school. He actually had to quit because he couldn't get it under control."

It was the same thing he'd told Dallas the day before. Verbatim.

"All the stress you're under can't be good for it either."

Well. That was a new twist. "Which is why we should head out and set ourselves up poolside," Dallas said.

"Are you sure?" Paul approached from behind and made another grab for him, but this time it was only to rub Dallas' shoulders. "You need me to go to the pharmacy? Or look up a doctor for you?"

"I'll be fine, baby," Dallas told him. "Let's go downstairs."

Dallas covered Paul's hand with his. Someday, after they'd enjoyed a few more weekends together (and a lot more naked encounters) it would be clear Dallas was in good health, and he'd need to come up with a new excuse…though he could probably get some mileage from "the stress must've caused a flare-up." For now, though, no matter how much Dallas felt like he was taking advantage, he'd need to accept this Paul's doting.

Which was nothing short of adorable.

***

According to the National Weather Service, sunset would occur in Bermuda at precisely 20:25. Paul was certain of that. He'd triple-checked the time. And then he'd quadruple-checked that his watch was set accurately. And then he'd set an alarm. Even so, he paced back and forth across the empty tarmac as if the motion of his feet could encourage the planet to rotate more quickly and bring on the precious darkness he was waiting for.

"Any minute now," Kaye called from the aircraft's doorway.

Paul planted his hands on his hips and glared at the western horizon. His watch beeped three times. Sunset. Even so, the Atlantic had a glow about it that was nowhere near as dark as Paul had hoped it would be. It began to dim. Paul scanned the horizon for a single bright light, the beacon Marlin had been trying to tell them about in his final communication. He could make out a dusting of stars, maybe, although one didn't particularly stand out from another. He scanned the night sky, did a quarter-turn, scanned some more, and then a bank of halogen lights flared to life with a startling pop and obliterated his night vision.

"That's no good," Kaye said.

"Why is it that when we need something to work, like the radio, or the Internet, or anything even remotely useful—it's toast? And yet, when we actually want something to shut down, surprise! It's on an auto timer!"

Kaye shrugged and shook her head in disgust.

Paul did his best to keep his voice level, though it would have felt awesome to scream in frustration. "Okay, so I find the circuit breaker and shut it down."

"I don't want you electrocuting yourself. Maybe you should wait until tomorrow's trip and disable it while it's still light out."

"It's fine," Paul said. "I'll be able to figure out an electrical panel. I've got my flashlight." Kaye pondered his statement for a moment, and he added, "You didn't see anything wrong with Marlin running around after dark."

"You've got it wrong." Kaye tossed Paul her flashlight so he had a spare. "I just knew he thought he was invulnerable. And I had no hope of convincing him otherwise."

"I'll be careful. I always am."

Paul found a sizable conduit housing the electrical cables that led to an array of outdoor lighting. He followed it to a juncture where it fed into a thicker conduit, looped around a hangar, and then connected to a cable housing that was larger still, as big around as his thigh. He followed that to a galvanized panel just outside the baggage area. It was locked, but a keyring hung from that lock, and a clipboard with an inspection checklist lay on the ground beneath it. The key turned easily. Leaving the access door shut, Paul eyed the enclosed panel carefully, preparing himself for a snake or scorpion or black widow to spring out at him when he opened it. Not that he had any knowledge that such wildlife made its home on the island, but he'd made a point of saying he'd be careful, and he didn't want to end up looking like an idiot. He stepped back and angled his body away, presenting the smallest possible target, then tapped it open with the rubberized edge of his flashlight. Nothing crawled, wriggled or sprang out. Even so, he paused for a moment to wait for his heart to stop thudding.

Not to make sure he didn't end up looking bad, he realized. But because if anything horrible actually did befall him…what would happen to Kaye?

What would happen to Dallas?

Paul refused to abandon them—like Marlin had.

He studied the panel. It was labeled in English (one can never presume these things) and compared to the instrument panel of a commercial jet, fairly straightforward. It seemed reckless to simply shut everything down. What if he needed to recharge the flashlights sometime during the night and he couldn't get it back online? No, he'd focus on the lights, he decided, and only those. With four clicks, he shut down the lighting for the runway, taxi lane and hangars, then gazed up at the night sky while his eyes adjusted. Better. But not perfect. He flicked off a few more switches and the service road and parking lot went dark. Another click, and the terminal's interior lights went dark.

Behind Paul, something flashed white, then green. He turned and found the airport beacon atop the control tower still going strong.

```
travelers in dark,
when the blazing sun is gone
find the tiny light
```

Paul's heart resumed its hyperactive thudding, and even picked up its pace. The rotating beacon. That was it. The key…it had to be. What else could that message possibly mean? He flipped on all the lights again, and the empty airport lit up. "Paul?" Kaye called from the aircraft a few hundred yards away. Distant, but as the only other human voice on the island, distinct. "Did you find something?"

He called back, "I don't know. I'm going to check." And while he briefly considered being all Marlin about it and jaunting off without bothering to mention what he was doing, he decided it was best if Kaye knew—even if she probably wouldn't leave the aircraft even to do recon. "It's the tower—the beacon."

"Be careful!"

No, he'd probably die injured and alone if he fell off the damn tower attempting to reach the damn beacon. But at least Kaye and Dallas would know precisely what he was trying to do, and why. For such a small airport, Wade International kept its control tower in a hard-to-reach spot. Paul had to pass the private hangars, cross the runway and the taxi lane, and then hike across a hundred yards of scrub. He'd started off in a huff, but soon realized he'd better keep his eye on the ground to keep from twisting his ankle on a hunk of rock or a discarded bottle. Though the night air was chill, he'd worked up a sweat by the time he reached the tower.

It was unlocked.

Shift change, protocol, Paul didn't stop to marvel at the fact that he wouldn't need to rifle through the empty cars and dig up a tire iron to pry open the door. What mattered was that any moment now, he would get to the bottom of the turbulence once and for all. He darted up the stairs, then paused in the empty control room that smelled like burnt coffee. The room was octagonal with windows all around, a 380-degree view of emptiness. Monitors flickered, and the radio band from the weather service played in a continual loop, small and tinny, through an empty pair of headphones that had fallen on a nearby chair. The idea that maybe it wasn't a loop—maybe he wasn't alone—sent a creeping sensation up the back of his neck. He spun around, heart jolting when he spied motion, only to realize that it was his own reflection in the tower's window, looking back at him with wide, terrified eyes.

As he willed his heart to stop pounding, the headphones beside him announced the temperature and windspeed in a computerized voice.

Too bad he wasn't a rock climber. Then he'd have access to some kind of harness to keep him from falling off the tower. It was unnecessary, though. A metal walkway circled the top of the tower, and a set of rungs set between a pair of windows led to the flashing light on top—the modern equivalent of a lighthouse, although instead pointing down to illuminate the sea, the spread of its light pointed up at a 10-degree angle to the horizon to alert incoming aircraft to its location. The lighting element was hot and smelled like cooking metal, but when Paul poked his head over the side of the tower, he found that it was angled in such a way so as not to shine in his face and blind him. Moving even more carefully than usual, he crawled up over the edge, found his footing, and shone his flashlight into the strobe light's housing, looking for that one key element that would bring the whole mystery together. And then he shone Kaye's torch in, too.

But other than an old bird's nest and a handful of dry leaves, there was nothing to discover. Not a damn thing.

CHAPTER 21

Once they landed in Fort Lauderdale, Dallas watched Paul emerge from the cockpit. Initial enthusiasm over seeing Paul safe and whole was dampened by the troubled look on his face. Whatever it was he'd tried out there in empty Bermuda, it hadn't worked out. Someday this would stop surprising Paul, but in its own way, that would be a shame. The day he stopped being disappointed at his failure to solve the mystery would be the day his hope had died.

If they were in Bermuda, Dallas could lift his spirits by angling him into the galley and stealing a kiss. But propriety weighed more heavily on this Paul, and cornering him into a public display of affection would do more harm than good. They walked to the car in silence. Paul loaded his rollerbag into the hatchback, then paused and sniffed the back of his hand. "Pineapple?"

"Piña colada."

"Lotion?"

"Bubble bath."

Paul gave a humorless little laugh. "Great. My brain's out there bashing its head against the wall and my body's taking a bubble bath. Alone?"

Dallas raised an eyebrow in reply.

Paul shook his head. "Great."

They climbed into the car, exited staff parking and headed home for their afternoon break. The lie that would save Paul an immense amount of worry had been perilously close to spilling out. *No, I did*n't *join you, I left you all by your lonesome in that big* ol' *bathtub.* But if, on the off chance, Paul believed it, all he would need to do was take a whiff of Dallas to know the truth.

And this Paul wouldn't forget, either.

Dallas' home was not far from the airport, so it wasn't until he'd turned onto his street that Paul found it in himself to talk about his night. "So I figured it was the rotating beacon. You know, the flashing light on the control tower? I mean, think about it. *When the blazing sun is gone, find the tiny light.* Up close, it's huge. But if you're a pilot looking down at it from the sky, it's one tiny light among dozens of other tiny lights that all look basically the same. The color and the flashing pattern is the thing that tells you that what you're seeing is an airport. If you're a pilot…right, as if Marlin ever thought like a pilot."

Dallas began to pull in to his driveway and found another car was already there. He didn't recognize it, but it wasn't particularly threatening, a tiny white Honda a few years old with a USF bumper sticker. Chantal's school. He supposed he should have mentioned the fact that he had a teenager at some point in the past week. He supposed it never seemed like the right time. And he supposed it was shady of him to wish he'd floated it by Bermuda Paul first to gauge his unfiltered reaction. "My niece is here," he said. "I raised her since she was six."

Paul absorbed the extremely succinct explanation. "Oh."

Not exactly a gushing acceptance…but Paul Cronin wasn't a gushy kind of guy. Not outside Bermuda.

Dallas cut the engine and popped open the hatchback. "I haven't told her yet. Everything that's happened this week. You, Marlin. It never seemed like the right…I mean, you and me, we were only official as of yesterday."

Paul dropped his hand to Dallas' knee and said softly, "It'll all work out." Here, in the face of his own disappointment, he still found comfort for Dallas. No, he wasn't as effusive about it as he might be when his censors weren't in place. But these shy glimpses of his depths were just as sweet.

If Paul was okay with it, that left only Chantal's reaction to worry about. They'd had a pretty good Easter together, despite Uncle Carl getting into a knock-down drag-out argument with his new girlfriend. They'd carried on so loud the police had to break it up, to Dallas' mortification and Chantal's wry amusement. But with finals coming up and all of Flight 511's foolishness, neither of them had texted each other in over a week. Dallas knocked on his own doorframe and called out, "I'm home, Miss Thang." No, Flight 511 wasn't responsible for their lack of contact. It was Dallas' focus on Paul, plain and simple. Maybe someday when Chantal found a serious boyfriend, she'd understand.

Dallas rounded the corner and found a boy making a peanut butter sandwich in his kitchen. A six foot tall, hazel-eyed black boy built like a brick shithouse.

Well, then. Apparently he and his niece both had something to say.

Chantal pounded down the hallway and swung into the kitchen breathlessly. "Uncle Dallas? This is..." her eyes darted over Dallas' shoulder and her expression shifted as she took in Paul. And then she recovered, almost seamlessly, and said, "my boyfriend, Terrel."

"And this is Paul," Dallas replied, unable to keep the lilt that implied "*my* boyfriend" from his voice. He left it implicit though. Since he was the parent, his tone needed to suggest the delivery of information rather than a request for consent.

Knowing Chantal, she probably wanted to play it cool, so she refused to stare. Unfortunately, her curiosity was getting the better of her, and her gaze kept hopping around the room, but most of the time landing on Paul. "We met at work," Dallas supplied. Given their AVA uniforms, that much was obvious. But stating the fact seemed to level out a conversation that threatened to veer into a tailspin.

"And we met in Environmental Economics," she said. Which would explain the matching hemp bracelets. Chantal—the girl who'd insisted on the 18-carat gold pendant for her high school graduation—was now, less than twelve short months later, adorning herself with clay beads and jute.

"My schedule's still the same," Dallas said gently. "You drove four and a half hours to get here, and I'm back on a plane to Bermuda this afternoon."

"I know. But I wanted to see you. And Terrel has a car." Chantal looked like it just now occurred to her that the drive time, not to mention the gas money, could have been put to a much better use. "And he offered."

Paul edged past them, dragging his rollerbag sideways. "I need to check my email," he said apologetically. "And we should probably wash a load of shirts."

"I'll get the shirts. You can hop online in the bedroom."

Paul blushed crimson as he sidled out of the room under the gaze of Dallas and Chantal. Terrel slapped a piece of bread on his sandwich and said, "I'm gonna go, uh, eat this outside." Judging by how awkward he sounded, he was probably blushing just as hard as Paul, though for him it didn't show.

"How long you been with Terrel?" Dallas asked, once he and Chantal were alone.

"We were friends first. A group of us. I didn't think to say anything to you about it, you know, 'cos we were just friends last semester, and most of this semester too. But then we set up this study group, and one night everyone else blew us off, and it was just him, and just me…and when we were alone it seemed so…" she shrugged. "Like it couldn't have been any other way."

It was never easy for Dallas to see Chantal with a boy; he knew damn well what teenage boys could be like, and his protective nature ran deep. But given that her pairing up with someone was inevitable, friends to lovers was the best possible scenario he could wish for her. Had Dallas ever had that? Not that he could remember. He'd grown up too fast and run with a crowd of friends who sized up every new man they met as potential hookup material.

"Paul and I are still figuring this whole thing out," he said.

"Oh."

Dallas had intended to leave it at that—after all, he was the adult, it was his home, and he shouldn't have to explain himself to a teenager. But Chantal's "oh" had an entirely different quality compared to the "oh" Paul gave in the car. Paul had sounded like he was standing by to see what else would unfold, and reserving opinion until he had the lay of the land.

Chantal, by contrast, sounded distinctly relieved.

Dallas led her to the breakfast nook, an outdated little corner of the room that might have looked sunny and cheerful thirty years ago when it was new, but now seemed worn and tacky. He sat her down, then bumped her farther onto the bench so he could slide in beside her, rather than across from her. He took her hand in both of his. "The whole time you were growing up, I never brought men home. It didn't seem right."

"I don't buy into the rhetoric that gay parents aren't just as good as straight couples, and I never expected you to—"

"Let me finish. I was never serious enough about a man to take it to the level where I trust them around any child of mine. It was my choice, and I'd do the same again. But you're at school now, the house is empty, and there's no reason for me to be single. Especially not when I meet someone as special as Paul. Him and me, we do have plenty to figure out—but whatever this is between us, it's serious."

"What's there to figure?"

"It's not easy working for an airline." Especially one that flew through the broken part of the Bermuda Triangle. "With most people it's an obstacle, but we got that in common. He lives in DC, though, so when he's here, he's staying with me."

"So it's a once-in-a-while thing."

She wished. Even though she wasn't saying it out loud, and even though she'd never admit it, *Why you gotta get with the world*'s *whitest white guy?* was written all over her face. "We're on the same crew," he told her. "We spend the whole week together." The fact that he spent more time with Bermuda Paul was not a detail he was prepared to elaborate on. Besides, they were really the same person. Basically.

"Well. It'll take some getting used to. But I'm happy for you." She didn't sound happy…but she did sound like she might attempt it.

They both went quiet to look up at Paul as he entered the room with a basket of laundry. He was wearing the same blue polo shirt he'd worn last night in Bermuda. But last night the main impression Dallas took away from it was how fine that color looked with his peaches-and-cream skin.

Today, the shirt's most prominent features were the wrinkles and folds the luggage had left in the fabric. Funny, what a difference self-confidence made. "There was a grease stain on your sleeve from yesterday," Paul said. "I put that on top so you can pre-treat it to keep it from setting." He put the basket on the countertop and took a few steps closer to the breakfast nook, then looked right at Chantal, despite the fact that she was sitting bolt upright, just waiting for an excuse to sass him. "Wow. I didn't assume you were blood relatives—I mean, you could be related by marriage or something—but you have his eyes. Exactly." He then pinked, as if he hadn't realized how awkward that would sound out loud, said, "Anyway…" and retreated to the bedroom.

Chantal toyed with the salt shaker for a moment, then said, "Hard to be critical of someone who notices your eyes."

Dallas wasn't sure if he should take it at face value and presume that Paul had managed to flatter her, or if she meant something deeper—that what mattered was the way Paul *saw* Dallas, had actually committed his features to memory, and was looking for something that went beyond a quick lay and a good time.

The four of them ended up having a relatively relaxed lunch together. Despite the fact that Chantal's boyfriend had just eaten a sandwich (and possibly more than one) Terrel was at that age where his primary talent was making food disappear. Of course he was up for pizza, though he and Paul practically had to arm wrestle to determine who would pay for it. Terrel won the honor when Dallas reminded Paul it was best to stop tempting fate with his credit card, referring to the Bermuda spending spree, only briefly, as a "bank error."

Terrel turned out to be quite the high-minded intellectual, in his painfully young and overly-earnest fashion. And the way he gazed at Chantal when she wasn't looking seemed light years more evolved than the looks of the high school boys who'd wondered how far they could get, what with her bedroom door mandatorily open and strict Uncle Dallas watching TV in the next room. No, Terrel had substance to him, as much substance as a twenty-year-old could have. A hell of a lot more than Dallas had at that age, when all he cared about was clothes…and parties and weed and boys.

Once they'd eaten, finished their laundry and suited up for their next trip through the turbulence, Dallas took Chantal aside and kissed her on the forehead. He said, "You gonna be here tomorrow when I get home from work?"

"Can't. Exams. Gotta leave early in the morning."

Which she should have been studying for, and not driving across the state on a whim. But Dallas didn't remark on it. She'd never start making better decisions if he didn't allow her go get some practice in. He didn't comment on the sleeping arrangements, either. She was mostly grown up now, and no doubt they would do what they wanted whether they were in Dallas' house, Chantal's dorm room or Terrel's apartment. Best not fuss over it.

He drove to the airport in silence, just thinking. Chantal. So different than she used to be. He knew it was going to happen, someday she'd grow up, but that nappy ol' hemp bracelet, that was the detail that Dallas kept coming back to. And her plain T-shirt and jeans, and her hair natural, brushed back in a simple ponytail instead of its usual elaborately straightened bob with the ends curled under. But mostly, the bracelet.

As they pulled into the airport parking lot, Paul said, "I had a nice afternoon."

"I'm glad. Me too."

When Dallas parked the car, Paul caught his hand and held it there over the arm rest. "I didn't want to kill the mood or anything back at your house, but I'd better tell you now, so you hear it from me, and not…well, you know, in Bermuda. I called Bernadette while I was putting together the laundry. She said Marlin's service is Saturday morning. I told her we'd be there."

Dallas had wondered if Paul might linger in Fort Lauderdale—if not the whole weekend, maybe Friday night. He'd been hoping for at least that one night together, him and Paul—all of Paul. But not like this.

The belief that Marlin was actually gone was slow to sink in. Dallas had seen his empty house, been glared at unhelpfully by the cops, spoken with his ex-wife. But given the mindbending shift he witnessed every time he flew, would it be so far-fetched to hope that Marlin's death had actually been one big mistake? That he was off-roading in a swamp somewhere when he managed to lose his cell phone, get himself stuck twenty miles out, and all this time had been hiking back toward civilization?

No. If Bernadette had arranged for a cremation, then it was highly unlikely Marlin was currently fighting his way through the mosquito-infested mangrove. And the service, well...that's where Dallas would have to admit to himself that this whole situation was actually real.

Dallas' heart felt too heavy for his body to contain it. He squeezed, and only then realized that Paul had never let go of his hand.

CHAPTER 22

From the parking lot, Dallas sized up the East Shore Unity Center. He hadn't expected Marlin's church to fit his preconceived notion of "churches." He'd been presuming it would be modern, since he couldn't imagine the New Age lingo flying back and forth across a traditional pulpit. He didn't visualize light streaming in through stained glass windows and a pipe organ churning out hymns. But what he hadn't been prepared for was the sense of deja vu it evoked. Like the storefront Baptist church in Montgomery his Auntie Esther had repeatedly dragged him to the summer he was eight, this church of Marlin's was located in a strip mall.

As he hesitated in an attempt to get his bearings, another car pulled into a space marked *Reserved - Funeral.* When the driver got out, she slung a cheap imitation Fendi bag over her shoulder and strode purposefully to the nail salon next door. Beside him, Paul sighed.

"Thank you for coming with me," Dallas said.

Paul had spent the evening online trying to figure out how to return the key from his crash pad in Boston, since rent was coming due. He paid nearly as much for a bed in Boston as Dallas did for his entire 2-bedroom rental home in Lauderdale, and his new schedule meant he wouldn't need it anymore. He'd never met Marlin, and as far as Dallas could tell, he didn't care for religion. Plus, he hadn't been back to DC for a week. Most other pilots in his shoes would make their apologies, skip the service and catch a flight back to take care of their business. But no. Instead, Paul sat with the oppressive South Florida sun angling through the passenger window, looking slightly wilted in his borrowed suit, and forced a smile. "You don't need to thank me. You shouldn't have to do this alone."

Dallas had told himself he wouldn't cry—and here he was, about to well up before he'd even made it across the parking lot.

Paul seemed as if he would like to hold Dallas' hand, had it been the time or the place to do it. He settled for walking close and brushing the edge of Dallas' sleeve with his fingertips. Dallas pinched the bridge of his nose in an effort to stem the threatening tide, fortified himself with a good, deep breath, and ventured in.

The similarities to First Church of Christ of Dallas' childhood ended at the strip mall door. Marlin's church looked more like a flea market than a house of worship. Chairs were mis-matched, as if they'd been donated one by one or discovered at garage sales. One corner held chunky, colorful toys on a carpet printed with cartoon characters. Book shelves lined the far wall, with hand-lettered signs taped up that read, *2 at a Time - Honor System* and *We Need Current Non-Fiction* and *No Highlighting the Pages, Please.* A long banquet-style folding table dominated each side of the room. One was covered with plates of cookies and brownies, fruits and cheese, casseroles and sandwich wraps.

The other held Marlin Fritsch's mortal remains.

It held flower arrangements too—some tacky and professional, some strange and freeform, likely homemade—and it held mounted photos propped on stands. On one side, a big enlargement of the AVA photo in uniform from his business card, the print blurry since it had probably been done at the corner drug store. On the other, a picture of him with a terrible mullet, looking young and cocky. But all the flowers and all the photos in the world wouldn't have made a bit of difference. Dallas couldn't tear his eyes off the small silver canister in the center of the table. The urn.

He turned from the table, hoping to fix on something else so as not to be seeing that awful little jar, and was relieved to find Bernadette standing in the corner in a fitted black skirt suit and sassy Mahlo Blahnik pumps, arms crossed beneath her bust, lips pressed together tight. He made his way to her with Paul by his side. She didn't seem to know anyone else, so even though they'd only met once before, she relaxed as if some old friends had just shown up to support her. It wasn't that Marlin's people seemed standoffish—just that they clearly knew each other so well, were so engrossed in the conversations they were having with one another, that anyone who wasn't part of their crowd became an outsider by default.

And then Captain Kaye showed up in full uniform, right down to the hat (which she never wore at work), and the mingling congregants immediately knew how to categorize her. They splintered off from their groups to approach her, to inquire about Marlin's last days at work and see if he'd confided in her while they were alone in the cockpit, to wonder aloud about the question that was really dogging all of them that day: *Why?*

Half an hour after the service was scheduled to begin, a middle-aged white man in a suit that was too snug across the back encouraged people to take a seat. Kaye sat beside Paul, Bernadette beside Dallas. The man in the suit was eventually the only one standing—pacing, really—and when he began to speak, only the authority with which he commanded the room marked him as a preacher.

"One of the five basic teachings of Unity is that we are all spiritual beings. We're eternal—we exist before we take a body, and we do not cease to exist after we transition out of it."

Dallas stared. Not only was it disconcerting to hear someone talking exactly like Marlin always had, it was weird to wrap his head around how gay this preacher man clearly was. He knew Marlin well, and spoke at length about how he was such a great guy—upbeat, generous, dynamic and fun. Apparently Marlin regularly took members of the church out to the marina for mini-cruises after Sunday service, and he gave guitar lessons to a few kids in the congregation too. Everyone genuinely liked him. And as far as they could tell, he was happy.

"Which is what makes it so difficult for us all to understand..." he paused and gathered himself, then plowed on, though his voice had grown thick and tears were creeping down his cheeks. "We know Marlin has returned to Source. We're not mourning for him. It's us—his physical friends, who are missing him right now—we're the ones who've got it hard."

A buzz startled Dallas. Paul, too, flinched. The cell phone in Paul's front pocket vibrated between them. Paul's cheeks flushed. He clapped his hands over the buzzing in his slacks to try to muffle the sound. It wasn't exactly loud, but it was audible. Marlin's friends didn't make a huge deal out of it—they really didn't seem like the type to be sticklers for propriety in their sandals and shorts—but they did shift in their seats. The preacher paused, momentarily distracted, and seemed to have forgotten whatever else he'd meant to say. He sought his ideas for a long, awkward moment, and then decided that maybe he was done talking, after all. "And now, if anyone has a fond memory of Marlin, the rest of us would be honored if you'd be willing to share it."

Paul pulled the phone out and began swiping at the screen. "It was supposed to be off," he said under his breath. "I swear I turned it off."

Kaye frowned at the phone, then stood up and said, "I can start." The preacher gave her a "by all means" gesture and sat himself down to listen in a pale oak chair that looked like it had been rescued from a dining room set sometime in the eighties. "I've been working with Marlin for the past year," Kaye said. "And being a commercial pilot, knowing that all those passengers are counting on you to handle whatever situation may come up and keep them all safe…it's stressful. I remember once, after a really rough flight, we were standing there together just outside the cockpit, and I'd had it—I was ready to pack it all in and start looking at retirement. Then Marlin pointed out through the cabin door at the clouds, and he said, 'But look at that amazing sky, Kaye. As long as there's still beauty in the world, things can't be all bad.' Marlin was the most positive person…" she trailed off and turned to his photo, as if it might give her some hint as to what he'd been thinking, and then to the urn, the awful urn. "We'll all miss him," she said, and took her seat.

A murmur ran through the congregation as a few members tried to gather the wherewithal to speak next, and a buzzing sound from Paul's pocket cut right through the murmurs. "For crying out loud," he whispered. He pulled it out and jabbed the screen, and the buzzing stopped.

"I'm so sorry."

Whereas someone like Auntie Esther would have shot Paul a look that would singe off his eyebrows, the Unity folk just shrugged and gave wan smiles that seemed to say, *These things happen.*

As Paul pocketed his phone, a girl sitting off to the side shot up out of her chair, like she'd finally convinced herself to speak but needed to force herself to go through with it. Dallas might not have recognized her if he hadn't just seen her photograph on Marlin's fridge—Caitlin. Barely older than Chantal, by the looks of her. Dallas had never met her in person, though Marlin's autopilot had shared photos of a weekend camping trip with Dallas once, gushing about what a "great girl" she was…until just a few weeks later, when things "didn't work out."

Hard to imagine her roughing it in the forest now. Her skirt was short, her shimmery top was clingy, and her silky straight blonde hair hung as perfectly as a department store mannequin's. "So…Marlin was the whole reason I started coming to church," she said. "I always thought church was kind of nerdy and old-fashioned, but I figured if someone like him was so pumped up about going, it couldn't hurt to check it out. And so I never would have met any of you if it hadn't been for Marlin." She paused and looked at his official AVA photo as if she might, at the last moment, figure him out…but then she could only shake her head in bewilderment. "At first I thought he might be giving me a pickup line—he seems that way, you know, like he's trying to be all smooth. Except then, after we hung out a few times, I realized that it wasn't an act. He really is that way, totally sure of himself. Or, uh, he was." She sniffled. "But then I realized that when we were doing stuff together, it didn't actually matter to him if I was there or not. I mean, he thought it was nice, I guess. But at the same time, he didn't really need me. He'd be just as happy to stand there and stare off into space and just…think." She took another look at his photo and said, "Was I wrong? I thought he didn't need anyone else. He seemed like he was happy. Maybe I didn't know him at all. Maybe none of us ever really know anybody."

She sat down just as suddenly as she'd stood, and she buried her face in her hands. The very concerned young men on either side of her patted her shoulders consolingly. Saddened by the sight of the poor child so distraught, Dallas slipped his hand toward Paul's—only to be jolted back by the buzzing of his phone. Paul fumbled it from his pocket. "I turned it *off*—you saw me."

Dallas slipped him a set of keys and whispered, "Why don't you go run it out to the car?"

Paul breathed, "I'm sorry," grabbed the keys, and sprinted for the door in a crouch like he was dodging sniper fire. The church folk just shook their heads mildly.

Once the door shut behind Paul, someone else stood, a white lady around Kaye's age—a white lady who looked awfully familiar. "What I'll remember the most about Marlin was the way he ate his SpaghettiOs," she said. Dallas wondered where he knew her from. The grocery store? He could picture her as a checkout clerk. "Straight from the can. Didn't heat them up or anything. Said it reminded him of camping." Or maybe she worked at the telephone company, where Dallas paid his bill in person in case he needed to debate the types of monumental triple-charges he got while Chantal still lived at home. It was probably safe to start paying that bill online now, he supposed. "He was always so busy, driving through things or climbing over things or jumping across things. But when he wanted a change of pace, and he decided to stay still for a minute, he'd hole up in front of his TV, crack open a can of room-temperature SpaghettiOs, and set himself up for an all-day Gilligan's Island marathon." She smiled at his AVA portrait as Dallas took in her profile and tried to place her face. Maybe the bank. He and Marlin did use the same bank, since it was so convenient to the airport. But why would a bank teller know so much about Marlin's habits? Even Dallas didn't know about his taste in canned pasta.

"Such a character," she sighed. "A little too impulsive, I suppose. But he talked the talk and he walked the walk. It takes a lot of courage to carry that off."

Once she'd sat down again and the congregation was murmuring amongst themselves to decide who'd speak next, Paul slipped back into the room. He planted himself next to Dallas and shot him an embarrassed grimace. A teenage boy stood and talked about Marlin helping him pick out his first used car. An older lady said Marlin always bought magazine subscriptions from her when she was selling them for her granddaughter's school. Marlin had touched so many lives, which struck Dallas as strange, because he never talked about it. Or maybe he would have, if Dallas had spent more time with the whole Marlin Fritsch, and not just his autopilot.

Once the pause after the last remembrance stretched long, the preacher stood again and said, "Did anyone else have something they wanted to add?"

He didn't seem to be talking to anyone in particular, but Dallas couldn't help but glance at Bernadette, who'd been conspicuously silent. She kept her eyes planted straight ahead, though, and the fine lines on her brow and the corners of her mouth looked set. Dallas supposed he wasn't the only one who wasn't ready to leap up and declare how much Marlin had meant to him. He wasn't the only one who didn't really know how to process the loss.

The service wrapped up with a reading from the New Testament (which surprised Dallas, since he expected something a little more esoteric) and then an invitation from the preacher to stay for snacks. About three dozen people in all were there, which seemed like more bodies than the tiny church normally needed to accommodate. Kaye, who wasn't what you'd call a people-person, looked none too comfortable in the crowd. She stayed and shook hands and accepted condolences anyway. Marlin had no parents, no siblings, no children, no girlfriend or wife, only some cousins who hadn't seen him since high school. Bernadette wasn't trading on whatever relationship they'd shared years ago, so Kaye became his primary relative by default.

Maybe Dallas could have stepped into that role, too. Kaye had made a statement by showing up in uniform, but it wasn't anything a flight attendant would normally do, not without a specific request from the family. And since there was no family to speak of....

"I haven't seen you two around here before." The gay preacher man clapped Paul on the shoulder as he came to offer a handshake. "I'm Rev. Ralph. Or just plain Ralph is fine."

"I'm Paul. This is my partner, Dallas."

Dallas did his best not to preen over the way the word *partner* had flowed out so easily. Maybe even a touch forcefully. Because Ralph had zeroed in on Paul as soon as the service ended, not that Dallas could blame any red-blooded homosexual for scoping him out.

As Dallas and the Reverend spoke about how they knew Marlin, how they'd miss him, how their lives would seem a lot duller without him in it and how they felt privileged to have known him at all, Paul seemed awkward, shifting his weight and glancing around like he didn't quite know where to look. So it was a surprise to Dallas when Paul said to the Reverend, "You know, we were thinking, if anyone needs help clearing out Marlin's things, we're free the rest of the weekend."

Ah. He didn't actually want to help, though he might end up doing so inadvertently. Mostly he wanted to look for Bermuda clues. Dallas supposed it was okay for an action to do double-duty, taking some of the burden off Marlin's ex while chipping away at their bigger problem. Would Marlin have wanted it that way? Probably. Figuring out the turbulence phenomenon was his life's work. He'd be "stoked" to have someone carry it on.

"How sweet of you!" Ralph gushed. "That would be fabulous. Give me your number and I'll set something up for tomorrow." Paul handed over his card, and Ralph gave the tiny AVA photo on it close scrutiny, then said to Dallas, "Nothing quite like a man in uniform, is there?"

Once he excused himself to go see to the rest of the guests, Paul leaned in and whispered, "The condo association called me *four* times in the past hour. If my last check to them bounced, I'd just as soon blow them off—they'll get their money soon enough. But what if there's an actual emergency? You know, a burst pipe, or a break-in, or a fire."

"Hush now," Dallas murmured, before Paul began imagining earthquakes and hurricanes and plagues of locusts. "Let's get going, and you can find out what they actually want before you get yourself worked up over nothing."

"Really? You don't want to stay, and uh…?"

"I don't think so." Dallas glanced at Marlin's AVA portrait and tried to recall if his sparkling eyes were blue, or maybe green. When they were spending five nights a week together, it had never seemed particularly important. Now Dallas' memory of him was already eroding. The portrait was no help, either. The poor enlargement was too jagged and blurry to tell. Dallas' heart ached. If there was closure to be found, it wasn't at the East Shore Unity Center. "Just needed to pay my respects."

The noontime heat enveloped them like a steaming wet towel as they stepped out into the parking lot, made twice as sickening by the chemical polymer smell wafting out of the nail salon next door. Dallas' heart, already heavy from the service, sank even more…until Paul's hand found his, and their fingers intertwined. Hand in hand, they walked to the far end of the lot. Not speaking—no need. Handling Marlin's death was horrible, but how much worse would it be if Dallas had needed to do it alone? He sent up an earnest prayer of thanks, and then glanced over to look into Paul's eyes and find solace in his companionship, when a movement across the street caught his eye instead.

A woman—the woman from the service, the bank teller or cashier or whoever she was—approached a dowdy sedan parked across the four-lane. "Paul, do you know that lady?"

Paul turned to look, and an eighteen wheeler rolled up and idled, blocking their view. "Who?"

"Behind the truck." Which should move any time now. Any time. "A white lady, maybe sixty or so, with hair that looks like a wig."

"You've just described my mother and all her friends."

"I know her from somewhere." They waited while the truck idled, and a cloud of black diesel smoke belched out of the smokestack. When traffic finally moved, the sedan was gone. Dallas supposed he could get her name from Ralph later on by recounting the SpaghettiOs story, but it was one of those niggling things that just didn't want to let go. "Remind me to ask—" he turned toward his car and spotted the sedan around the corner, even closer now than it had been before. "There! In the silver car."

"Which one?"

Dang it, there were at least five other silver sedans all around her. "With the hair." Oh, that was helpful—and now she was getting away. "Right there by the steakhouse."

"I can't tell."

The lady pulled into a turn lane, where just as soon as a gap in oncoming traffic came up, she'd be gone, maybe for good. Dallas was searching, trying in vain to capture some detail about her that might help him describe her later, when she dug out a pair of clip-on sunglasses and snapped them onto her prescription frames.

And a chill ran through him despite the sweltering heat. He remembered that gesture. He'd met her before—more than once.

She'd been on his first flight to Bermuda.

CHAPTER 23

Paul turned up the AC as Dallas steered out of the parking lot with one eye on the woman in the silver sedan. Within moments, she pulled onto the highway, merged into traffic, and was gone. Dallas shook his head.

"Are you up for lunch?" Paul asked, since there was nothing to be done for it short of punching it into gear and embarking on a high-speed chase...and he didn't think Dallas' slightly dented hatchback was up for the challenge. While he wasn't particularly hungry himself, he figured they should probably eat. Better a drive-through where they could be alone with their thoughts—with each other—than the potluck back at Marlin's church where the atmosphere was too thick with confusion, grief and forced optimism to choke anything down.

Dallas stared at the entrance ramp until a car horn blasted from behind them, then he shook off whatever was bugging him and drove. "What're you in the mood for?"

"Anything, you pick. I've gotta see why the condo association was playing redial roulette."

"Chinese?"

Paul hit the callback button. "Sure, fine." The phone rang three times and a man answered. Paul recognized the voice—it was the husband from the married couple that comprised half the association's officers. Aaron Haskin was treasurer and his wife Sylvia was president, though Paul always suspected Aaron was really calling all the shots and Sylvia just went along with him to keep the peace. "This is Paul Cronin. You called?" Tempting to add, *four times...during a funeral.* Aaron's sense of entitlement to other people's time and attention had always rubbed Paul wrong, and he didn't want to give the guy the satisfaction. Plus, given that his check had probably bounced, he wasn't really in a position to get snippy.

"Mr. Cronin. I was beginning to wonder if you were making some sort of statement by ignoring our letters."

"A...statement?"

"We sent it five times—the last one through registered mail."

"I haven't been home all week."

"Oh." He shuffled some papers. "I see the office signed for it."

"Right." The office he was currently sitting in had signed for the letter he was wondering if Paul had received. "I have them sign for all my stuff. Since I'm a pilot. And I'm usually not there."

"So what you're saying is that you haven't read any of the correspondence."

Paul rolled his eyes. Was the guy even seeing the irony here? *His own secretary* had signed for it. "I haven't read anything. If you could email me a copy, then—"

"This is official business, Mr. Cronin. I'm not going to send it over the Internet."

What would they prefer, then—carrier pigeon? "Then we'll have to straighten it out on the phone. There was a temporary freeze on my accounts, but the bank tells me it should all be clear by Monday."

"What accounts?"

Breathe. Just breathe. "Let's back up a few paces and start again. Did my fees clear?"

"Why?" Aaron demanded. "Did you stop payment?"

The fact that the *treasurer* didn't know off the top of his head whether or not there was an issue with Paul's check was not exactly comforting. "Of course not. I had some international charges on my debit card and the bank put a stop on it." Paul hoped he didn't need to mention yet again that he was a pilot. That would be like dropping the fact that he was a member of Mensa in casual conversation—no way he could come out looking like anything but a tool.

"Let's see..." more papers shuffled. "I have your check right here. Haven't made the deposit yet."

That was a relief. Paul paid his bills long before they were due—and he'd never bounced a check in his life. But if the condo fees weren't the issue.... "Then what's the problem?" Please, please, please, don't let it be a leaky toilet in the unit upstairs.

"Section 12e of the bylaws," Aaron replied gravely.

After an uncomfortable pause in which it became apparent Aaron wasn't going to enlighten him, Paul said, "Which is?"

Aaron cleared his throat and read: "Signs, banners, advertisements and emblems of any kind may not be displayed on doors, windows or mailboxes."

Paul waited for him to continue on—maybe to the next page, which was lost on the desk amid all of Paul's registered mail—but as the silence stretched, Paul realized he was done. Finally, he had to admit, "I have no idea what you're talking about."

"On or about the twentieth of May, you placed an emblem on the lower right corner of your living room window."

An emblem? What the hell was that supposed to—Paul's breath caught as he realized, picturing his front window in his mind's eye, exactly what Aaron was talking about. The "emblem" in question was approximately two inches by three inches. His favorite bartender had slipped one to everyone last time he'd shown up for happy hour. "The rainbow sticker?"

"The content is irrelevant," he said loftily.

The hell it was. That's what the crack about "making a statement" was all about. And another thing—Paul couldn't imagine anyone reporting it if he'd stuck a Jesus-fish decal to the glass. "It fits in the palm of my hand—you can't even see it from the street."

"There's a twenty-five dollar per day fine associated with the infringement."

If Paul had indeed bounced a check, even though it had actually been his autopilot at fault, he would have gladly accepted the punishment and paid the fine. But twenty-five dollars a day for a tiny sticker in the corner of his window? "I'm not paying that."

"You signed the charter, Mr. Cronin. You're not in a position to pick and choose which of the provisions you feel like obeying."

"Is that all?" Paul said coldly.

Aaron huffed and puffed for a moment, then said, "I'll be sure to deposit your fees first thing Monday morning," and hung up.

Paul seethed. Possibly for a good long while. Eventually, though, he realized he'd been staring at a glove box and the smell of fried rice was wafting in through the air conditioning vent. He looked up and found he was in the Happy Wok parking lot—and he felt anything but happy. Dallas was watching him calmly, allowing him to pull himself together.

"I have first amendment rights," Paul said.

Dallas nodded knowingly. He must have picked up the general gist from Paul's half of the conversation. "Take a look at whatever you signed before you go Stonewall on their asses. And if you think they really are targeting you, then decide if it's a battle you truly want to take on. Especially considering how difficult it would be to do any business with a lawyer when you spend most of your week in a place where no one exists but you and Kaye."

"I need to deal with this in person," Paul sighed. "I'm sorry. I hate leaving you alone, after this morning—but if I don't handle it now, it's going to drag out another week. I'll check the flights, see if I can be back by tomorrow morning to help with Marlin's house."

Paul pulled up a schedule on his phone, but before it loaded, Dallas' fingers slid across the screen, blocking his view. "I'm thinking there might be another empty seat on your flight. The question is whether you're up for company."

Really? Dallas would do that for him? Paul let his breath out slowly and nodded.

They found a flight to Philadelphia that they could catch if they wolfed down their kung pao chicken and didn't bother stopping at home to change. The last row was empty since it didn't recline, and it felt like their own little world. Dallas spent the entire flight drawing lazy circles on the back of Paul's hand with his forefinger. By the time they connected with their flight to DC, Paul's righteous anger had transmuted into something more like purpose. That, and the desire to rumple his neatly made bed with Dallas.

It was twilight by the time the cab dropped them off in front of Paul's building, and compared to the sprawl of seedy single-family stucco homes, Georgetown felt vibrant and exciting when Paul imagined viewing it through Dallas' eyes. Gearing up for battle over a little sticker—maybe it really wasn't worth it. Not in the grand scheme of things, not when the fabric of reality was warping out there over the Atlantic. So maybe, he decided, he and Dallas could simply enjoy one another.

He let them into the vestibule and emptied his overstuffed mailbox, glad for the second pair of hands, then led Dallas upstairs. It felt strange to be crossing his threshold without a rollerbag bumping over the carpet strip—especially accompanied by someone he was actually excited to be with. They dumped the mail beside the door, then Paul gave Dallas the 25-cent tour. Granite countertops, custom. Bamboo flooring, very green. The view, old architecture and twinkling city lights. Dallas stood beside Paul, arms loosely around each others' waists, and looked down at the 3-inch piece of vinyl on which the course of their day had pivoted. "Ain't hardly nothing," Dallas said, "is it? Maybe it's the little things that count, though. If you got to make your point, I'll back you up. However I can."

A feeling surged through Paul, as sudden and heated as the rush he'd felt over the sticker—but bigger, and broader, and much warmer than that. And a heck of a lot less familiar than anger. "I…" love you? *No. Too soon.* "…appreciate that. You're totally amazing."

Dallas replied with a kiss—sweet, but then deepening into something more, something tinged with urgency and need. Paul couldn't help but wonder if he should have thrown caution to the wind and just blurted out what he'd actually been thinking. But the last thing he wanted to do was ruin things before they'd had the chance to get started. And Dallas didn't seem to mind hearing he was amazing, either.

Dallas' hands slid down his back. Paul felt his body react when each touch left a shimmering vapor trail of sensation behind. Even his hand tingled as if Dallas had found a new erogenous zone during the flight, and his caresses had started a build that then gathered all day, and was now hurtling toward a dizzying apex. Paul slid the knot from Dallas' tie and worked open his shirt's top buttons with trembling fingers. He followed with his tongue, tasting the salt of Dallas' throat, sweetened by an elusive hint of cologne.

"It is *killing* me to not be able to touch you," Dallas murmured. Paul almost asked what was stopping him—but of course Dallas didn't mean now. He was talking about Bermuda. They managed to fumble themselves onto the couch, Paul lavishing kisses on Dallas' throat, Dallas with the seat of Paul's trousers balled in his fists. Maybe, Paul decided, he should let the rainbow sticker slide after all. No doubt there'd be plenty more chances to stand up for himself. Right now, fixing the turbulence should be his priority.

Paul felt his thigh brush a prominent bulge, and his heartbeat raced. Tonight, now, they'd lose themselves in one another's bodies, and the rest of the world could fall away, and take its judgment with it. He reached down and cupped Dallas' hardness, and Dallas moaned into his hair. He grabbed Dallas' belt and unhitched it...and then the pounding started at his front door.

"I know you're home—your lights are on." Denny. "And you dropped a Vitamin Warehouse postcard on the floor."

Maybe it was more of a civilized knock, and maybe it was just his own heart Paul felt pounding against his ribcage. But he jumped up off the couch as if he'd been caught...doing what? Kissing his own boyfriend? In his own home?

"Hel-lo? Are you in the shower? I don't hear the water running."

Dallas rearranged himself, then buckled his belt. Then he raised an eyebrow at Paul.

Paul just shook his head.

The knocking turned into banging. "Aren't you coming to dinner? If it's just me and Richard, he might think it's a date."

"Don't flatter yourself," Paul muttered. The banging stopped, but twin points of shadow remained in the sliver of light at the bottom of the door while Denny lurked there on the other side of the plywood. Paul was hoping Denny might go away. But he also suspected it was too much to hope for.

"Come on, Paul," Denny wheedled. "First round is on me."

What? Paul wondered if he was being punked. Denny never offered to pay for anything.

"Unless you want to stand Richard up and stay in. Maybe you could convince me. If you're really nice."

Paul stomped over to the front door and yanked it open before Denny could come up with anything even more embarrassing to yell through it. "What were you doing?" Denny said, oblivious to the fact that Paul must surely look like he wanted to jam some junk mail into his mouth to shut him up. But then he did see Paul—all of a sudden, all at once—and said, "Since when do you own a linen suit?"

"I'm busy," Paul said firmly.

Which Denny ignored. "It's really not you, dearie. Too Cuban. You're nowhere near trendy enough to pull it off."

Paul had been body-blocking Denny from squeezing through the door, but at the sound of himself called "dearie" in that condescending dentist-voice, he decided to take a stand on something after all. He turned to the couch, looked at Dallas, and gestured toward Denny with a sweep of his arm. "Dallas, this is my neighbor, Denny Armstrong." He turned back, looked Denny square in the eye and said, "This is my boyfriend, Dallas."

Denny snorted. Loud. Then cleared his throat, took a steadying breath…and tittered.

Instead of arguing, or defending himself, or insisting Denny elaborate on what was so funny, Paul gave him a level stare in return.

Denny looked Dallas up and down, then eyed Paul again. "I guess that explains the coordinating outfits." He smoothed the front of his tailored shirt and cracked an ambiguous grin. "I guess that explains a lot of things."

"Anyway, we already have plans tonight." Paul grasped the door and angled Denny toward it. "But say hi to Richard for me."

"Oh, believe me," Denny drawled, with one final look of appraisal for Dallas as he swung out into the hall. "I will."

Paul clenched the doorknob so hard his knuckles went white, and he fixed his eyes on the table beside the door, glaring at a gap in his coordinated desk set where Denny had "borrowed" the matching pen and never returned it. He wasn't sure if he felt humiliated, or mortified, or angry. It was one thing to be sneered at by Denny, but another thing entirely to see it happen to Dallas. "I'm so sorry," he managed to say, though he spoke to the hole where the pen should have been because he couldn't bring himself to look at Dallas.

"Can't say I'm warming to your friend," Dallas said. "But ain't nothing you did wrong."

"No, I've known how awful he is for a while now. I should have told him off a long time ago."

Dallas allowed Paul to wallow in shame only for a moment before he mercifully changed the subject. "So what do you want to do about the sticker?"

"I have no idea."

"Do you know where your condo agreement is? We'll start with that."

With the stack of mail several weeks old to go through, Paul's filing system wasn't completely up-to-date. But important documents—no problem. They'd all been labeled, filed and alphabetized ages ago. He had his contract out in thirty seconds flat. Dallas looked through the fine print, while Paul took in the wine rack, the hand-knotted wool rug, the entertainment center, all with as much detachment as he'd give a motel room.

Dallas set his hand on Paul's shoulder and squeezed. "Sorry to break it to you, baby, but you did agree on this piece of paper not to hang any signs. Lawyer up if you want, but it won't do you any good."

"I suppose not."

"So I can peel it off? We'll put it on my bathroom mirror."

Paul turned away from the sticker and looked fiercely into Dallas' eyes. "I hate this place." The feel of the words in his mouth was suddenly so right, it was the most fitting thing he'd said all day. He repeated, "I hate it," and decided it was true.

"What about your granite countertops and bamboo floors?"

"Fuck 'em."

Dallas held his gaze calmly, unruffled. "Well, we can probably start back to Florida tonight. But make yourself useful while I check for empty seats. Pack up some clothes." He pulled out his phone and swiped through pages for a few moments, then slid a glance toward Paul that was a lot more promising than Paul thought he deserved. "Enough to stay a while."

They would have made just as good time back to Fort Lauderdale if they'd set the alarm for 3 a.m. and headed out early in the morning. Instead, Dallas arranged for a late night flight with a two-hour layover in Atlanta and a four-hour stop in Orlando. Paul stood at the terminal window and gazed out over the tarmac as the first hint of sun peeked over the horizon while Dallas stood in line for overpriced coffee. Paul thought about seeing that sunrise from outside, from empty Bermuda, and wondered whether there even was a way to solve the problem of the turbulence, or if it was just a matter of flying through it until he couldn't stand it anymore and then handing over the reins to the next unlucky pilot. Then he wondered if that was what Marlin had just done.

His phone rang just as he thought his predecessor's name, and the irrational idea that maybe Marlin was calling from beyond the grave momentarily spooked him. But at least this time his phone was actually on—he'd deliberately turned it on once they taxied up to the MCO gate. He glanced at the screen. Denny…at 5:13 a.m. Paul was inclined to let it go to voicemail, but his morbid curiosity as to whether Denny was up really late or really early got the better of him, and he answered.

"You'll go to any length to prove a point," Denny slurred, "won't you? I hope you're proud of yourself."

"What?"

"You think you're cool now? Is that it? So hip…so urban."

"Yeah. I'm really cool."

"You're not home…where are you?"

"Stop lurking around my place!"

Denny belched through his nose, then said, "I will absolutely die if I find out you let Homeboy jam his dick up your ass."

Paul's stomach heaved. If there'd been anything in it, he suspected he might have actually thrown up. He swallowed the metallic taste of adrenaline, and said, "It's none of your business."

"God only knows what you'll catch."

"I'm hanging up now."

"Wait—just...just wait, Paul. Listen. I get it, see? You're the high-minded one of the group, the secular humanist, the guy with all the lofty ideals. You always were—we all know it, okay? Now stop slumming around and come back home where you *belong*."

"You know what? I don't care if you're drunk-dialing—it's no excuse. You're just saying what you really think." He hung up on Denny, turned off the phone and slipped it into the pocket of his borrowed linen suit. Turning, he saw Dallas striding across the terminal with a pair of coffees in his hands and a tender hint of a smile on his face. Go back to DC? Every day it held less and less appeal. As far as Paul was concerned, Denny knew nothing about the concept of belonging, nothing at all.

CHAPTER 24

Federal Aviation Administration guidelines state commercial pilots must be allowed eight hours uninterrupted rest time between duties. Luckily, Paul wasn't climbing into a cockpit that morning—he was tackling the cleanup of Marlin Fritsch's house. Or, more accurately, he was hoping to find the real black box and somehow encourage Bernadette to allow him to keep it, all the while doing his very best impression of clearing out Marlin's stuff.

The sight of a rented dumpster on the front lawn brought Paul vividly awake—the sight of the thrift store truck, too. "They started already," he gasped. "It's not even eight o'clock and they're throwing things away."

"Breathe," Dallas said. "It's all there. You'll get a chance to see everything. We can split up and cover more ground."

They found Bernadette in the living room, wearing a tank top with a Chanel logo across the chest, a pair of jeans that looked like they'd been ironed, and a pristine pink bandanna that covered her hair. She was holding a set of nun chucks by two fingers, at arm's length, as if she thought they might be diseased. Two of the teenagers who'd been getting guitar lessons from Marlin were eyeing the weapon dubiously. "I don't want it on my conscience if some kid ends up buying it and bashes his—oh, hi, guys. Thanks for coming. I'm already sick of playing the sell-donate-toss game." Her objective, she explained, was to clear out the personal stuff, the un-sellable stuff, and leave the rest for an auction house to attempt to liquidate. There were also "keeper" piles forming by the back door. The teens were splitting Marlin's CD collection, and one of them had snagged a guitar stand and a pile of paperbacks.

Perfect.

Paul decided he'd just need to focus on sounding mildly interested in keeping the black box once he did run across it, but not enough to cause anyone else to wonder why he wanted it so badly. Since it would be full of things from Bermuda, he could say it had sentimental value. And even if she wanted to sell the box itself, all that really mattered was getting his hands on the contents.

Dallas immediately took his place as Bernadette's sounding board, and the relieved teenagers shifted into carry-mode, moving mounds of clothes and books they wouldn't have to make any decisions about. That left Paul to his own devices.

He began in a spare bedroom. It looked like the teenagers would feel right at home there, since the walls were covered in Harley Davidson posters and the smell of incense lingered. Cheap shelving had been erected in front of the posters and filled with stuff. The Harley posters with the chesty bikini women in them were just as likely to be obscured by mounds of collected miscellanea as the posters that were just bikes with Photoshopped glints on the chrome. There was a black plastic storage tub buried beneath a pair of rollerblades and a slushy maker, the sight of which got Paul's hopes up, but only for a moment. It was full of shells and sea glass. Nothing more.

The bedroom closet seemed promising, until he saw it was so thick with spider webs that it was unlikely to have been used anytime recently. Still, he figured he'd better look. Fishing tackle and gardening gear. And in a big steamer trunk underneath it all (which looked brown, but might have been black, once) a few old quilts with tufts of batting and shred hanging out where mice had gotten to them. In other words, nothing.

Paul sighed. One room down. The rest of the house to go.

Keeping away from everyone else so they didn't actually notice how little he was doing, Paul scoped out both bathrooms and the living room. Dallas and Bernadette had the main bedroom, so Paul trusted that Dallas would keep his eyes peeled for anything black, box-like, and stuffed with

Bermuda research. A quick glance into the garage showed tools and gear stored in stacks of bright plastic milk crates, red and orange and green. According to the teenager with the hair in his eyes, the attic was more of a crawlspace and probably wouldn't have anything important stored there. The Florida sun beating down made the temperature unbearable, and anything kept there would quickly disintegrate. No basement, either. Still, Marlin had been a collector, and what space he did have was full of crap and clutter. Paul's initial panic at seeing things hauled away eventually gave way to a sort of relief, since nothing he'd seen looked like a black box. He was about to expand his mental image of the box—maybe it was lacquered, or maybe it was smaller than he'd been envisioning it—and was standing in the middle of the living room, puzzled, when another helper showed up.

"I've got liquor store boxes," Rev. Ralph sang out, then stopped abruptly as he spotted Paul from around the teetering tower of corrugated cardboard in his arms and said, "Dashing Pilot Paul…I didn't realize *yo*u'd be here so early." He dropped the boxes and made a show of patting down his thinning hair and smoothing his eyebrows.

Paul never thought he'd be a sucker for campy, harmless flirting. Then again, maybe he'd never been on the receiving end of it. There'd be a price to pay for the attention, though, positive or not. Paul's ability to sift through Marlin's things while everyone else was distracted was now compromised. Once Ralph got the teenagers set to boxing up the smaller bric-a-brac, he found Paul and said, "So what can I help you with?"

Paul's initial urge was to get rid of Ralph—send him out for more boxes, or maybe to pick up some pizzas for lunch. But then he realized that Ralph knew Marlin as well as anyone did, and maybe he knew the house, too. "Marlin had some keepsakes from Bermuda…mostly papers and clippings. I'm worried they're going to get tossed out."

Ralph rolled up his sleeves and said, "Then let's see if we can't find them."

How simple. It wasn't even necessary to lie.

"Why don't we start in the kitchen?" Ralph suggested. "It looks like he used it as an office. There's a lot of paperwork stacked around the table."

A lot of paperwork was an understatement. Newspapers. Magazines. Junk mail. Evidently Marlin Fritsch never threw anything out. None of it seemed to relate to Bermuda, though, so Paul tried to ignore the sinking feeling that he was never going to find anything, to instead simply keep his nose to the grindstone and sort.

He was at it so long that his back protested when he sat up to stretch it. Ralph was seated across from him in a kitchen chair with a pile of paper on one side and a recycle bin on the other, efficiently scanning and tossing. His fingertips were black with ink. Ralph glanced up and said, "So how are you holding up?"

"Me?" Paul said. Ralph had sounded so concerned, he actually felt guilty for his lack of grief. "I didn't know him. Dallas is the one who worked with him."

"He was very fond of Dallas. Kaye too."

That surprised Paul. He'd taken Marlin for being too madly in love with himself to notice anyone else.

The sorting continued—they were making headway, which was good—but they were nearing the bottoms of their stacks without finding anything from Bermuda, which was not so good. As Paul's heart sank, Ralph spoke again. "It's a good thing Dallas has you for support. Losing a friend can be just as bad as losing family. When you're gay, sometimes birth families can be iffy, so our friends fill that role. They're the family we choose."

Paul kept his head down, kept sorting, but he hardly registered what he was tossing into the recycle bin. What did it say about his own choices if he had friends like Denny?

"Here, split that pile with me." Ralph held out a hand. He was done with his own huge stack of paper and was ready to help Paul divide and conquer his. Paul grabbed a thick stack of papers and passed it over, but didn't say anything. He didn't trust the way his voice would sound—not now that a total stranger was here trying so earnestly to help him solve his problems, no questions asked, while he wouldn't have even dreamed of asking his own friends....acquaintances...whatever they were.

Paul got to the bottom of his pile, finding absolutely nothing related to Bermuda. He stared at Ralph's hands dully while Ralph flipped through his last few pieces of mail.

That was that.

"Let's haul the recycling into the garage," Ralph said, with enough hearty cheer that Paul suspected his crushing disappointment must have been showing on his face. "Get it out of the way. Then we can set our sights on our next target."

Although Ralph's optimism (especially in the face of his own grief) should have been encouraging, he had no way of knowing what was really at stake. Finding a box of mementos was one thing—figuring a way out of the turbulence was another. For Paul, the idea of some unbridled part of his personality sabotaging his fledgling relationship with Dallas was torture, not to mention the fact that being forced to accept that this phenomenon, which couldn't possibly exist, was somehow real. For a skeptic like Paul, it was a philosophical sucker punch—every damn time it happened. Still, although Ralph was ignorant of the stakes, having some sort of anchor back in the real world was better than wondering if the whole flight crew was steadily losing their minds, so Paul hefted his recycle bin and followed Ralph out to the garage.

"Maybe we should check out the living room next," Ralph suggested. "Keepsakes are the type of thing he would've wanted to show off to his guests. Or maybe the bedroom, if they're more personal, something he'd look at in private."

"I guess." Paul held the door open with his foot while Ralph squeezed through it, then bumped it with his hip so he could follow.

"I hope it's not too forward of me to say, but I get the sense something's bothering you. And devilishly handsome exterior aside, I am a minister. If you need someone to talk to…."

Paul felt he was probably in the minority of people who didn't associate anything good with the word *minister*. However, his initial assessment of Ralph as an upbeat, intelligent, self-aware person had him actually considering opening up—if not about the specifics of Flight 511, at least in general terms about his feelings of inadequacy, discouragement…and even, at times, despair. He set down his recycle bin, wondering where he could even begin. But when he turned to Ralph, the look of concern on the minister's face was completely overshadowed by the massive wall of papers, photos and scraps looming behind him.

Paul's breath caught.

Ralph glanced over his shoulder and touched his fingertips to his throat in an imaginary pearl-clutch. "Oh, my." For a long moment, they simply stood and stared, taking in the avalanche of color and texture, hundreds upon hundreds of slips of paper, fliers and brochures, Post-Its and receipts. Finally, Ralph said, "The garage is the last place I would've looked. Just goes to show how Source energy will come through for you when you're clear on what you want."

Source? Hardly. It took up the entire wall. They were bound to run across it at some point. Paul approached the massive collection. Was it the Bermuda research? It couldn't possibly be anything else. But why call it the…? Ah. The frame. A thick black windowbox of a frame. Paul supposed he should be excited, eager to go through the collection. But mostly, he felt ill. Overtired, worn out and used up. This gigantic mass of crap was just one more thing he needed to cope with, and his patience was running on fumes.

"So…should we box this up?" Ralph asked. He was keeping up the pretense of normalcy, but he had to know this was no keepsake or memento, that it was something sinister and bizarre. *Had* to. "Or were you going to find a way to transport it all in one piece?"

Paul's overwhelm grew. "I don't think we have the room." Not in the car, and not in Dallas' little rental home.

He wanted to throw his hands in the air and say, I've *had it.* I'm *done.* Every time he thought the solution was in his grasp, it slid farther away: to the belly of the cargo hold, or at the top of the control tower, or now, among a mass of thousands of scraps of paper. Not only was it too much, but he wouldn't risk bringing it into the cockpit with him and somehow altering it in empty Bermuda. He only had the few hours between flights in which to sift through it. And the weekends. Plural. Because the thought that *this* would certainly be the week in which he circumvented the turbulence suddenly seemed pathetically naive.

He'd had enough. Unfortunately, walking away and leaving Dallas to deal with the turbulence alone was simply not an option.

Ralph subtly cleared his throat. Paul offered his best attempt at maintaining the normal veneer Ralph had established. "I think I need to, um… maybe I should take some pictures of it first. Before we dismantle it. So I can remember it…how it was."

"Okay."

Paul pulled out his phone and snapped a photo, and then he realized how he'd probably never make heads or tails of it with all those tiny bits of information. He needed closeups. He needed a grid. He approached the black box and began on the upper right, taking shots as close up as his phone would manage without blurring. Then, overlapping slightly, he aimed lower and snapped another.

"I'll go get us some empty boxes," Ralph said. Several minutes later, once Paul was done, Ralph trooped back into the garage. He'd left his breezy attitude behind, though. Now he seemed serious and subdued.

To his surprise, Paul actually felt guilty for using Ralph to find the black box. "Listen," he said, hoping to offer some sort of explanation that wasn't too horrible of a lie, "we really need to understand what was going on in Marlin's head. This might help."

Ralph scanned the bulletin board and nodded slowly. "I get it. But we attract the versions of people that we're in Alignment with, so maybe the answer can't be found in the things Marlin left behind. Maybe it's inside us."

And so the mumbo-jumbo talk began. Paul simply nodded and got to work taking down the papers and notes, since he really wasn't in the mood to argue. It took a while, since they worked slowly, keeping clumps of scraps and receipts and slips of paper together wherever possible, being careful to retrieve anything that fluttered to the floor. They didn't speak, and Paul eventually lost himself in his task, watching the blur of words and images go by as he transferred them from the black box to the cardboard box. He'd found a detached sort of rhythm, pulling and packing, when the torn book page he'd stacked in his box caught his eye.

When the blazing sun is gone,
When he nothing shines upon,
Then you show your little light,
Twinkle, twinkle, all the night.

Recognition—he'd seen that first line before. It appeared in Marlin's email. Paul should have felt triumphant. Here, among all the masses of paper, he'd actually stumbled across the clue he was searching for. However, there was no sense of triumph, only the sick, cold miasma of failure. Because it wasn't a scientific observation he'd found, a technical measurement, an intelligent theory, or even a creative insight. The page had been torn from a children's book.

And the title of the page was *Twinkle, Twinkle Little Star.*

Paul crumpled the page in his shaking fist. Marlin's final message... was gibberish.

"Are you okay?" Ralph said. He was watching Paul very closely.

As Paul held the minister's gaze, realization dawned on him. Although it might be grasping at straws, he'd better take advantage of Ralph's influence while he had the chance. And he'd better use that influence to get some straight answers out of someone who might actually know what was going on in empty Bermuda. "Tell me," Paul said, "do you know what Bernadette is planning to do with the ashes?"

Ralph answered cautiously. "She hasn't decided."

"Because I think they belong in Bermuda." Paul indicated the box of island "mementos" with his eyes. "Don't you?"

Ralph planted his ink-smudged hands on his hips, mulled the idea over, then said, "Why?"

"Not for me—but for Dallas. For Captain Kaye. It's totally fitting. They're the ones who were close to Marlin, and the three of them shared

Bermuda together."

"In Unity, we teach that people aren't the same as their bodies. The ashes are just ashes, and anything you do with them would be symbolic. The essence of who we know as Marlin isn't contained by this dust he's left behind."

Maybe. Maybe not. There was only one way to find out.

"Symbolic," Paul said. "Exactly." He'd never been good at hiding his emotions, and Ralph was far too shrewd to think he wasn't holding something back. Still, the suggestion should make sense. It was logical. Not that Paul trusted anyone from that strange church to defer to logic....

When Ralph finally answered, he nodded reluctantly and said, "You'll need a death certificate for customs."

Not where Paul planned on taking those ashes, he wouldn't.

CHAPTER 25

"I'm sorry," Dallas told Bernadette, "I wish we could stay longer. But it's past midnight and we fly out tomorrow, so we need to go home and get to bed."

"No, that's fine." Bernadette's voice shook. Over the course of the day, she'd moved through several stages of grief while she got Marlin's things ready for the auctioneers. Anger, denial...Dallas wasn't exactly sure what was supposed to come when. Just that she'd now reached the stage that involved a lot of crying. "You've been such a big help dealing with this house. I'm really...grateful." Her voice broke as she turned to the side, knuckling away tears and the last few remaining traces of mascara.

"You need to get your rest, too." They'd all worked hard and cleared a lot of clutter. Even after the teenagers reached the limit of their attention spans and drifted off, Paul and Ralph found a second wind and managed to sort the kitchen, the utility room and the entire garage. "Truck's full now anyway," Dallas said. "You need me to make a phone call?"

"No." Bernadette squeezed her eyes shut, pressed her lips together, and took deep breaths through her nose. "No. I've got it. You've done so much. I...."

Dallas gathered her into his arms. She resisted at first, but finally the dam broke and she wept, stiff-shouldered and helpless. Once she cried herself out—at least for the moment—she pushed off him, embarrassed. "Anyway, yes, I think you should go. I'd rather be alone right now."

"You can always text me," Dallas said. "I'll answer soon as I can."

She nodded hard, arms wrapped around her middle as if she was moments away from another wave of grief, and her body angled like the last thing she wanted was for him to see it. He stepped out of the bedroom and gently closed the door behind him.

Paul and Ralph were hauling a stained area rug to the dumpster. They'd both sweated through their clothes—Ralph rather unglamorously, poor thing, but not Paul. No, Paul was all damp hair, flushed cheeks, and glistening skin just begging for Dallas to slide his fingers across. It felt disrespectful to think such a thing given how they'd spent their day mopping up after Marlin's suicide. But emotions had run so high and raw, Dallas was beyond caring.

When they said their goodbyes and Paul actually left the preacher man with a sweaty hug, Dallas nearly had to pick his jaw up off the lawn. He knew Paul didn't think much of the church. What a relief that Paul could be open-minded today—because while he had plenty of fine qualities, flexibility was not usually one of them.

Cradling a box of papers on his lap, Paul stayed quiet on the way back home, which was also a relief. He didn't say a word until they pulled into the driveway, when he turned and touched the front of Dallas' shirt, still damp with Bernadette's tears, and said, "You're all wet."

They could barely get through the kitchen door fast enough.

They clutched at each other, grabbing at clothes, kisses landing off-kilter. Dallas backed Paul into the counter, working open his jeans. Paul's fingers raked down the back of Dallas' T-shirt, as if he was so desperate to lose himself he couldn't even be bothered to strip it off. They kissed more firmly then—hard, breathy, tongues filling each other's mouths, until Paul turned his head and gasped against Dallas' cheek, "I think your neighbor hates me."

Dallas grazed his teeth along Paul's jaw and made his breath catch. "How come?"

"He was making a face when we were groping our way up the driveway."

"He's Haitian. That's how he looks at everyone."

"I just didn't know if it was a gay thing or a racial thing."

Knowing old Giroux, probably both. But Dallas wasn't going to let it stop him from living his life. "Don't worry about it. People gonna think what they want anyway." He pressed his lips to Paul's before more protests could happen. The last thing Dallas wanted to worry about right now was the world outside that kitchen door. It felt too hard to navigate, especially on days like today, days where everything seemed to gang up and prevent them from being happy. Right now, the only thing he wanted was to forget about the funeral, forget about the turbulence, forget about everybody's disapproval, and lay Paul down in his bed. He broke the kiss and said, "Let's go in the bedroom," and the trip up the hallway was twice as bad as the driveway. This time there was furniture to knock over—an end table, a fake plant, a wastebasket that scattered wadded-up paper all over the bedroom floor.

Once Paul tossed his glasses on the nightstand, Dallas found the bed, fell sideways and pulled Paul down on the mattress to face him. They kissed and grappled until they were breathing hard, and there was nothing left to do but peel off their sweaty clothes and peel open a condom. Paul shoved Dallas onto his back and straddled him. Dallas was glad enough to not have the conversation of who'd be doing what tonight. It was better to just watch Paul rise up on his knees and settle back, breathing hard, wincing as he was penetrated while Dallas lost himself to the delicious tightness. He kept himself still so that Paul could set the pace, until finally they were good and situated and he could get in on the action with some thrusts of his own.

Paul closed his eyes and wet his lips, tilting his head back to ride out the storm. It was just like he'd looked in Bermuda, soaking in the big hotel tub, flushed and sensual, with piña colada bubble bath collapsing all around him. But it was even better here, now—touching him, exploring him. All of him.

Spent, both physically and emotionally, they slept in each other's arms with the sweaty sheets twined around their legs. It was almost an afterthought to set the alarm…but even *gettin' some* wasn't enough to make Dallas slip up and forget. They didn't need to be up and about for their afternoon flight until noon, but he wasn't taking any chances. Lateness was not an option. Not with Flight 511 now a duty for them both.

The alarm turned out to be unnecessary. Dallas woke at eleven to the smell of coffee and bacon. He found Paul in the kitchen, looking totally at home in T-shirt, shorts and flip-flops, moving through the room with spatula firmly in hand like he'd been doing it for ages. Although Dallas did his best to conjure up images of Paul's fancy condo and visualize him in that setting, the granite countertops and shiny chrome appliances felt strange. More like a fake half-kitchen in a home center, waiting for Paul to step out of the display and into the real world.

Dallas sat himself down in the breakfast nook, and Paul set down a cup of coffee in front of him, just like he liked it. Cream, no sugar. "You're in a good mood," Dallas observed.

Paul assembled two plates of bacon and scrambled eggs, only losing a few bits of egg over the edge of a plate in the process. "Yeah. I suppose I am."

While Dallas would've liked to think the good mood was due to his bedroom finesse, he suspected the box of papers and junk Paul rescued from Marlin's garage was more likely the reason. "You found something?"

"Maybe. Probably. I guess...we'll see."

Dallas didn't press. Hopefully whatever Paul's new theory was, it wouldn't require scaling tall buildings or risking electrocution. Although Dallas had been living longer with the foolishness in Bermuda, and although Paul was the last one to join the team, figuring a way out was obviously something Paul simply needed to do.

It was a relaxing morning and a leisurely ride to the airport. Paul marched out onto the blistering hot tarmac to begin his inspection while Kaye performed her exacting quadruple-check of the cockpit. Dallas found the cabin as immaculate as he'd left it—he'd grown accustomed to having exclusive use of the same plane, which was unheard of in commercial jets—and so he could take a moment and just gaze out the window and watch Paul doing his thing, looking all capable and smart. And maybe...a bit on the thin side.

Bacon and eggs aside (they'd spent all those calories the night before) a man shouldn't have to live on baloney on white bread, and no way would Paul indulge in any Bermuda food for his supper. Good thing the best sandwich kiosk in the terminal was a short ways from Flight 511's gate. Dallas jogged up the skybridge and ordered the most elaborate sub on Fazzio's menu, with prosciutto and beef and three kinds of cheese, but he held the oil and vinegar to make sure the bun didn't end up in Bermuda in a big, soggy mess. A few packets of mayo and plenty of napkins later, he was ready to plant a decent meal for his man.

Kaye was making notes on her checklist when Dallas peeked into the cockpit. She eyed the sub. "That's quite a sandwich."

"Make sure you tell Paul I bought it in Florida, so he don't get funny about eating it." He unzipped Paul's flight bag to swap out his dinner. The bag was full, but maybe without the baloney, there'd be enough room to slip the sub in without too much squashing. Notebook, T-shirt…Dallas pushed them to the side. But what he found beneath them was not a pair of plastic-wrapped sandwiches at all. It was hefty. Silver. Rounded.

Marlin's urn.

Dallas bolted up from his crouch, gasping so violently that Kaye flinched back and snapped, "What?"

There were no words, at least none that Dallas could string together. He pointed instead, vaguely aware that he didn't seem to be able to catch his breath. He'd thought empty Bermuda was a shock. But it was nothing compared to this.

Kaye had him by the shoulder, nudging him out of the way so she could rise out of her seat enough to see for herself. "What the…?"

What kind of monster would sneak around with someone's mortal remains in his rollerbag? Dallas had thought he knew Paul—he'd trusted that man with his car, and his home…and with Chantal.

"Oh my God," Kaye whispered.

Trust? What a joke. Dallas didn't actually know Paul. The guy in Bermuda who shared his room, the sweet one who took bubble baths and gave back rubs? That Paul wasn't even real. And on Bermuda Paul's coattails, the real Paul had coasted right into Dallas' heart.

"Here," Kaye said, and Dallas became aware that she was gently prying open his fingers to take the now-crushed sub from him. "It's okay."

"It's *not* okay."

"Just breathe," she said. "When you think about it…maybe it does make some kind of sense."

"What does?" Paul said from the cockpit door. When Dallas jerked away from Kaye to face him and the open flight bag could be seen, his eyes widened. Other than that, he stayed remarkably calm and controlled. Like the smooth and practiced liar he was. "Okay, don't be mad."

"Don't be—" Dallas scoffed. "You crazy."

"I knew you wouldn't like it," Paul said quickly, "but logically, with the turbulence—"

"I wouldn't *like* it? That's my friend in there, all that's left of him. Does that mean anything to you?"

"It does. Of course it does. I'm not taking this lightly—but there's nothing to lose by trying."

"Oh, there's plenty to lose. What the hell you playin' at?"

"Well…if the superego splits off from the rest of the personality, or the mind splits off from the body, when we go through the turbulence with the ashes…."

"If he was buried, would you go dig him out of his grave and prop up his body in the co-pilot's seat?"

"It's not like—look, I needed to talk to him, okay?" Paul tried to catch Dallas' hand, but Dallas jerked it away. "That last email Marlin sent, it wasn't a clue. It was nothing."

"So that gives you the right to shove his remains in your bag, next to your deodorant and your spare underpants? You don't know what's gonna happen when you fly that urn through the turbulence. It could be nothing at all. Or it could be bad."

Kaye took Dallas by the arm, and he did allow it from her. "You're angry. It's understandable. But at this point, the best option is to bring the urn with us. What else can we do? Leave it in a storage locker? In the trunk of your car?"

Since as far as Dallas was concerned, Kaye's word was law, her firm, clear explanation allowed him to actually think. Crew lockers could be busted open, and so could cars. Besides, it was like an oven in his hatchback. The last thing he needed was some kind of morbid lingering smell to keep reminding him of the moment when Paul showed his true nature. "We can't leave it behind."

"Then hit the pause button on this conversation," she said. "There's thirty-one passengers boarding in just a few minutes. If we're settled on bringing it to Bermuda, there's nothing more to discuss."

Airline delays happened all the time. If it were any normal flight, Dallas wouldn't have let the matter drop. This was Flight 511, though, and it always left on schedule. The crew didn't want to find out firsthand what might go wrong if it didn't, and somehow the weather and mechanics always fell into place to accommodate the flight.

And just like always, today's flight boarded on time, and taxied up to the runway on time, and took off on time. Luckily Dallas had done it often enough that he could simply go through the motions, checking that everyone was strapped in, their devices were off, and that nothing would come loose and crush anyone during the turbulence. Those tasks were all second nature and hardly took any concentration at all. Mainly, he was worried about where he wanted to be when the turbulence actually hit... though, of course, there really was no debate. The autopilots could take care of themselves for a night. There was only so much Kaye could eat in fourteen hours. And if Paul destroyed his credit rating, well, maybe it'd be some small kind of justice.

Once drink service was complete and the passengers were settled with their coffees and sodas, Dallas tapped on the cockpit door. The pilots buzzed him in. "I'm coming with you," he said simply.

"That's fine." Kaye blew on the suction cup of her manual compass and fixed it to the control panel. "But no freaking out during the flight—either of you. No matter what happens. Our number one priority is staying calm and landing the aircraft safely. Anything else, and I mean *anything*, we will deal with once we're on the ground."

The remaining minutes before the turbulence felt like they would never end. In his anger, Dallas stormed up and down the aisle several times before he realized the passengers were flinching away from him when he passed…and they were on their very best behavior. Not one had so much as unbuckled a seatbelt. He made his way to the galley, crossed his arms, and glared at the cockpit door before one of the passengers wet themselves. *Nothing to lose by trying.* Like hell. This was no flattened cockroach in a margarine tub they were dealing with—it was a human being, a *person.* A soul.

Which apparently didn't matter to Paul. He didn't like church? Fine. Dallas hadn't gone to service since he was sixteen, and Reverend Mason declared that laying with another man made him an abomination. But turning your back on church was a far cry from not believing in anything.

Kaye's voice on the intercom jolted him out of his memories. "Dallas… report to the cockpit."

It was time.

The commuter jet was small and its cockpit felt cramped, especially when Dallas had no desire to lay his eyes on Paul, and even less to see the urn. He folded down the jumpseat, strapped in, and looked fixedly up at the ceiling.

"I think maybe we need to open it," Paul said, not to Dallas (he knew better) but to Kaye. "If somehow his mind can make a body appear when he goes through the turbulence…."

"In that case, he shouldn't be in your lap, either. He'd end up jamming the controls."

Something nudged Dallas in the arm. Something hard and cylindrical and horrible. He picked out a single bolt in the ceiling and stared at it very, very intently. "Dallas?" Paul said. "We're almost there."

Although every fiber of his being was straining against it, Dallas forced himself to look at Paul—to look at the terrible urn—and to hold out his hand and take the damn thing.

"Open it," Kaye said.

Dallas' gorge rose. Hadn't he done enough? Paul was the one who thought he knew everything—shouldn't Paul be the one to open it? But he'd already turned away to fiddle with the controls. "Static," he said into his headset. "Electrical systems offline."

"Pneumatic pressure dropping," Kaye replied, then turned and glanced over her shoulder at Dallas. "Did you hear me?" The plane bumped once, then again. The sensation was different in the cockpit. More concussive. More raw. "Open it."

How the hell could he? Dallas tried to will his hands to move, but they felt as inert as the silver canister they held. The third bump, the *critical* bump, would be on them in less than a second. After a year, the rhythm of the turbulence played through Dallas' mind with the familiarity of the Donna Summer record that carried him through junior high. This time around, the interval seemed to sustain—to suspend—while Dallas considered the possibility of what might happen if he couldn't force himself to open that urn. What if the turbulence did shake out a new body for Marlin, only to have it topple over dead with an urn in its belly? What if the compression of the closed canister resulted in some kind of gruesome explosion? Opening the urn might be the hardest thing he'd ever done, but the alternatives were worse. He grasped the top, and he twisted.

The ashes weren't just laying there in the urn—they'd been packed in cellophane. Also, they didn't entirely look like ashes. They were chunky, pebbly. Bones? Teeth? He jerked it out from under his own nose as if he could un-see the texture just as the third bump hit, the big bump, and the bag inside the urn snapped open. Particulate sprayed out, engulfing the cockpit in a gritty haze of ash.

And then everything went white.

Dallas squeezed his eyes shut and did his best to not breathe in—and especially not to suck in the deep breath of air a person normally takes when they're about to hold their breath. Bad enough to be covered in his friend's remains. He didn't want to inhale them.

The navigation system bleated and rang—Dallas had forgotten how chaotic the turbulence was inside the cockpit—and his sense of self-preservation got the better of him, forcing him to open his eyes.

The cockpit was filled with white light. Not the steady, opaque white of the big turbulence bump, but an echo of that light, a reflection passing from one mote of dust to another, blossoming like Christmas lights, filling the cockpit with sparkles. Dallas blinked, eyes watering, and the dazzle began to fade.

Filling his field of vision instead, was Marlin's face.

His eyes were the color of Castle Harbour at dusk, and they were wide with wonder. Although they seemed to be trained right on Dallas, there was no recognition there, not initially. But then the directional gyro's warning buzzed. Marlin blinked and focused on Dallas…and then he smiled. "Dallas?" His tone was hesitant. Puzzled. "Whoa. I just had the most badass dream."

CHAPTER 26

It worked.

Paul was tempted to pinch himself to make sure he wasn't dreaming, but his skeptical dream-self survived pinches all the time. He stole a glance over his shoulder. No blood and guts, no ash cloud, no bloated, drowned corpse. Just a guy, a dark-haired guy in a uniform identical to Paul's. The cockpit was a tight enough fit for two people, let alone four. Marlin stood with his back pressed into the curvature of the cockpit wall, his hands on Dallas' shoulders. And Dallas stared up at him from the jumpseat, wide-eyed with shock.

That was all Paul could see, in the stolen moment before he turned back to the console to get back to the business of landing Flight 511.

If it weren't for the automated weather report in his headset, he probably would have been startled by the thrum of his own heart. Here, now, he would finally have his answers—and then he would hopefully be able to make things right with Dallas.

The landing gear touched down with a smooth tap. Paul focused hard on making his landing look effortless, since all those people jammed into the cockpit had their eyes on him. Kaye took the yoke and taxied to the terminal—and Paul wondered, briefly, why she even bothered when they could just circle around and position the aircraft at the start of the runway. Old habits died hard.

A series of clicks powered down the engines and switched off the repetition of the recorded windspeed in Paul's ears, and then there was silence. Which was broken by Marlin, saying, "So, you're my replacement!"

"That's Paul," Kaye said.

Paul turned in his seat and tried to come up with an appropriately assertive reply, but Marlin thrust a handshake at him before anything came to mind. "I'm Marlin…sweet landing." Without waiting for a response, he turned to Dallas, looked down at a mangled sub beside the jumpseat and said, "Fazzio's? No way. Will you split it with me? I'm totally starved."

"Take it." Dallas handed Marlin the sub. His voice was gravelly, and his hand shook.

Marlin cradled the sandwich against his chest, buzzed open the cockpit door and strode out into the cabin. Dallas followed, then Paul, then Kaye, crowding into the galley. "So we're alone," Marlin said, not like he thought it was weird, but maybe like he didn't take anything for granted. He flipped the actuator and the stairs powered down, and the jet fuel scent of the airport wafted in on a gentle island breeze. He took a deep breath and smiled.

The eerie afternoon silence of the airport was already familiar to Paul. Flags snapped atop flagpoles. Gulls shrieked overhead. Waves lapped in the harbor. But Marlin standing there on the tarmac not three feet away from him wolfing down a flattened sub—that was not familiar at all.

"Are you okay?" Dallas asked, sounding as if he thought such a state of being should be impossible.

But Marlin nodded heartily as he chewed, and once he'd swallowed, said, "Awesome."

"And you remember what you…" he glanced at Paul, who Marlin had recognized as his replacement.

Marlin had just bitten off another huge chunk of the sub, so instead of answering, he simply kept on nodding.

"Why?" Dallas' voice broke on the single word.

He looked so stricken that even Marlin went somber. He swallowed, wrapped up the uneaten sub half, and said, "I thought it was my duty as the Guide. I figured if I could go back to Source, I wouldn't be stuck looking at the problem though my physical eyes, and I'd see the path so

I could lead the rest of Flight 511 out of the turbulence. Now I see…man, the experience of *knowing* would just blow your mind…I see we're all the Guide sometimes. Or the Keeper, or the Leader." He strolled over to the aircraft and ran his fingertips over a series of rivets on the fuselage. "Back here on the ground, I never found the answer, not because I wasn't looking hard enough." He gave a shrug, and gave up on suppressing his smile, too. It broke over his features, impish and self-deprecating…and, damn it, charming. "Turns out I was asking the wrong question."

"Which was what?" Kaye called from the cabin door.

Marlin turned as if he had expected her to follow him outside, and only just now remembered she never left the aircraft. "You can come down. It's okay."

"I'm staying right here."

"But there's no reason to. Reality won't disappear. We're all sharing this experience, not just you. And why would staying in the cabin make any difference to the permanence of your surroundings, anyway?"

"Well," Kaye frowned. "Staying in the cockpit during the turbulence is what brings us here to begin with."

"That's the cockpit. Not the cabin. And it happens out there over the Atlantic, not here in the airport."

He actually made sense—more sense than Kaye. Paul was stumped.

"Maybe so," Kaye allowed. "But there's no room for experimentation. If I step off the plane and I'm wrong…" she looked at Marlin uncertainly. Hadn't he done the same thing, in a much more decisive way, at the bottom of his swimming pool? Now, afterward, he seemed pretty pleased with himself. At least at the moment.

Marlin stepped up to the foot of the stairs and held out a hand as if he was inviting Kaye to dance. "I never got to share Bermuda with you. Either it was one of us with the other one's autopilot, or you in the cabin with me checking out the lay of the land. Come with me, Kaye. Just this once."

She swayed. Wavered.

"Nothing bad will happen," he said. "I promise."

The atmosphere between them was thick with apprehension, but finally

Kaye accepted his hand, and stepped down from the jet. She let out a shaky breath, and Marlin jiggled her hand, laughed, and kissed her hair. "Rock and roll! Now that we're four-strong invincible, let's go for a spin."

He strode into the arrival area, past customs, and out into departures. A black convertible was idling at the curb with its trunk open and a suitcase beside it. "Tight ride." Marlin closed the trunk, then opened the passenger door for Kaye. "Milady, your carriage awaits."

Paul climbed in back beside Dallas, glad for the fact that he wasn't being called upon to speak, because what could he say? The Marlin of his imagination, a strutting pseudo-spiritual jackass of a manly-man, turned out to be nothing more than a big friendly dork. That realization rocked him nearly as much as the turbulence had, because how could he have been so sure, and yet so utterly, incredibly wrong?

Marlin pulled away from the curb, popped the CD out of the car's stereo system and cranked up the radio instead. A Beach Boys song threaded through the wind. "Weird how the automated stuff keeps right on going," he called back over his shoulder. Paul had thought the very same thing every time a weather report droned past his ears. "Once the power plant fizzles out, I imagine they'll start shutting down."

Could that happen overnight? It never had before.

Marlin crossed The Causeway with his left elbow propped on the car door and the wind whipping through his wild dark hair, singing along without knowing the song's words, and without particularly caring. The ride was only a few minutes long, just across Harrington Sound. Marlin drove through a large parking lot, then coasted to a stop directly in front of the aquarium building. He swung around to face the back seat and flashed his goofy smile. "Let's go see who needs a *Get Out of Jail Free* card."

The interior of the white stucco building was cool and dimly lit. The glassy sheen of tanks covered the walls. "Don't worry about the fish," Marlin said. "Either they're small enough to catch…or they're too big for the four of us to do anything about." He paused in front of a massive tank, its rounded face stretching high overhead, and pointed to a shadowy form slicing through the plant life at the far end of the water. "Wait for it…all he does is circle, so he'll come around…now."

The great white was there and gone in a second. Its sheer size was startling. Everyone but Marlin took a step away from the tank as it cruised by in its purposeful orbit.

"You want to free the animals?" Kaye said. "Why?"

"Because it's the right thing to do."

Dallas asked, "So what happens to the big ones?"

"I can chum Mr. Sharkey for a while…or I could find a rifle and take him out with a quick shot to the head. Although shooting through the refraction of the water is tough—I might miss, and that would be cruel… but maybe better than starving to death. Or I suppose I could just find some chemicals and taint the water."

"How long does it take for a shark to starve?" Paul wondered.

"No idea. Good thing the Bermuda Public Library is always open." Marlin turned to a nearby guard station and plucked a magnetic keycard from a jumble of office supplies on the desk, then headed down the hall and gestured for them all to follow. "C'mon in back. That's where I can really use your help."

So if the animals were freed, Paul thought, what would that mean once the crew flew back through the turbulence? All the animals would be gone from the zoo? That wasn't the way things worked at all. Nothing they did in empty Bermuda was permanent. "Why bother?"

Marlin glanced back over his shoulder, met Paul's eye and shared a secret "look." Paul had no idea how to interpret it. Marlin pushed open a set of double doors, and the bright afternoon sun slanted into Paul's eyes, dazzling him. "Most of the animals never made it here to begin with," Marlin said, pointing out a large and conspicuously empty open-air tank surrounded by tiered seating. A banner hung across the back, *Sea Lions - showtime: 12:30, 3:30, 5:30*. "The dolphins are gone. The manatees, the seals, the whales too. I used to think it was because they were mammals. Then one day I took a tortoise count and saw their oldest Galapagos tortoise—the one who all the kids get their pictures taken with—he'd disappeared in the turbulence just like all the people. So when I was back stateside I put it out on Facebook, posted that people should try talking to the tortoises 'cos they dug it. And the next time I took a count, the tortoise herd was down by half."

"How long you been doing this?" Dallas asked.

"Pretty much from the beginning, from the time I realized that if there were birds circling over the airport, there must be captive animals who'd starve and die if I didn't figure out how to spring 'em." He slid the keycard through a reader mounted beside a door that had been painted to blend in with the surrounding wall. "Good thing pets don't stick around. There'd be no way to let 'em all out and get back to the airport on time for pre-flight inspection."

The room beyond the locked door reeked. Mostly of fish, but other animal smells, too. Unlike the public areas of the aquarium, this staff room was all utility. A small radio in the corner played a modern dance beat, buzzing where the inadequate speakers couldn't keep up with the bass. Stainless steel tables lined the walls. They were covered in buckets and scales, scoopers and tongs. "I'll just feed the lizards and toads," Marlin said. "Then they'll be good for a few days and I can take my time getting back to them."

He paused beside a wooden box about the size of a nightstand and unlatched the top. A buzzing drone that Paul had taken for part of the dance music intensified, and a shuffling, rustling sound was added to the mix. It was the scent that wafted out of the box, though, that brought all the impressions together. Paul's most treasured friend through his high school years had been a hand-me-down pinktoe tarantula from his older cousin, so he knew that smell: crickets.

A plastic bag of crickets from the pet store was nothing compared to the teeming mass in the box. Dallas and Kaye both recoiled, but Paul stepped forward to see. The susurration of legs and wings and shifting chitinous bodies grew louder, until it sounded like waves lapping at the pier. Marlin met Paul's eyes over the top of the open cage, and Paul used the moment to attempt to get a straight answer out of him. "So when you land in Bermuda and you find fewer tortoises in the herd, it's not because you let them out on an earlier trip. It's because they've become more domesticated from being spoken to."

"Totally."

"Is everything you do in Bermuda undone when you fly back through the Turbulence?"

Marlin mulled over his response, then said, "Wrong question." He grabbed a measuring cup and scooped out a mound of crickets, clapping his hand over the top of the shifting mass. "Quick and dirty guide to the multiverse theory—let's say this is our reality." He held up the cup two-handed. A cricket squeezed from between his fingers, leapt, and pinged to the floor. "That guy? He was a possibility. And as soon as a possibility exists—*boom*—that universe fragments off from ours, and both of them play out 'til they're done."

Another cricket wriggled out from between Marlin's fingers. It jumped and lit on the leg of Paul's slacks. He picked it off and cupped it between his palms. "So this cricket is Bermuda? Empty Bermuda?"

"Yep. One of them." Marlin eased up his grasp and several more crickets leapt out. "Every time we go through the Triangle, it's a new Bermuda. We overnight, depart, and then that particular Bermuda goes on however we leave it. And the next time Flight 511 arrives—" another cricket popped out "—it's a different piece of reality. I could chase the little guy down, but even if I could catch him, chances are pretty slim that I'd get him back in my hand while I'm holding on to everything else."

"But all of us, the crew, we go back," Dallas said. "Right? We get put back together with our autopilots."

"And that's the cool part," Marlin said, while Paul lifted his hand and his cricket made a break for it. "Otherwise, how would we know we'd split off?" He elbowed the top of the cricket cage shut, then walked to the door and waited for Paul to open it and let him through. It led to a cramped hallway that faced the back of the reptile exhibits. Marlin stood beside a lizard tank and held the crickets while Paul unlatched an access flap. "Maybe that's why we fly to an unpopulated probability. Less confusing stuff to clutter up our heads."

"What do you mean, maybe?" Paul said. "Don't you know?"

"I'm still working through some of the details." Marlin was stunningly unconcerned. He thrust both hands into the glass enclosure and released a small flurry of crickets, then moved on to the next tank and waited for Paul to open it. Once they fed all the reptiles and amphibians, they tossed a big bucket of vile-smelling chum into the shark tank on their way back outside. There were wire enclosures to snip open and gates to unlatch, and although the aquarium grounds were small, by the time they were finished the sun hung low on the horizon.

"Aren't you glad you're not stuck in that stuffy old jet?" Marlin asked, flinging his arm around Kaye.

"Ugh. You smell like sweat and dead fish."

"It's part of my rugged appeal." He opened the convertible's door for her and then hopped into the driver seat once Dallas and Paul were settled. Though they were crammed in the back of a sports car together, Paul avoided looking at Dallas. He'd been so pissed off at Paul for smuggling Marlin's remains onboard, Paul was positive he'd blown any chance at being together. Now, maybe, there was some possibility of winning him back. Except the less Marlin explained, the more Paul began to suspect that there might not be a happy ending in store for First Officer Fritsch after all. And the less Kaye and Dallas asked about it, the more it seemed they were treading around questions that had answers they didn't actually want.

CHAPTER 27

They washed the stink of the aquarium from themselves in the kitchen of the Ocean Point Bistro, then dined on the terrace overlooking the sunset above Gibbons Bay. Plates brimmed with lobster, ribeye and baby greens, while bottles of Pinot Noir that cost more than Paul's smartphone graced the table. No one objected to eating the Bermuda food, not even Paul. Once Marlin assured them it wouldn't disappear in the turbulence and take their vital organs with it, the idea that they'd been denying themselves all this time seemed rather sad. Marlin insisted on cooking and serving—and he insisted on keeping up the chitchat, too. He steered the conversation deftly, getting Kaye to reveal she'd very nearly opted to go into nursing instead of aviation, and Dallas to talk about his regret that he'd never pursued anything beyond his high school diploma. But he didn't talk about himself, or his plans for the future. And he didn't say a word about what it was like to die.

A few hours later, the meal was a distant memory. Marlin went to retrieve another bottle of wine, and Paul excused himself and followed. Marlin gave the massive wine rack some serious consideration. "Maybe we should switch to something a little sweeter for dessert."

When he flipped open the price list to consult, Paul dredged up the courage to blurt out, "Your email…it was Twinkle Twinkle Little Star."

"You noticed!" Marlin turned and lavished his infectious smile on Paul. "That thing's got like seven verses, too—but I guess you must know all about it if you spotted the reference. How cool was it that I made it into a haiku?"

"Subtle."

Since he seemed so pleased, Paul forged ahead. "But what did it mean?"

Marlin crossed his arms, leaned back against the bar, and allowed his gaze to defocus as he remembered. "Travelers in the dark—it's us, right? But not just us. It's everyone in the physical. Because to live in the physical we need to forget we're Source so we can experience the contrast that causes expansion. When the blazing sun is gone—that means when you're not right in the midst of your contrast, you're not freaking out, you're calm—find the tiny light. That's Source. And it's like a star, too. It looks small to us, from here. But if we were to get right up in it, we'd find it as big as a sun."

"So sending out your haiku, you were telling the crew where you'd gone." When he drowned himself in his pool. "To Source."

"Exactamundo."

"Oh. Because I thought you were telling us how to stop the turbulence."

"It's not stoppable. But if you don't wanna fly it, then don't. We always have a choice—not just metaphysically speaking. When you get your weekly schedule from AVA, if you want to quit, then don't sign on."

Paul was no quitter. But if there was no stopping the turbulence, he at least needed to know why. "The expense of flying here and back is huge. Add that to the overnight cost, and it doesn't make any sense. Why us? Why this airline? Why fly over that patch of airspace at all?"

"Dunno. I was plenty busy trying to lead us through it, and ended up having to wrap my head around the whole multiverse deal. But why me, you or any of us got picked for this particular duty…maybe Scheduling could tell you."

"The computer program that shoots out the email?"

"No, no, they do it all by hand and plug it into a spreadsheet. Go to the Fort Lauderdale admin building and ask for Ava—she knows *lots* of things. Maybe she can shed some light on it."

While Paul would prefer for Marlin to be there for any face-to-face meeting with Scheduling, he had a strong suspicion that wasn't going to happen, not in this reality. "So feeding the lizards this afternoon, chumming the shark…that was all buying time. Because tomorrow, or the next day, or the day after that, you'll figure out how to introduce them to the wild."

"I was about to give up on Mr. Sharkey, but then I got an idea for caging him and tethering him to a fork lift. Not exactly elegant, but the bay's only a few hundred yards away."

"Because you're not coming back with us tomorrow."

Marlin pulled a bottle of wine from the rack, fiddled with the cork, then reached into the refrigerator and grabbed a wine cooler instead. He cracked the lid and drank, considered his reply for a moment, and said, "It doesn't make any sense to go back. In that probability, I'm non-physical now."

That much, Paul did understand. "You mean dead."

"I mean non-physical."

"Do you remember it?"

"I do." Marlin smiled to himself. "It was such a rush—a total trip. But I'm in no hurry to shed my skin, since I know Source will always be there waiting for me. And now I've got another chance to squeeze more juice out of the physical, too."

Paul had always presumed that once you were dead, that was that. He wasn't quite sure how to integrate Marlin's existence into his own worldview. It flew in the face of everything he knew—or thought he knew. Allowing himself to have hope was scary. Slightly comforting, but scary all the same.

"You know," Marlin said, "at dinner, you never mentioned what you wanted to be when you grew up."

"A pilot. I've always wanted to be a pilot."

"Not surprising. You've got that laser-sharp focus. Me? I hoped flight school would be a stepping stone to NASA. It would've been smarter to join the Air Force, but I thought soldiers were all a bunch of macho crewcut douchebags. And anyway, flying was cool, and aviation turned out to be enough to keep me occupied for a dozen years. Still, you know what the wildest part of the space program was, before our time, back in the sixties? Not launching a manned spacecraft—and you just *know* the Soviets must've had a few misfires they never let on about—but bringing the rocket jockeys back down to Earth. I used to think about those covered-up Comrades floating around in their capsules as the oxygen ran out, and wonder if they had any regrets." Marlin drained his wine cooler. "I don't. Not a one. Plus…I've got all the air I care to breathe."

Marlin turned his attention to opening the next bottle of wine. As Paul remained silent, contemplating the enormity of everything—the exclusive jet, and the extra fuel they lugged across the Atlantic—the vastness of the situation began to feel like a tiny dot of light swelling and expanding, with the potential to reach the size of a red hypergiant. Once he'd eased out the cork, Marlin said, "So, you're gay, right? 'Cos I've got this buddy, Ralph. A super-cool guy—very smart, very fun, and very single…."

"I'm seeing somebody." As he said it, Paul wondered if it was even true anymore. "I'm seeing Dallas."

"Really? I mean, that's awesome—I love Dallas like crazy—but I totally didn't pick up on the connection in your guys' body language."

Paul's heart sank. "He's livid that I smuggled your…" Paul realized what he was about to say, and to whom, but it seemed too late to put on the brakes. "Your urn. I smuggled your urn on board and I've never seen him so angry."

Marlin went utterly still, and Paul wondered if suddenly he regretted being a metaphysical Cosmonaut after all…and then he cracked a smile. He snickered, then he chortled, and then the guffaws overtook him. He doubled over, slapped his knee, clutched his belly, and laughed until he cried. And finally, when he knuckled away the tears, he said, "If you didn't go through proper channels, how'd you manage to get the urn past security without the X-ray guy stopping you?"

Paul couldn't think of a way to sugar-coat the answer, so as neutrally as possible, he said, "It's plastic."

A fresh fit of laughter overtook Marlin, and Paul gently pried the open wine bottle from his hand while he waited for it to subside.

***

Dallas crammed a handful of used napkins into the trash bag with enough force to split the plastic. Slimy. What the hell had the passenger in 4A done, hack up phlegm all the way to Bermuda and hide it under the seat? He checked the impulse to slam the disgusting wad of paper against the floor. And then he thought, fuck it.

Throwing things felt nowhere near as satisfying as he'd hoped.

From his post at the cabin door, Marlin said, "You don't actually need to clean up—the possible Dallas in the other Bermuda's got it covered."

Dallas kept his face turned away. "Maybe I want to." Damn it, he'd told himself he was going to hold it together.

"I'm not usually big on regrets and coulda-beens…but hurting the rest of the crew is the last thing I meant to do. I'm sorry."

Dallas grabbed some empty cups off 5B and C. Marlin handed him a new trash bag, then leaned across 3A to peer out the window at Paul, who was scrutinizing a vial of jet fuel for contaminants. "Listen, Dallas, if you can do one thing for me—I'd do it myself, but he's really in the zone out there—make sure you tell Paul I appreciate him bringing me along for the ride."

After the pilots closed the cockpit door, Dallas gave Marlin one final hug. Marlin squeezed him tight, clapped him on the back, and said, "This is gonna be awesome." As the pneumatic stairs folded up and the cabin door eased shut, Dallas stole one last look outside at Marlin, who touched his hand to his forehead in a jaunty salute.

It didn't take long to taxi to the runway—Wade International was tiny. By the time the jet gained speed for takeoff, Dallas could no longer stop himself from looking out the window. Marlin was jogging toward the end of the runway, waving. Dallas saw that wave at the airport all the time. It was the wave of someone embarking on the vacation they'd been saving up for their whole life. Dallas pressed his hand to the window as Flight 511 began its ascent.

Once he dried his eyes, he settled himself in the cockpit in time for the three big bumps. The return turbulence was typical. The autopilots had been on good behavior—none of the crew members were hungover, though Paul and Kaye had sunburn. The twenty-eight passengers who'd appeared in the cabin were strapped in tight. Nobody's handbag had become a lethal projectile. It was the best Dallas could have hoped for, all things considered.

Landing was smooth. Dallas, Kaye and Paul waited in the galley while the passengers pried their luggage from the overhead bins. "Here's what gets me," Kaye muttered as ground crew hooked up the skybridge, "I had no idea about the aquarium. I just figured once his research was done for the day he'd go and dick around all night."

"How could you have known?" Paul said. "Playing at the beach and herding tortoises probably leaves you smelling about the same."

Kaye didn't wait for the passengers to deplane. As soon as the skybridge was open, she said, "See you at preflight," and took off at a powerwalk just shy of a run. Her eyelashes looked wet. Maybe she'd make it to her car before the dam broke. Paul stood his ground, though, thanking the customers for flying AVA as they filtered out into the terminal. Once they were alone together, or alone as they could be with a staffed and populated airport humming around them, Paul caught Dallas' gaze and held it while he said, "I know I blew it—yeah, my idea worked, but that was never the point. It was doing something behind your back because I was worried you'd stop me."

Dallas wasn't even sure he knew what the point was anymore. He sighed deeply. "You didn't blow it."

"Really?"

Dallas glanced over his shoulder to make sure ground crew was occupied, then caught Paul's hand, wove their fingers together, dark skin and light. He gave a quick squeeze, and released. "You're not the only one to keep things to yourself. When I'm on autopilot, we get up to plenty more than candlelight dinners and bubble baths."

"Yeah." Paul gave his jaw an experimental click. "I kinda figured." He looked Dallas over and cracked a timid smile. "At least my other self has good taste in men."

Paul might have an edge to him, but he still had his moments. "Do you feel like you slept at all? You need to come home and nap before we fly out?"

"Actually, I need to go talk to somebody in the admin building…and I was really hoping you'd come with me."

CHAPTER 28

Paul usually dealt with AVA admin matters in DC. The Fort Lauderdale building was smaller and shabbier, done up in a navy and burgundy color scheme about twenty years out of date. He could have made a drinking game out of counting fake potted palms that needed a good dusting. The first floor was personnel and payroll, with plenty of uniformed flight crew and ground crew mingling with AVA office workers. The second floor, however, was nothing but a dimly lit lobby and a single desk that blocked access to whatever offices lay beyond.

It's only a desk, Paul told himself, but his body wasn't buying it—his stomach was in knots and his tongue was dry. The secretary in the headset watched him and Dallas approach, her expression bland. She couldn't have been a day over thirty, but she exuded an air of authority.

"I'd like to talk to Ava from Scheduling," Paul said.

The receptionist stared a beat too long, then said, "Last name?"

"I don't have any…I was just told to ask for Ava."

"Sir, we have over twelve hundred employees. I can't help you without a last name."

So, this was how it was going to be. Like when Captain Kaye requested flight data and was blocked every step of the way. The "everything's fine" that pervaded the airline when everything was obviously not fine. "It's not a common name," Paul said. "You mean to say the computer can't search by first name?"

"I'm sorry." She didn't sound it.

"Ava from *Scheduling*."

"If you don't have a last name, sir, there's nothing I can do."

"There is, actually. You could open up your company directory and find Scheduling—how many people could there possibly be in that department—ten? Twenty? Fifty? Probably closer to ten—and then you could look at the list for an Ava."

"There's no need to take a tone with me, sir."

"You must have a printed directory...the airline prints everything out. I've got enough AVA paperwork in my filing cabinet to build a bunker. Don't tell me there's no directory."

Dallas caught Paul's sleeve and murmured, "Easy, now."

Paul looked to the receptionist pleadingly. Her eyes were hard. He knew with sudden clarity that he could rant and rave, grovel and beg, and it wouldn't make a bit of difference. She wouldn't help. In fact, she was probably in the midst of hitting a hidden panic button to summon security. "You know what? Fine. I'll come back when I have a last name. *Thank you* for *all* your *help*."

He strode back to the elevator and, with great effort, only hit the button once, and with a restrained amount of force. Dallas stood beside him, watching the elevator dial. "You feel better now that you got your sarcasm out?"

"A little," Paul admitted. The elevator door opened and they stepped inside and pressed the first floor button. "It's just that Marlin told me there was no way to stop the turbulence...the only choice was to quit, and it seems to me that if I quit, they'll just find some other pilot to do it, and I'll be stuck flying all over the place and only get to see you on weekends, if that. So if I'm gonna fly out every day and sit there in empty Bermuda while some stupid, oversexed version of me is throwing himself at you, I at least want to know—" Paul's stomach lurched as the elevator rose. "What the...? I hit the down button. You saw me hit the down button."

"The first floor is lit."

"I swear, if anything worked the way it was supposed to anymore, I'd fall down dead."

"Don't even joke about something like that," Dallas said.

"What, my words have magic powers now?" Paul jabbed the lit button. "You know, Marlin almost sounded logical to me, back there in Bermuda. Maybe that's what I should be worried about."

The elevator shuddered to a stop on the top floor, number five. The doors slid open and a stale smell wafted in. The corridor beyond looked unused, deserted. Paul jabbed the first floor button again. A fluorescent light flickered. A massive wall-mounted clock ticked with a hollow echo.

"Nice." Paul was reaching for the button when a distant creak and rattle made him look up. At the far end of the corridor, a housekeeping cart turned the corner, pushed by a stooped woman who looked like she could have retired twenty years ago.

"Hold the elevator," she called out in Spanish-accented English just as the doors began to slide shut.

Paul considered only pretending to try…but come on, it was a little old lady. He'd feel like a massive jerk if he let the door shut on her. He pressed the "open door" button, and waited for the housekeeper and her creaky cart to join them. It took a while, since her version of hurrying was more of a shuffle.

"I'm sure we'll be able to find the name online," Dallas said. "Maybe email someone. Set up an appointment. If not today, then tomorrow."

"Okay. Right. You're totally right."

The old woman reached the elevator door, finally, and attempted to rock the cleaning cart over the threshold. Paul was unsure if he was supposed to help—she managed to do her job without him up to this point, after all—but eventually he and Dallas both gave the cart a tug to ease it in so they could all be on their way. "Basement," she said, and Paul hit the bottom button.

The elevator started its descent, then creaked to a stop. The doors opened on four. There was no one waiting. Paul sighed.

"Old building," the cleaning woman said, rather loudly. Paul checked to see if she had a hearing aid, but found she was listening to an MP3 player.

Paul did hit the "close door" button now. Which didn't seem to do much of anything. He hit it harder. "Just let it be," Dallas said. "You get yourself all worked up."

"Can you blame me?" Paul checked to see if the cleaning lady was about to bear witness to a racy lovers' spat, but she was staring straight ahead, nodding her head in time to her music. The doors shut, and the elevator went down. It passed three (miraculously) then opened on two. The dim hallway that led to the single desk with the world's least helpful receptionist behind it mocked them. The corridor was empty, of course. "All she had to do was look," Paul whispered. The doors slid shut. "That's what gets me. She didn't even look. I mean, really, how many Avas can there… be?" As he said it, his eyes lit on the Airline's logo above the button panel.

AVA.

With a sinking feeling, Paul realized that he'd allowed himself to get carried away with Marlin Fritsch's handsome smile and easygoing charm, just like everyone else. There was no "Ava." He'd been speaking metaphorically about the airline itself, a huge, faceless entity. This final clue—delivered in person—was another wild goose chase, yet one more way to make Paul look like a sucker for believing there was reason to be found in a cruel and arbitrary world.

And then the cleaning lady removed one of her earbuds and said, "Did you say Ava?"

Paul's heart stuttered.

"From Scheduling," Dallas said.

"Her office is downstairs. I'll show you."

The basement level was teeming with activity, as if gravity had caused the administrative personnel to settle there in a low-ceilinged cubicle farm. The color scheme here was putty and gray, a good decade or two worse than the rest of the building, and the air conditioning ran cold enough that the thinner-skinned folks needed to wear sweaters. Paul and Dallas crept along behind the shuffling cleaning woman, who paused at every waste basket to empty it out, whether there was anything worth emptying or not. Just as Paul wondered how rude it might be to ask the housekeeper to simply point him in the general direction, the old woman pulled out one earbud, stuck her head in a cubicle, and said, "Buenos dias,

Ava. You got some flight crew here looking for you."

"Why would they…?" Ava replied. Paul peeked around the corner and she got a look at him. "Cronin…employee number 7414563 from Flight 511. Come in."

I know her. Paul would have taken the sensation for déjà vu, but it was stronger than that, more like a word he'd conceived and immediately forgotten, hovering at the tip of his tongue.

Dallas, however, did a double-take and gasped, "It's you."

"Shh," she said. "You two gotta be quiet, so I can…." She closed her eyes, sniffed in a deep breath through her nose, then exhaled through her mouth in a "ch" sound. And then another. Paul took in as much of the cubicle as he could while her eyes were shut. The furniture, acoustical walls and carpet were all either gray or beige. The furniture was worn and dented, piled high with teetering stacks of manila file folders. Her personal items stood out among the piles of non-color: a faux Tiffany lamp in peacock colors; a paisley scarf in purples and golds draped over the back of her gray office chair; a bright blue sweatshirt with a folksy rendition of the American flag stitched onto the back in big, clunky, deliberately naive stitches.

The gate. That's where Paul knew her from—he recognized her "fashion sense." It was the woman in the mom-jeans who asked if they'd be flying over the Bermuda Triangle on his first flight out. Just as he placed her, Ava's eyes snapped open. She said, "They're here."

"Who are *they*?" Dallas asked.

"The spirit world."

"Ghosts?" Paul realized he sounded like an incredulous dick—and really, given all he'd seen, shouldn't he be a little bit more open-minded at this point? But moaning and rattling chains and going on about Christmas past was just so…fictitious.

Ava picked up a yellow pad of sticky notes and scribbled something on it. She looked at her drawing and laughed. "Not like this." She peeled off the note and handed it to Paul. It looked like a blob and a couple of scribbles at first, then it resolved itself into a cartoon sheet with a couple of holes cut out for eyes. "*Non-physical entities* might be a more general way of saying it. They send me pictures sometimes. Like jpg attachments in my head."

She scribbled something else on her pad, peeled it off and handed it to Dallas. "What's this?" he asked.

"Globes. A line of globes, like maybe they're on a shelf at a globe store—do 'globe stores' even exist? I can't imagine people wouldn't just buy 'em from Amazon and get the free shipping. That's what I see, though, a whole big row of globes. Touching. Does this make sense?"

"Maybe."

Ava scribbled some more, big looping circles, then a few squiggly lines. "Two of the globes are touching, and they're kind of...mashed in. What are globes made of, anyway? Plastic?"

Paul said, "It depends." He realized he'd been holding his breath, and the hair on the back of his arms was standing on end.

"They're mashed in where they're touching." She peeled off the sheet and handed it to Paul, then resumed scribbling. Her hand moved quickly, only enough time to make a looping mark, then she peeled off the next note so fast that she ended up sticking it to the side of Paul's hand rather than actually giving it to him. "Mashed in. They keep showing me that same picture. You're sure you get it?" Scribble. Peel. Scribble. Peel. Scribble.

Paul cocked his head to look at the top scribble, and realized it was the shape of the Atlantic Coastal Plain. Exactly. With a dent in it at the latitude of the turbulence. "I get it," he said. His voice sounded rough.

Ava scribbled on the corner of her desk blotter. Her ballpoint pen skipped, then ran dry. She found a fresh pen, scribbled a zigzag on the blotter until the ink flowed, then went back to her sticky note. The quality of the scribble there was different—spidery, organic. "Now they're showing me...do you play basketball? No, wait, it's the globe. You're kind of mashing it back into shape."

A flurry of scribbles and notes followed, a big stack of them, all showing ghostly, wavery hands and a globe, until Paul said, "Okay."

Ava turned back to Dallas. "Mr. Turner, employee number 2344212.

Flight attendant, right?"

"Right."

Scribble. Peel. Stick. "You're flying the plane. You and him."

Dallas turned the single sticky note this way and that as if he couldn't make out much of anything in it. "What about Captain Lehr?"

Ava's focus softened for a moment, and then she drew a slow, meandering line. It didn't look like anything from where Paul was standing. Then again, most of the notes didn't...until they did. Ava considered the drawing, then shrugged and handed it to Dallas. "I see her holding a baby."

Any other time, Paul would have laughed. Except he felt queasy, and the sweat on his palms was soaking through the sticky notes. "She's almost sixty."

"What can I tell you? That's what they showed me." Ava poised the pen over the pad, held it there for a moment, then said, "That's it. That's all I got."

If Paul were to listen to his body, he'd have to agree that the show was over. His state of heightened alert was ebbing now, leaving him with a weary sort of lassitude and the desire to be alone to talk things through with Dallas. They thanked Ava, who was already clacking through a spreadsheet on her ancient desktop computer, and she dismissed them with an awkward wave. The parking lot felt like it was a million miles away, too far to walk on rubbery knees, so Paul touched Dallas' elbow and steered him to the crew lounge instead.

The lounge was far from empty, but the other flight crew stayed in their own bubbles of conversation or isolation without paying Paul and Dallas any mind. A bank of three flat monitors showed the weather, the news, and the AVA flight schedule, but Paul only glanced at them. They represented the outside world, and right now he was more concerned about sorting through his own personal experience. A sofa facing the window was free. They settled there, looking out over the airfield. If Paul craned his neck, he could see his little ERJ-135 getting combed over by a pair of mechanics, neither of which was the guy who'd been sent to the emergency room by a ruptured brake line. Maybe that guy was still recuperating.

Dallas pulled out his phone and said, "I'm gonna check on Kaye."

"Seeing if she missed her period?" The humor sounded forced. Dallas quirked an eyebrow and dialed. Paul flipped through his sticky notes until he found the one of the dented coast and the ocean beyond. It was uncannily accurate.

Dallas kept his conversation with Kaye brief. When he hung up, he turned to Paul, gave him a "this is gonna be good" look, and said, "So Kaye just found out she'll be a grandma by Thanksgiving."

Paul realized that at this point, it would take an awful lot to shock him. "Okay."

He hadn't realized there were grown Lehr children. Maybe that was personal information their autopilots had shared.

Dallas pulled out his own stack of sticky notes, which was much shorter than Paul's, and considered Ava's last drawing. "I see it," he whispered. "There's the baby's little nose."

"I've met Ava before," Paul said. "She talked to me face to face, and asked if I was willing to fly through the Triangle."

"I have, too. Gave me a good once-over like I do with Chantal's boyfriends."

"Two weeks ago, I couldn't have imagined myself talking to a psychic without laughing in her face."

"Good thing you're willing to keep an open mind." Dallas ran his thumb over the sticky note. "I don't mind a skeptical man, and if I have to, I'll even put up with a stubborn man. But I can't be with a man who doesn't believe in anything at all."

"I believe my own eyes." Paul shuffled his stack of drawings. "We all spent the night in empty Bermuda with Marlin, and he came from somewhere, didn't he? I may not know where. But I saw him. He existed."

Dallas stuck Ava's drawings to the back of his phone and began scrolling through the pictures on it. "Looks like we had ourselves a party in the other Bermuda, too. Me, you and Kaye on the beach. And the urn. We must've spread Marlin's ashes there...whatever ground crew didn't vacuum up out of the cockpit."

"The urn was plastic," Paul said softly. "Marlin got such a kick out of that." Out on the field, a massive 747 taxied toward the runway. It seemed cumbersome and ungainly compared to their sleek commuter jet. "I really clicked with him, you know—which totally blew me away. I wish I'd had a chance to get to know him better."

"Maybe, in another cricket-life, you do."

Paul sighed. "He was a heck of a lot nicer than my drinking friends in DC." Hidden by the angle of the sofa, Dallas clasped his hand. Paul's awareness gathered in fingers and palm, and coalesced at the point where his skin and Dallas' touched. "You're a lot nicer, too."

"Is that a fact?"

"Don't tease…I'm trying to work up the courage to tell you I love you." Paul stole a sidelong glance to see what kind of reaction he got.

Dallas kept his eyes trained on the field, but allowed a small smile to play over his features. "Bermuda Paul beat you to it in the bubble bath… but I've been looking forward to hearing it from you."

"You really need to stop seeing that goofball." Paul let go of Dallas' hand to peel the sticky notes from the back of his phone, searching for the one he wanted. The elaborate doodle was abstract, but the strip of adhesive told him which way was up, and he stared at it calmly until he made out a front view of figures in a cockpit—one with a hint of a goatee, the other with glasses. Paul was in the Captain's seat, Dallas the First Officer's. "When you think about it, getting your commercial license is phenomenally doable."

"Me, a pilot."

"Absolutely. I've never seen anyone keep a cooler head in an emergency. Plus, I'd make sure you ace flight school the first time around, teach you all the math, the charts. We could have ground lessons at Wade International a couple of hours every day."

"You mean, after we're done setting the flamingoes and turtles free?"

Paul supposed so, but Mr. Sharkey was on his own, at least until they could figure out how to start a rumor among the aquarium employees.

Strategic placement of a fake brochure about keeping sharks happy and healthy with conversation might do the trick. "I'll bet Kaye wouldn't mind changing up the Bermuda duties. While you come to empty Bermuda, she could duck out of the cockpit for the turbulence and wrangle the autopilots instead."

"Something tells me they'd probably be pretty low-maintenance, too," Dallas said. "She'll be lucky to pry them out the hotel room."

A series of chimes and beeps sounded. All around the crew lounge, cell phones and the occasional pager were going off. Paul and Dallas both turned to see what the commotion was about, and found the other AVA pilots gathering around the monitors. Paul checked his phone. It was indeed turned on, but it held no new messages, which was par for the course these days. Although he suspected it was unnecessary, he went to check the monitors for himself.

The weather monitor showed the swirling, rainbow-colored mass of a small tropical storm off the coast of Grenada. It had turned sharply eastward, picking up speed. The flight monitor flickered as the word *DELAY* appeared beside several Caribbean and east coast flights, and the pilots of those flights shrugged and prepared to settle in and wait out the weather. Toward the top of the list, though, the particular flight he was looking for remained unchanged.

`BERMUDA - GATE A12 - 16:35 - FLIGHT 511 - ON TIME`

On time? Paul expected nothing less. These days, it took an awful lot to surprise him.

About this Story

Turbulence was originally run as a serial, with a monthly 3- to 4-chapter episode debuting in my newsletter. I had figured I could just write a silly little paranormal thing about the Bermuda Triangle that would take about a week of my time each month, then work on my other projects for the remaining three weeks—and then this story ate my life like the Triangle eats aircraft. The story turned out to require significant technical knowledge to write a realistic airport and cockpit. It also turned out to be thick with subtext about race, religion, orientation and class. I'm pleased with the final product—I just hadn't comprehended the dimensions of the approaching storm until I'd taken off. And then there was no turning back.

It's interesting to daydream about what might have happened to all the vessels that disappeared in the Bermuda Triangle over the years. I like to think they sailed off into an unspoiled part of the multiverse and lived happily ever after.

About the Author

Author and artist Jordan Castillo Price is the owner of JCP Books LLC. She writes paranormal, horror and thriller novels from her isolated and occasionally creepy home in rural Wisconsin.

Jordan is best known as the author of the PsyCop series, an unfolding tale of paranormal mystery and suspense starring Victor Bayne, a gay medium who's plagued by ghostly visitations. She's also conjured the vampire road-trip series Channeling Morpheus, a wild, sexy ride that's unflinchingly gritty.

Connect with Jordan in the following places:

JordanCastilloPrice.com

PsyCop.com

JCPBooks.com

Twitter.com/JordanCPrice

Jordan-C-Price.LiveJournal.com

Facebook.com/JordanCastilloPrice

CPSIA information can be obtained at www.ICGtesting.com
Printed in the USA
LVOW050350210213

320901LV00004B/496/P